Broken
Man
Broke

Also by Marcus Lopés

The Visit
Everything He Thought He Knew
The Flowers Need Watering

Broken Man Broke

Marcus Lopés

TORONTO, CANADA

Marcus Lopés
Toronto, Ontario
Canada

Publisher's Note: This is a work of fiction. Names, characters, places, and incidents are a product of the author's imagination. Locales and public names are sometimes used for atmospheric purposes. Any resemblance to actual people, living or dead, or to businesses, companies, events, institutions, or locales is completely coincidental.

First Edition

Book Layout © 2019 BookDesignTemplates.com
Cover Design: Lieu Pham
        www.covertopia.com

Broken Man Broke / Marcus Lopés

Issued in print and electronic formats.

ISBN 978-0-9958294-5-9 (softcover).--ISBN 978-0-9958294-6-6 (PDF)

To Myrtle Stewart Gillis

Broken
Man
Broke

Part I

September 1997 – December 1999

New Beginning

SUNDAYS HAD LONG BEEN ORDINARY AND routine, almost melancholic. A day of gimmicky rituals he tried to escape. Like going to church when he didn't really believe. Or the weekly family dinners that he didn't enjoy, but living at home he couldn't escape them. Or ransacking his grandmother's bedroom, while she was still alive, for the bottles of scotch and gin she hid.

This Sunday was anything but ordinary or routine. Certainly not melancholic. This Sunday was about new beginnings, where repressed desires would be allowed to unfurl. This Sunday had the power to transform him and his life.

If he could be daring and bold.

If he could let himself believe in something.

If his mother could let him go.

Scott Davenport, standing on the sidewalk near the back of the silver Range Rover, ran his hand over his shaved head. "Yes, Mama, I'm listening."

"Watch your tone, mister," Margaret Davenport said, and started rummaging through her shopping-bag-size purse. She pulled out a crumpled tissue and dabbed it at her moist eyes. "Promise me you'll call. At least once a week. And don't forget to eat…"

As his mother slipped into her teacher's voice, Scott was already daydreaming about the new world that awaited him. Eighteen or soon-to-be, he was in a new city to which he would willingly give himself over. Ready to transform from boy to man. All he needed was for his parents to get into their car and drive away. Then he would be on his own at last, and free to do as he pleased. And he had big plans for his freedom. The snapping of fingers brought him out of his dream-state.

"You're not even listening," Margaret chided.

"I am —"

"Then what did I say?"

Scott dropped his gaze. *Probably something about Jesus protecting us from the devil. Probably...* He lifted his head. "God, er, Jesus … that I should let Him —"

"You weren't listening," Margaret interrupted. "I don't want you drinking. You're here to get an education."

"Mama —"

"Don't Mama me." She stomped her foot. "And be careful. The devil's going to tempt you at every turn, but I don't need any more grandchildren yet." She gasped, her eyes wide open, and covered her mouth with her hand. "Oh, dear…" Her hand fell away. "Just be careful then." She reached out and drew him into a crushing embrace. "Oh, my baby."

Scott loosely returned the hug. "I'll be fine, and I'll be careful."

"Find a church." Margaret blinked magnificently. "There's got to be a decent Baptist church nearby."

"We should get on the road," Terrence Davenport said as he watched the tears roll down his wife's pumpernickel face. "If you need anything, just call." He extended his hand to his youngest son, leaned in, and added in a whisper, "And call home. It'll make my life easier."

Scott, letting go of his father's hand, fumbled to hang on to the roll of money being slipped to him. He shoved the bills into his jeans pocket. "Thanks, Dad. You know, I'll try to find a part-time job."

"No, you won't." Margaret raised her finger and drew an 'x' in the air. "You focus on getting those A's."

Terrence slunk to the passenger door and opened it. "All right, let's roll."

"Your father will put money into your account every two weeks," Margaret said as she settled into the seat.

Scott grinned.

"Margie!" Terrence unintentionally slammed closed the passenger side door. "Good luck, son." He made his way around to the driver's side and climbed in. "We agreed on once a month!"

Taking a couple of steps backwards as the engine roared, Scott's heart thumped as the car rolled down the narrow street. This wasn't just a dream anymore. It was real. The rush of excitement had him trembling, to the point where he thought his bladder would burst. It didn't. *Go, just go,* was his silent wish when his parents' vehicle stopped at the intersection. Then, as it veered right, his mother stuck her arm out the window. He waved enthusiastically as they disappeared out of sight.

Finally.

Alone.

And free.

The bright September sun toasted his already caramel skin as he walked along Willcocks Street towards New College residence, the place he'd call home for at least the next eight months. The buildings along the route — some built with large grey stones, others with brown brick, or the newer structures made of steel and glass — were like a puzzle to him. When he came to a construction site, he slowed down and, with an almost child-like wonder, locked his gaze on the metal crane rising towards the heavens. Idle now, tomorrow it would come to life, bring together so many pieces — metal, brick, wood, concrete — to form something whole. He wanted to feel whole, or that he was a part of something. Seeing his reflection staring back at him in the street-level window, he picked up his pace. He didn't recognize himself, convinced that there was a part of him that didn't completely exist.

Now he hoped to unearth that missing part of him. That was why he'd fled to Toronto. He had to stop questioning who he was and search for a way forward. Deciding on a field of study would help him with that, right? Give his life direction? Maybe. Deep down, he knew that what he needed was to just be himself, stop worrying about what others thought. That meant living out some of his secret fantasies. Had his mother sensed that 'darkness' in him? Was that why she didn't want him living off campus? A lot had changed since she'd been to university, yet so much had stayed the same. But the parties, according to news reports, were wilder. New drugs popped up almost weekly. At least in residence there were rules to be followed. Off campus, Scott could do as he pleased. And what she wanted was for him to stay in Ottawa, under her watch. But Scott had to get away and him living in residence was the compromise. As far as his mother was concerned, that was safest for both him and his soul.

Crossing over Spadina Avenue, Scott thought about the emotional goodbye at the car with his mother. He was used to her sentimental ways, but that hug was different, like it had a certain transformative power. His lips curled into a smile as he turned onto the pathway leading to the entrance of his residence building. *She tried to purge the devil from me, reclaim my soul. Didn't work.* Smirking, he raced inside and sailed up the stairs to the third floor, prying open the heavy metal door. Animated voices assailed him from all sides as he made his way to his room midway down the corridor. Parents carried boxes and suitcases into their children's new homes. Mothers had tears in their eyes. Younger brothers and sisters screamed and laughed as they ran up and down the hall. He ended up stuck behind a tall guy carrying two boxes with a half-full garbage bag balanced on top. The bag fell, and Scott intervened to catch it. "Got it."

The man stopped in front of the door directly across from Scott's room. He made a play for the doorknob but was unable to reach it and looked hopelessly at Scott. "Could you get the door?"

"Sure." Scott took a step forward, pushed the door open wide, and stood off to the side to let the Eddie Cibrian lookalike pass through.

The guy set the boxes down on the floor by the window, then made his way back towards Scott, who was still propping the door open. He took the bag, tossed it on the bed, then extended his hand. "Troy. Thanks for saving the day."

"No worries," Scott said, accepting the firm handshake. "I'm Scott." He covered his ears with both hands at the screaming and laughter booming in the hall. When it subsided, he slipped his hands into his pockets as he and Troy stared intently at each other. "I should go and try to settle in a bit."

Troy ran his hand through his brown hair. "Are you first-year?"

"Yes. I'm thinking about majoring in English or philosophy. Maybe even political science. I'm not really sure yet."

"Ah … a thinker."

"Hardly," Scott said with a slight edge, catching the hint of condescension in Troy's eyes. "What about you?"

"Biology major. And afterwards, med school."

The confidence with which Troy spoke, like he had his life all planned out, made Scott squeamish. Nothing about his own future was clear. "Well, good luck with that." He backed out of the room, crossed the hall, jammed the key in the lock and pushed down on the door handle in one sweeping movement. More yelling and laughter had his head spinning, and he scrambled to close the door to block out the rowdiness. Looking through the peephole, he saw Troy nodding and smiling at the other students passing through the hall. When it seemed like Troy's gaze was trained on his door, he backed away. Heat burned in his cheeks, the way it did every time he ogled a *hot* guy on the street and got caught. Was Troy, like Scott, assessing the significance of their exchange? Was it significant?

Scott collapsed on to his bed. Anxiousness replaced his earlier excitement. "This is home?" His eyes roved the tiny room with cement walls, the space cold and lifeless — the way he imagined the cells at some secret government detention centre. Maybe it wouldn't be that different from his last year at home when his bedroom had become his prison. And, oddly enough, the only place he could be himself. This room was different. Without his photos, plaques and books, it let him strip away the memories of a childhood he wanted to forget. And maybe it would also be the place that would allow him to become the man he hoped to be.

Suddenly, he could see Troy's tall frame in the doorway and that had him wondering if they'd become friends. Scott never felt like he'd been a friend to anyone, or anyone to him. So, no, he and Troy wouldn't be friends. They'd be the type of neighbours who smiled politely at each other without ever knowing the meaning behind those inquisitive eyes.

He slid his body backwards until his back rested against the cool wall. Already sensing the change occurring in him, the anxiousness began to ebb. This was his time to prove to his family, and perhaps more so to himself, that he could stand on his own. Be a man. It was the only way to shed his mother's perception that he was still her baby in need of mothering. Hadn't he proved that already by working two jobs over the summer, earning a good chunk of spending money for the year? Or by being awarded the scholarship that covered his tuition? His parents paying for his residence and meal plan didn't mean, not to him anyway, that he needed to be coddled. He worried that his parents weren't proud of him and, worst of all, that he was still a disappointment. Yet he was the one, not his brothers, who was going to university. He had a plan, too, to get a master's degree. But it didn't seem like enough to please his mother, who focused so much on him being gay — like that was the whole of his identity when there was so much more to him.

After a time of just sitting there, Scott moved off the bed and began to unpack. He plugged in his CD player and hit the 'Play' button. "For the love of God," he groaned as Mahalia Jackson belted out, 'As the Saints Go Marching In.' Somehow his mother had inserted the CD without him knowing, her subtle message understood: Jesus is my help. Let Him be your help. He removed the CD, replaced it with Tracy Chapman's *New Beginning*, hung up his clothes and made the bed. Afterwards, he taped posters of Martin Luther King Jr., Pierre E. Trudeau and John F. Kennedy Jr. to the walls. *Any surprises in here?* he wondered, opening the box with his dictionaries and notebook. He twitched, picked up the pocket-size version of the *New Testament* and threw it in the waste bin. After arranging the books on the shelves above the desk, he set up his toiletries in the bathroom, thankful that he didn't have to share. His grades made him eligible for the 'Quiet Floor' with all single rooms, and his mother agreed to pay the extra cost. *Can this be home after all?* He'd just unpacked the cleaning supplies when three solid knocks on the door had him staggering towards it. Opening it cautiously, "Oh," slipped out, then he swallowed hard.

"Interested in grabbing a beer?" Troy asked, placing his hands on each side of the doorframe.

"I'm not old enough yet," Scott said.

"Then how about grabbing a bite to eat?"

"I'm on the meal plan and the food's supposed to be good."

"Let me explain how this works." Troy scratched the top of his dark full mane. "I'm new here, you're new here. You helped me out earlier, so that kind of broke the ice between us. I don't know about you, but I don't know anyone here yet. So you say, 'Yes, sounds like fun,' grab your wallet and keys, and maybe you've made a new friend on your first day in residence."

Scott took a moment to assess the guy standing before him. Something in those hazel eyes instilled equal measures of calm and suspicion. Maybe not suspicion, but a certain hesitancy. He couldn't imagine Troy playing a part, or even willing to for that matter, in one of his secret fantasies. So, what was it that made Scott suspicious? He had no fucking idea. "Sure," was his reluctant reply.

Troy led the way to the stairwell. They barrelled down the three flights of stairs and edged their way through the crowded lobby before emerging outside, squinting at the scorching afternoon sun. Ten minutes later, they were on Bloor Street and ordering drinks at The Soho. Troy handed a twenty-dollar bill to the cashier.

"Thanks," Scott said, moving to collect his latte at the far end of the bar. Then he made his way outside to the small, street-side patio and secured the table being vacated by a grey-haired man. He was nervous. Troy made him nervous, but why? At six-foot-one, he was taller than most people, but Troy towered over him. That made him feel small, insignificant.

"Where are you from?" Troy asked as he fell into the metal chair across from Scott.

"Ottawa. You?"

"Calgary." Troy lifted his paper cup into the air. "Cheers!"

Scott picked up his drink. "Cheers."

"Why'd you choose U of T?" Troy leaned back and stretched out his pale, hairy legs.

Scott tapped his fingers against the lid of his drink. "The scholarship, a chance to live in Toronto … be away from home and family."

"I get that. I just want to be myself and not have to pretend to be someone else."

Scott raised an eyebrow. *What does that mean?*

Troy brought himself forward in his chair. "Did you leave anyone behind?"

"I'm not sure what you mean."

"I mean … were you seeing anyone?"

"Oh! No. It was a clean break."

"Lucky you." Troy eased back in his chair. "I thought Derek would follow, but in the end he stayed in Calgary. Wasn't ready to leave the nest."

Scott looked down, holding his gaze to his lap. *Oh my God!*

"Don't worry," Troy said, "this isn't a date."

"Edward went to McGill." Scott levelled his eyes at Troy. "It wasn't serious between us. I needed to be farther away than Montréal. Too close to home."

Troy smirked. "I thought so."

"But this still isn't a date," Scott said with emphasis. "Just two friends out for a coffee together."

"Now we're friends?" Troy chuckled. "Philosophy, English, or you mentioned political science?"

"Probably English."

"What are you going to do with an English degree?"

"Teach, proofread, write." Scott offered a faint smile. "Not all doctors can write."

"Ha-ha."

The afternoon slipped away as they laughed and joked, sharing stories about their families, cautiously revealing their hopes and dreams. They were surprised by how easy it was for them to talk to each other, how unexpectedly they had let their guards down. They headed back to the university in time to eat before the cafeteria closed. Afterwards, they spent the evening in Troy's room, listening to music and drinking beer while playing Gin Rummy.

Scott glanced at his watch, then his eyes widened. "Is it really two?"

"Yes," Troy confirmed and dealt the next hand.

"I better go." Scott slid off the bed.

"Oh, come on." Troy pointed at the piece of paper next to him. "I'm like twenty points away from finally beating your ass."

"We'll finish the game tomorrow."

"It'll take ten minutes. Less if I've dealt myself a perfect hand."

Scott started for the door. "I'm tired. Goodnight, Troy."

"Scott…" Troy bounced off the bed and cornered him at the door. "Do you ever just…"

"Do I ever just what?"

Troy scratched the back of his head. "Get off with a guy? Just to —"

"Are you…" Scott chuckled. "I don't know if you're drunk or just horny. Either way, it doesn't matter. Today was fun, but —"

"I'm sorry," Troy broke in. "It's been nice talking to someone who gets me. Like I said earlier … not having to pretend to be someone else."

"You can be *you* with me," Scott insisted. "But hitting on your new best friend is weird."

"New best friend? Huh." Troy's lips spread into a broad smile.

Scott opened the door. "We'll finish the game tomorrow. And so you know, in my family I'm known as the comeback kid. Be prepared to have your ass kicked." He stumbled across the hall and, his heart racing, jammed the key in the lock. Pushing the door open, he turned around and his gaze locked on Troy, who'd stepped into the hall. *Okay. He's pretty damn hot, but we just met. And I think he gets me, too. So, having sex would screw that up. Right? Besides, I want to try to* just *be his friend.* Scott waved, then rushed into his room and bolted the door. Part of him was tempted to storm back into the hall and into Troy's arms. What was wrong with a little companionship? Everything. Sex changed everything. The other part of him checked that urge because, really, he didn't know what he wanted. Except to be himself. But who was that?

Undressing, he glimpsed the *New Testament* in the garbage. "Fuck!" He retrieved it, opened the cover and read the inscription: *Jesus loves you! And so do I! Mama.* He hid it in the desk drawer, climbed into bed and drew in several deep breaths. A startling calm washed over him. Another shift. Despite what he wanted to believe, he wasn't alone. In such an unexpected way, a new friend had come into his life. That gave him hope for the days ahead … no matter what life threw at him.

The Secret

TROY HAD JUST PULLED ON HIS UNDERWEAR when there was a knock on his door. "Always so goddamn early." He moved to the door and opened it wide. "I still have fifteen minutes, Davenport."

"Whoa!" Scott raised his hand to his eyes. "I'll wait in my room."

"Get your ass in here." Troy grabbed Scott by the arm and pulled him inside. "You can help me decide on what to wear."

"God, we'll never make it to the party."

Troy slipped into the bathroom to finish styling his hair, trying for those carefully styled curtains that only David Beckham could really pull off. He came close, though. He strutted back into the main area of his room, his eyes landing on Scott, who stood by the window. His gaze travelled down Scott's back to the round bubble butt. He couldn't help himself, couldn't stop it. Something about his new best friend always had him hard like a baseball bat. Like now, the outline of what he was packing clearly visible in his white briefs.

Scott spun around and raised an eyebrow. "Are you ever going to get dressed?"

Troy saw how, for just a moment, Scott's eyes had lowered. That had him wanting to whip out his cock right there and start jerking. Was Scott *now* interested? Or was it more that a gay man couldn't resist looking? He wanted Scott to rush him, pin him down, devour him. His heart's desire since they'd met, and it tormented him every night as he lay in bed fantasizing about the things he'd let Scott do to him.

"What about this?" Troy picked up the blue and white checkered shirt.

"Sure," was Scott's emotionless response.

"Or this?" Troy held up a solid navy-blue V-neck T-shirt.

"It's a house party, Troy." Scott checked the time. "It's not like you're off to meet the Queen."

"I want to look good."

"You always look good."

Troy's lips curled into a smile. There it was, what he loved about his best friend. Scott always lifted him up, made him believe he was extraordinary in a world of mediocrity. Yet it still didn't seem like he stood out, not in the way that Scott did. But that wasn't true, and a complete reversal of his days at boarding school. After the first week of classes, students crowded into his dorm room on Wednesday nights to play poker. He'd already received three warnings from the crotchety Residence Advisor and been threatened with expulsion. Walking to class, people shouted "Hello" at him, or stopped to shake his hand or high five him. He *was* the popular kid, or at least one of them, and liked by everyone. And he loved it. But he still searched for a deeper connection, like the kind he had had with Patrick. Longed for someone who could find that special space inside him. Actually, he'd found that, but the person he wanted to inhabit that place didn't notice him. Not in the way he wanted.

Scott pulled out the desk chair and fell into it. "I could use the time to study for next week's midterms, so I'm good not going to this party if you can't decide what to wear."

"This!" Troy picked up the T-shirt and pulled it on. When his head poked through the neck hole, he caught Scott checking him out again. That sent his heart into overdrive. He stepped into his jeans, taking a moment to adjust the bulge still in his underwear, and involuntarily flicked his eyebrows at Scott.

"Oh, don't look at me like that," Scott roared. "We had *that* conversation already. If you need to get laid, you better find some silly ass drunk at the party."

"You want it," Troy teased, zippering up his jeans. "You know you do."

"Someone's feeling better."

After a short silence, they burst out laughing.

But, really, Troy wanted it. He wanted Scott, now more than ever, since the night when Scott had taken care of him. It was a week ago, but to Troy it was like it had happened yesterday.

He'd heard the knock on the door, but the way his body ached he couldn't move. That was why he'd left the door unlocked.

"You decent?" Scott asked from the doorway.

"Yes," Troy croaked.

Scott came into the room. He carried a tray and set it down on the desk. "Are you hungry?"

Troy coughed, phlegm corralling in his mouth, and he spat it into the tissue-filled waste bin by the bed. "Not really."

"You should eat something." Scott eased himself on to the edge of the bed and placed the back of his hand to Troy's forehead. "At least your fever broke."

"I just ... can't ... get warm," Troy stuttered.

"Sit up. I want you to try a little of this soup. It's chicken noodle. My mom always made it for me when I was sick. And it should be easy on your stomach." Scott reached for the tray and set it on the bed between them. Then he lifted the bowl and held it close to Troy's face.

Troy, his hand shaking, moved the large spoon back and forth from his mouth. The whole time his eyes were glued to Scott. They didn't say anything. Barely six weeks since they'd met, they didn't have to speak when they were together. The warm soup settled his stomach, but halfway through he set the spoon down.

"No one's ever done anything like this for me," Troy said.

"It's what friends do." Scott placed the bowl on the tray, which he then returned to the desk. "We look after each other."

"You could be out ... on a date."

"With who? Danny Pintauro? The only date I've had lately has been with my right hand."

"T ... M ... I."

"Like you're a prude."

They laughed.

Scott stood. "Can I get you anything else?"

"Do you have to go?" Troy asked, panic rising in his voice. "It's just ... so lonely. I'm going crazy staring at these walls." He shifted to his right, making room in his bed for his friend.

Scott scratched his head and, after his mouth went dry, settled into the bed. With his back pressed up against the wall, he snatched off the desk James Joyce's *A Portrait of an Artist as a Young Man*, flipped to the bookmarked page and cranked his head at Troy. "You've only read to chapter two? The test's on Monday."

"Read some to me."

"Read to you?" Scott stifled his laugh. "Only because you're sick. Just don't fall asleep like you do in class."

As Scott started to read, Troy listened to the deep, at times chromatic, voice that cast a spell over him. Without thinking about it, he lowered his head onto Scott's shoulder and left it there. Scott didn't seem to mind. Then Troy drifted off to a dream world where he and Scott were in love and eager to give themselves over to each other in bed. The pillow crashing into his face broke his reverie.

"Where'd you go?" Scott asked, starting for the door.

"Nowhere." Troy tossed the pillow on the bed, then crossed quickly to the desk as the heat flared in his cheeks. No way he'd let Scott see how his face transformed into a tomato. He picked up the bottle of Eternity for Men and sprayed. "Ready."

"You're a horrible liar." Scott opened the door. "And don't be surprised if I'm gone by eleven."

"Sure." Troy pulled the door closed and locked it. "I bet you'll score tonight." *And if you do, let it be with me.*

"Ha-ha."

Troy lingered a moment, letting Scott go ahead of him. One more time, he trained his gaze at Scott's ass, and there was that spontaneous boner again. Was it just a crush or was it something more than that?

No, it wasn't just a crush. Yet he didn't have the courage to do the thing he wanted to most: make a play for Scott.

He couldn't risk the cost … at least not yet.

***

"I'M GOING TO CALL IT A NIGHT," SCOTT SAID.

"What?" Troy glanced at his watch. It was ten minutes to one. "Already?"

"Not really my scene." Scott took a step forward, but Troy's hand on his shoulder pulled him back.

Three hours after they'd arrived, Scott was ready to escape the crowded house on Croft Street, located a few blocks west of campus. For the past hour, longer than that, he hadn't talked to anyone. He stood alone in the living room, wedged between a black milk crate serving as a makeshift end table and the rickety IKEA bookcase. The walls vibrated to the thumping music. The air had a bluish tint from the cigarette and pot smoke spiralling above the crowd. He coughed every time he couldn't sidestep a big whiff of the smoke that rushed into his lungs. The stench had his stomach spinning faster than the teacups he always rode with his mother at the county fair. Occasionally, a screech or high-pitched laugh thundered over the music, dominating where many conversations colliding in the air could not. People, moving from one room to the next, squeezed in front of him, sometimes bumping into him and almost spilling his drink. They never said a word, barely looked at him. Like he didn't exist.

Scott was at the party only because Troy had coaxed him into it. The host, a muscled redhead named Evan Lorde, was one of Troy's poker buddies and had walked off before Troy could introduce them. No wonder Scott, at times, thought he was Troy's sidekick. In superhero terms, Troy was Batman and Scott was Robin. No one ever wanted to play with Robin. Troy was the one everyone flocked to while Scott, by the end of the second week of classes, had garnered a reputation for being a loner. Or was that loser? No one understood the pressure on him to succeed, what he had to prove — not necessarily to his parents but to himself. And while he'd never admit it to his mother, he shared her point of view: he was there to get an education, not party it up, and dedicated himself to the cause.

"I don't know anyone here besides you." Scott, looking coolly at Troy, shouted to be heard. "These are your friends, and it's not like I'll be missed."

"People, guys, want to get to know you." Troy took a swig of his beer. "You have to, I don't know, look interested and put yourself out there more. You may not realize it, but I get that you want to do well and that's why you study twenty-four-seven. News flash! There's a bold, new world outside of the library. C'mon, have a little fun." He leaned into Scott's ear. "Wallflowers don't get laid."

Scott placed his hand to Troy's chest and shoved a little harder than he had intended.

Troy, trying to hang on to his beer, tumbled backwards and crashed into the guy behind him.

"Jesus!" was the deep, guttural bark that cut through the air. The blond spun around, his eyes on fire and glued to Scott.

Scott held the gaze, and something inexplicable about those deep-set arctic blue eyes with their dramatic eyebrows made him swoon over the otherwise average-looking dude before him. He recovered quickly as the guy's angry glare softened. In that moment, he couldn't hear the thumping music or the raucous conversations swirling about him. His full attention was on the blond, who was wiping his beer-covered hands on his jeans. Their gazes locked again. Scott's imagination ramped up, him and that guy swept away in a dark room. Somewhere they couldn't see each other as they played out his secret fantasies.

"I pushed him." Scott swallowed hard. "It's my fault. I'll buy you a new shirt if —"

"What about me?" Troy asked, pointing to the dark spot on his thigh.

"It's just beer," the guy said, his voice gruff, his eyes still on Scott.

Troy raised an eyebrow and then, without saying another word, slunk away.

"I'm Anthony."

"Scott."

They shook hands.

"Is this how you always pick up guys?" Anthony grinned. "Spill a drink on them so they have to take off their clothes?"

Scott's mouth hung open. "No. It was an accident."

"Sure it was." Anthony flashed a coy smile, then drained his beer. "So…"

"I'm about to head out," Scott said, forcing the words that seemed contrary to his will. He wanted to shore up his sexual experience with men but didn't seem to have the nerve. "Sorry about —"

"If you're sorry … buy me breakfast."

Scott's heart raced. "What?"

"In the morning, you can buy me breakfast." Anthony flicked his eyebrows. "There's a diner down the street from my apartment."

Scott's cock twitched and he looked down. This was exactly what he wanted even though he knew it was wrong. Maybe not 'wrong,' but misguided. He'd only been with Edward and didn't want to come off as a novice. But he was. Did he have the courage to go home with a stranger?

"You're cute."

Scott raised his head.

Anthony took a step forward. "Can I kiss you?"

"Right here?"

"Why not?"

Before he could say anything else, Scott's body went rigid as the weight of Anthony's tongue crushed his. He kept his eyes open, surveying the crowd to see if anyone was watching, as he savoured Anthony's bitter taste. This wasn't like him. And he didn't want to be the guy everyone later whispered about for getting hot and heavy with a stranger. The kiss gained momentum, a longing so deeply buried in him surging with the force of a tsunami. Scott finally closed his eyes and just then Anthony pulled away.

"I take it we have a deal ... about breakfast?"

Scott chewed the inside of his lip. "Sure."

"We should go then." Anthony reached for Scott's hand. "It's going to be a long night."

They edged their way through the crowd and, near the front door, Anthony stopped to chat with a friend. Scott waited patiently, his eyes roving the hallway. His gaze latched on to Troy, who towered in the kitchen doorway and threw him a sneering smile. *What's that about?* But the thought was broken when the pressure on his hand increased, and he smiled as Anthony led him away.

The blaring music fell away as the door closed behind them. Still holding hands as they walked down the street and stealing sidelong glances of each other, Scott's heart cartwheeled wildly in his chest. He knew nothing about Anthony. Not his last name, where he was from, or if he was a student. But why, then, did he believe — even if he couldn't explain it — that this was the guy who would change his life?

Thanksgiving

THE TAXI CRAWLED DOWN THE LONG STREET with large houses that all looked the same, except for the colour of the siding and shape of the front doors. Sandwiched together on small lots and fenced off from each other. Perfectly manicured lawns. In the backyards, swimming pools tended by local pool cleaning companies. A suburban oasis, home to affluent families — doctors, professors, entrepreneurs — who'd tried to corner themselves off from the influences of inner-city life. Had they succeeded?

The yellow and black cab stopped at the bottom of the driveway to number 259. Scott reached for his wallet, but Troy was already handing over cash to the driver. He grabbed his knapsack from between his feet and scrambled out of the vehicle. He stood there a moment, watching the leaves float down a tranquil Hunters Run Drive, then focused his attention on the two-storey house in front of him. The house where he'd spent his youth, the house his father had built. Nothing had changed. Yet in the six weeks he'd been gone, he'd been hoping for some sort of transformation. Why?

A car door banged shut, and at that very moment Scott's stomach roiled. He was home again. With Troy Muir tagging along. Things *were* different. So was he. He knew it deep in his gut. Had *he* been transformed?

The anxiety that had built up during the train ride — a journey that seemed long — was back. This was his first trip home since leaving for university, and he'd brought someone with him. A friend. A confidant. A protector. Would his mother believe that they were just friends? When he called to ask if Troy could come for Thanksgiving, she'd tried to probe him for information on their relationship. But he said he was late for class and abruptly hung up. He couldn't explain — not yet, and not even to himself — why, despite the newness of their friendship, that his bond with Troy was special, real and deep. Just not romantic. But if she knew the truth… It was way too soon to go there.

Scott went rigid at the hand pressing into the square of his back.

"You all right?" Troy asked.

"I'm fine. Why?"

"You look … off."

"I'm fine," Scott said quickly. "Come on." He started for the house, relieved at least that only his mother's black Honda Civic was in the driveway. It was Friday night, which had long been his parents' date night. And if he had to venture a guess, they were probably having dinner at Red Lobster.

"I don't know," Troy said with a hint of suspicion. "You're not acting like you're fine."

Scott unlocked the door, shoved it open, then looked at Troy. "I've never brought anyone home before. I mean, not since I came out. You and I know we're not dating, but my mother…"

"It'll be fine." Troy cupped his hand to Scott's shoulder. "I'll lay on the ole Muir charm."

"That makes me feel so much better."

They stepped inside, the house silent and carrying a latent distrust. Lavender filled Scott's nostrils, and for the first time in years he felt like he *was* home. The purple flower was everywhere — in the vases on the occasional table in the foyer, the coffee table and dining room buffet. If he'd been a girl, would his mother have named him Lavender? In the kitchen, he found a note on the counter telling him there was a lasagne in the fridge and how to reheat it. Had his mother forgotten how much he had cooked with his grandmother growing up before drink got the better of her? He chuckled, put the lasagne in the oven and then gave Troy a tour of the house.

When the tour was over, they returned to the kitchen and sat at the table, Scott dodging Troy's gaze.

"You ever going to tell me what happened the night of the party?" Troy asked.

Scott's lips curled into a smile. "What do you mean?"

"You know what I mean." Troy leaned forward. "Don't be an ass."

"Do you want the short version or the play-by-play?"

Scott was stalling. He'd never imagined going home with a stranger. How many articles had he read about serial killers that always had Jeffrey Dahmer's face splattered on the page? Enough to make him weary of random hookups. But that night, Anthony's boldness lit the embers of desire, and as much as he wanted to resist him, he couldn't. The last thing he wanted, too, was to be the guy who shared every detail about his sexual experiences. Didn't want to be the one everyone laughed at or mocked. No, he didn't want to be known as the campus slut.

"Your silence tells me everything," Troy said askance. "Must've been shitty."

"It wasn't shitty." Scott looked down, counting backwards from ten in his head. Damn it, he'd taken the bait. "Anthony's a nice guy. We have fun together. I can talk to him."

Troy's eyes narrowed. "Are you dating?"

"Maybe. I don't know." Scott levelled his gaze at Troy. "I don't really know how to tell if we're dating."

"Are you screwing anyone else?"

"No!"

"Is he?"

Scott held his breath. "Actually, no. He said he wanted to 'see where this goes.'"

"Scott has a boyfriend." Troy slouched down in his chair. "That didn't take long."

The oven timer dinged and Scott rose. "Please don't bring it up this weekend. My mother, God love her, is still uncomfortable talking about the whole gay thing. I'm not going to tell her Anthony's my boyfriend after two weeks of dating. That would send her into a tailspin."

Troy drummed his fingers into the table. "You think he's 'the one?'"

"I don't know." Scott removed the lasagne from the oven, cut out two large squares and set them on the plates his mother had also left on the counter. "He's just —"

"He's just what?' Troy interrupted, his tone sharp.

"Easy to be around."

"Fuck, don't fall too hard for a guy you barely know."

"I'm not. I'll take it slow." Scott handed one of the plates to Troy. Seated again, he added, "Try not to swear. My mother's kind of ... devout."

"I don't swear. Fuck, don't make it sound like I have a potty mouth."

Scott bristled. "That's what I mean. And don't go all Perez Hilton on me, either."

"Now that's just rude," Troy said, devouring his meal.

They laughed. That was what Scott wanted his mother to see. His and Troy's friendship, that they understood each other. A friendship that manifested during their first week at university when they both ditched the frosh week activities to explore the city. They binged on Chinese food in Kensington Market, and visited the Royal Ontario Museum and Art Gallery of Ontario. Despite Scott being underage, the bouncers at most of the bars on Church Street let them in without checking their IDs. Troy had become to Scott, in a real, deep way, like a brother. That was why Scott wanted this weekend to be perfect. He wanted his parents to see how grown up he'd become.

The faint thud of the front door closing carried into the kitchen. Scott chewed the last piece of his lasagne. An acidic taste crept into his mouth when his parents appeared a moment later, a stony silence immuring them all.

"Mom, Dad," Scott said, breaking the tension, "this is Troy."

"Troy?" Margaret looked wide-eyed first at Scott, then Troy, and finally back to Scott.

"A pleasure to meet you, Mr. and Mrs. Davenport," Troy said, moving across the room to shake their hands.

"*This* is Troy?" Margaret asked, the shock in her voice undeniable.

"Yes, Mama." Scott sighed. "Remember our conversation on Monday? I told you —"

"Yes, but..." Margaret scrunched her eyebrows. "You never said he was —"

"So tall," Terrence cut in. "You must be six-three, six-four?"

"Six-five," Troy said.

Terrence simulated dribbling a ball, faking right, then left. "Ever play basketball?"

"Tried tennis for a while." Troy imitated an overhand serve. "Didn't have the agility for it."

"Well, if you'd have tried basketball, I bet you'd have been the next Larry Bird."

Troy scrunched his eyebrows. "Who?"

"Did you eat?" Margaret asked, eyeballing Scott as she reached for the floral apron hanging on the back of the door.

"Yes," Troy said. "The lasagne was delicious."

Scott manoeuvred around the kitchen island, away from his mother. "Troy and I are going to watch TV for a bit."

"Don't stay up too late," Margaret said, tying the apron strings around her waist.

"We won't." Scott stopped at the doorway. "I put Troy in Frank's old room."

"Oh. I thought…" Margaret, her mouth open, turned to Terrence for direction but all he offered was a languid shrug. "All right."

Scott waited a moment to see if his mother would say anything else, but she started busying herself in the kitchen. Like he wasn't there. *She doesn't like him*, he thought as he left the room and caught up to Troy in the hall. Really, he didn't know what she thought. She sported that unflinching poker face that always made his father, and him, fold.

Falling onto the sofa in the den, Scott's heart sank. What did he have to do to earn his mother's approval?

He had no idea. No fucking idea.

***

"SCOTT NEVER SAID HE WAS WHITE," MARGARET said, collecting the dirty dishes from the kitchen table, when she and Terrence were alone.

"Oh, Margie, you're too much." Terrence leaned in and kissed his wife on the cheek. "But … you said he was Scott's boyfriend."

"I assumed…" Margaret, after placing the dishes in the sink, threw her hands in the air. "Maybe, or, well —"

"Maybe they're not out yet as a couple."

"A couple." Margaret weighed that up, the horror twisted in her round face. "A couple? A couple? Oh, dear Lord. Oh, dear Lord." She fanned herself with her hand.

"Oh, Margie, calm down. Breathe." Terrence stood behind her and massaged her shoulders. "Forget what I said. You know I don't know much about *that* or how it all works. Whatever it is, let's just hope he's happy."

"A couple?" Margaret leaned her head back to rest on Terrence's shoulder. "Lord, I believe…"

***

IT WAS THE NEXT MORNING, AND SCOTT couldn't wait any longer. Troy had been in the bathroom almost an hour, and he knew his mother was holding breakfast for them. She wouldn't eat without them. He tapped twice on the door. "Are you ready yet?"

"Fuck, give me a minute," Troy grunted from the other side.

Scott drew in a deep breath, held it for five seconds, then pushed it out slowly through his nose. He repeated the exercise until the door flew open. "What did I tell you about swearing?" he said through gritted teeth, then led the way downstairs to the kitchen.

The doors to the dining room were open, which was odd. The room was reserved for special occasions like holidays and birthdays, not an ordinary morning breakfast. Not even at Thanksgiving. They moved towards the voices and, at the dining room doorway, froze. They didn't know what to think of the scene before them. And it took a moment for Margaret's, "Sit down," to register.

They pulled out chairs across from each other and shifted their gazes between his parents seated at both ends of the long rectangular table. His mother had prepared a feast. Pancakes. French toast. Scrambled eggs. Strawberries. Melon. Bacon. Sausages. Currant scones. Baked beans. The type of meal she'd get up at four in the morning to prepare on Christmas and Easter.

"What's so special this morning?" Scott asked, spreading the navy-blue napkin over his lap.

"My baby's home," Margaret said, smiling. "That's special enough."

"Well, you really shouldn't have gone through so much trouble. But thanks." Scott went to load up his plate but his mother slapped his hand away.

"In this house," Margaret said, pointing her index finger at him, "we say grace." She reached for his hand, then Troy's, and nodded at Terrence before closing her eyes. "Dear Heavenly Father, we thank You for waking us up this morning and starting us on our way. We know that by Your grace and mercy, You will bring us through this blessed day. Thank You for returning Scott home safely to us, and for, er, oh dear I've forgotten his name … Stretch Armstrong. May You guide them in their studies. Thank You for my loving husband, Terrence. Be with us all as we partake of this food, that it will nourish our bodies and our souls. This we ask in Your precious, holy name, amen."

"Amen."

"Stretch?" Scott howled, and placed his hands to his cramping sides. "It's Troy."

"Well…" Margaret remained calm and unfazed. "He's tall and lanky, so Stretch it is."

Laughter erupted around the table.

"I hope you like the pancakes," Margaret said to Troy as he shovelled a forkful of food into his mouth. "They're Scott's favourite."

"Delicious." Troy chomped on a strip of bacon. "Best home-cooking ever."

"Well, thank you." Margaret reached for her orange juice. "Scott never told me how the two of you met."

"I picked him up in a bar," Troy said.

"Oh, Lord, have mercy." Margaret's glass slipped through her fingers and hit the table with a hard thud but didn't spill.

"Troy!" Scott's eyes were on fire. "That's not true."

"I'm kidding," Troy volunteered while lathering butter on a scone. "We live across the hall from each other, and Scott helped me when I was moving in."

Terrence gave Troy a thumbs-up. "Good one."

"Don't encourage him." Margaret shot Terrence a cool look before returning her attention to Troy. "And you're from Calgary. Don't you mind being so far away from home, from your family?"

"Nah," Troy said before driving more food into his round mouth.

Margaret twitched. "'Nah?' Have they substituted slang for English in this university of yours?"

Troy finished chewing. "No, ma'am. I don't miss Calgary. I don't really think of it as home."

Scott tried to catch his mother's eye but she purposely avoided him. She was a retired high school English teacher who'd been affectionately known as Mrs. Demonport for her strictness, especially when she supervised detention. Proper language usage mattered to her, and words like 'nah' and 'yeah' weren't tolerated. She could be ruthless, in a loving teacherly way, and he sensed that ruthlessness coming on. His mother was about to subject Troy to a brutal interrogation, as if he were a prisoner at Guantanamo Bay.

"Tell me about your family," she said. When Troy didn't respond, she cleared her throat. "I know I'm not talking into thin air."

"I have an older brother and sister," Troy said, "and a twin brother."

"There's two of you?" Scott faked disbelief, but he knew all about Troy's twin and the rift between them.

Troy stuck his tongue out at Scott, then turned to Margaret. "I got the looks, he got the attitude."

Scott pretended to choke on his food.

"And your parents?" Margaret asked, slicing up a sausage link. "What do they do?"

Troy fixed his gaze on Scott, who ignored the help-me-out-here look. "My father works for the Alberta government, a deputy minister or something like that. My mother's a social worker, or she was. Now she teaches at the university. Or she did. Maybe she still does."

"A teacher?" Margaret gave a slight nod of the head. "I'd love to meet her."

"You must be looking forward to Christmas and seeing your family," Terrence said, part question, part statement of fact.

"Nah…" Troy sat up straight. "I mean, no, not really."

Margaret set her cutlery down.

Scott cringed. He recognized that look, impertinent and sassy, with a hint of annoyance. That meant one thing: she was about to be *moved* by the Holy Spirit. He bit his lip, knowing nothing he said could stop the wrath about to be unleashed.

"Sometimes it's easier to love your family from afar," Troy said.

"Young man, I've never heard such rubbish," Margaret said. "Family is all we have in this life. When you're down and out, family is there. When you're in need, family is there. When you're alone, family is there."

"My parents divorced when I was twelve." Troy spoke with an unexpected edge. "They've remarried. I've spent most of my life at boarding schools. I'm used to being on my own and, er, there isn't a home to go home to, not really. I was always the one who stayed behind in residence during Christmas and March Break. Sometimes one of my teachers would invite me to spend the holidays with their family." He shrugged. "I'd like to believe that family is everything, but that hasn't been my experience."

"You mean you're not going back to Calgary at Christmas?" Scott asked.

"No." Troy downed his glass of milk. "I've already made arrangements to stay on campus."

"You'll spend Christmas here," Terrence decreed, avoiding eye contact with his wife, "with us."

Troy beamed. "I'd love that."

"Yes, well, I suppose that'd be okay." Margaret reached for Troy's hand. "But you mustn't give up on your family."

"When you meet my brothers tomorrow, you might think that a campus Christmas is the more attractive offer," Scott volunteered.

"Scott Christian Davenport!" Margaret picked up her fork and pointed it at him. "Don't you dare badmouth your brothers."

Troy stifled his laugh. "Christian?"

"I give new meaning to the word," Scott whispered, but loud enough for everyone to hear.

"Terrence!" Margaret's eyes were wild with disbelief. "Speak to your son."

"Scott, why do you egg your mother on?" Terrence drove the last piece of his pancake into his mouth. "You know how she is."

Scott and Terrence laughed.

"You are incorrigible, Terrence Davenport." Margaret tried not to smile. "Incorrigible."

"And that's why you love me so." Terrence grinned.

"I'm going to show Troy around the city," Scott said, then dabbed his serviette to his lips. "Tonight, we're going out."

"Out?" Margaret shuddered. "Out, where?"

"To the movies," Troy interjected so that Scott wouldn't have to lie. It wasn't a lie, just not the whole truth. "We're going to the late show."

"I don't want you seeing any movies where there's cussing or violence or sex," Margaret said.

"Then we'll stay home and watch *Bambi*," Scott countered.

"Scott…" Terrence drawled in his rough tone that indicated his displeasure.

"I want you home straight after the movie," Margaret ordered.

"It's Saturday." Scott fiddled with a corner of his napkin. "Afterwards, we're going … dancing."

"Dancing?" Margaret's voice pitched high and cracked. "Oh, no. You go to the movies and you come straight home. There's nothing good in those sin-filled, sweaty, sex-thirsty 'establishments' you call bars. No. No son of mine —"

"Margie…" Terrence flicked his thick eyebrows at his wife, then turned his attention to Scott. "Curfew's at two. Our house, our rules. Don't come home drunk. And if you get into trouble, call us."

Margaret slumped down in her chair. "Terrence!"

Terrence stood and collected Margaret's empty plate. Standing next to her, he said, "How quickly we forget some of the stunts we pulled when we were their age." He kissed the top of her head before heading to the kitchen.

"Two o'clock." Margaret's tone was sharp like a drill sergeant. "And not one minute later." She stood and left the room.

Scott and Troy scooped more food onto their plates and ate in silence. They listened to the whispering in the kitchen, Scott especially trying to make out what was being said. What did his parents think of Troy? Did they believe they were just friends? *Everything's all right*, he thought, but he was nervous again. *Just enjoy the moment.*

He thought about them popping in and out of the shops in the Byward Market, touring Parliament Hill and dancing the night away at The Temple. Instantly, his nervousness ebbed. He looked at Troy and, when their eyes locked, they exchanged faint smiles.

That was the moment he knew: everything would be all right.

Doubt

SCOTT LAY THERE ON HIS SIDE, WATCHED THE bare chest rise and fall, the rhythmic snoring almost as calming as the April rain steadily pelting against the window. He didn't know what time it was, maybe four thirty or five. Darkness still hovered outside the bedroom window. He'd been awake for some time, something in his dream that startled him, left him breathless and sweaty.

Studying the sleeping beauty next to him instilled a calm. This wasn't a dream. Without really searching, he'd fallen in love, met someone who made him feel alive. But a lot of people — mostly Troy and his mother — kept telling him not to rush. "He's the first guy you've seriously dated," Troy had said bitterly. "Don't you think it's dangerous to be moving so fast?" The only 'danger' was letting someone else's doubts sway him from what he knew to be true. What kind of life would that be? False. And there were no set rules to love, none that guaranteed a happy ending. All he could do was go with the flow. Yet sometimes he did wonder about the lightning speed of their relationship, but Anthony had reeled him in. And he was hooked. It wasn't just the explosive sex, either, although that pleased him. Anthony's quiet presence had a mystical, almost cathartic, power that protected him from the rising tide of chaos in the world.

No longer able to hold back, Scott ran his hand through Anthony's hair, sweeping the longish bangs out of his face. How had he ended up here? How had he been so lucky?

"Why aren't you sleeping?" Anthony murmured, his eyes closed.

"Couldn't. Bad dream." Scott leaned forward and kissed Anthony's forehead. "Instead, I'm watching a beautiful man sleep."

Anthony opened his eyes and smiled faintly. "He's not sleeping now."

"Sorry, I…" Scott rolled onto his back and stared at the ceiling. If everything was perfect in his life, why did he feel 'off?'"

Anthony propped himself up on his elbow and placed his hand on Scott's chest, pulling gently on the curly hairs. "What's keeping you up?"

"Nothing."

"You're lying." Anthony pinched Scott's nipple.

"That hurts!" Scott swatted Anthony's hand away.

"Then tell me what's the matter." Anthony straddled Scott's waist. "Or I'll do it again. Only harder."

Scott slid his hands inside the bedcovers, cupped his hands to Anthony's beefy butt cheeks and squeezed. Just the weight of Anthony on him had his manhood twitching. And massaging that ass, he'd already forgotten about Anthony's question, clearly set on other intentions. "Jesus!" he cried at the pain burning in his nipple.

"Talk to me," Anthony spat.

"I'm not sure…" Scott bit his lip. "I think I made a mistake."

"About what?" Anthony asked, panicked. "About us?"

Scott grinned and, holding on to Anthony's butt, brought himself forward until their lips met. "You're the one thing I'm absolutely certain about. I don't want the semester to end. I mean, going back to Ottawa —"

"We'll find a way to be together," Anthony broke in. "Maybe not every weekend, but often."

"I hope so. I'm already looking forward to September and being back with you full-time. God, I'll miss you." He fell backwards, pulled his hands from under the covers and rested them on his stomach. "I think I made a mistake about school, my major. I don't want to study English."

"Don't you want to be a writer?" Anthony slid off Scott and settled onto his side. "You told me how much you wrote during high school, and that you even wrote a novel."

"I did. But it doesn't … call to me."

Anthony placed his hand on top of Scott's. "Are you saying that because it's hard to make a living as a writer? Because it's not easy. But that doesn't mean it's impossible."

Scott pushed himself up in the bed, drawing his knees and the bedcovers to his chest. "There's something I never told you. Remember back in February when I started going to that study group? It wasn't a study group. I joined the student Liberal Association. I've been attending rallies, volunteering a couple hours a month at our MPs office, and at the last minute I signed up to run for secretary. Found out yesterday that I won."

"Why didn't you say anything?"

"We've never really talked about politics. I didn't want that to be the thing that drives us apart."

Anthony squeezed Scott's hand. "I wish you would've told me. You don't have to keep anything from me, but…" He slid his body closer to Scott. "Are you saying you want to be prime minister? Because that would be *hot*."

"I don't know." Scott shoved Anthony playfully and grinned. "I don't like what's happening to the country. The Bloc Québécois in Quebec, the Reform Party in the West. The country deserves better, and somehow I want to make a difference. Troy thinks I'm crazy."

Anthony withdrew his hand. "Troy knows?"

"One night we arrived back in residence at the same time. He'd just gotten out of class and I'd been at the monthly Liberal Association meeting. And when he asked me what I'd been up to I … I couldn't lie to him." Scott chuckled. "I knew he was from Calgary and that that's the conservative heartland, but I never… He nearly had a stroke when he found out I was a card-carrying Liberal. Honestly, I don't know how we're still friends."

"Troy's wrong," Anthony said with an edge. "You're not crazy."

"Right? That's why switching to political science makes sense. Do I want to be prime minister some day?" He pushed his pursed lips from side to side. "Maybe. All I know is that something in the body politic has to change. It's too negative and divisive. Maybe I could run for city council, or join the civil service."

"You can do whatever you want. You're smart, talented and sexy. I'd vote for you." Anthony held his breath. "Have you told your parents about your plans?"

"No. My mother…" Scott stretched out his legs and straightened the sheets. "My father wanted to run for office, but she was dead against putting the family's life under such scrutiny. I never thought we had anything to hide or be ashamed of. Well, maybe my alcoholic grandmother. Boy, could she be inventive with expletives when she was drunk."

They laughed.

Anthony reached for Scott's hand. "Well, you don't have to tell them you want to enter politics. Just say you want to study it, understand it better."

"True."

"And fuck anyone who says you're crazy."

Scott slid down in the bed and pulled Anthony on top of him. They kissed, their lips pressed together, mouths opened slightly but no tongue. What was he waiting for? Why was he holding himself back now? And when Anthony's hand cupped the back of his head, trapping him in place, he pulled away.

"What?" Anthony asked.

"Do you think I'll ever meet your parents?"

"Way to kill the mood." Anthony rolled back onto his side of the bed. "How did we go from talking about you changing majors to my parents?" After a short silence, he looked at Scott. "I'm sorry. You know that's complicated."

"I do." Scott shifted onto his side, then yanked on the sheets to cover his exposed ass and keep it warm. "I'd just like to see where you come from."

Anthony smiled wryly. "One day."

"Sorry. I won't bring it up again. When you're ready, let me know." Scott wanted to touch Anthony, but something made him hesitate, pull back. Instead, he slipped out of the bed.

"Don't go," Anthony pleaded.

Scott spotted his underwear sticking out from under his bunched jeans, snatched them off the floor and stepped into them. "I'll let you sleep."

Anthony crawled across the bed, grabbed Scott's hand and pulled.

Scott fell forward, pinning Anthony underneath him, their faces millimetres apart. His body shuddered when Anthony's arms tightened around him. They kissed, just long enough for Anthony's tongue to trace the back of his upper teeth, but kept their eyes open. *Damn, he's beautiful.*

Anthony smiled broadly. "Stay with me."

Moving Day

IT WAS HAPPENING AGAIN. LIKE SOMEONE HAD hit 'Replay.' Scott grasping at the freedom that dangled above his head. Another Sunday that was anything but ordinary or routine. A day that held the promise of something new and bold.

He had survived his first year of university and the long summer in Ottawa that followed. Now he was back in Toronto, the city that had claimed him and where he could, finally, be himself. He still thought of that first night with Anthony, and the graceful lovemaking, as the most remarkable moment in his life. It unleashed an avalanche of desire that tested his limits. He worried that their time apart would have pushed Anthony into someone else's bed. But on the pretence of visiting Troy, who had remained in Toronto, he spent almost every second weekend with Anthony. And their time together proved that their appetite for each other was insatiable. With classes starting in a week, Scott was hungry for the man who'd hooked onto him, and eager to play out his few remaining fantasies.

A car horn honked and Scott, pacing the sidewalk, spun around. His heart careened into his throat as the silver Range Rover, drawing behind it a cargo trailer, pulled up to the curb. While he was grateful that his parents had collected furniture for his new flat, he was — like a year ago — keen to be on his own again. Free.

"Oh, my baby," Margaret said, hopping out of the vehicle before it came to a complete stop and charging towards Scott.

"Hey, Mama." Scott returned his mother's bear hug.

"Let me look at you." She pulled away and sized him up. "Are you eating? You look thin."

"I've only been gone a week. And, yes, I'm eating."

Scott had wanted to return earlier, but Anthony had already given up his flat and travelled to Barrie to visit his parents before the move. If anything, he was exhausted from crashing on the lumpy sofa in the house where Troy had rented a room for the summer. It gave them time to catch up, hang out the way they used to before Anthony appeared on the scene.

"Hey, hey, Momma D," Troy cheered as he came out of the house and walked straight into Margaret's outstretched arms.

"So good to see you, Stretch," Margaret said as they separated. "Are you taking care of my baby?"

"I don't need taking care of, Momma D," Scott mumbled. He thought his mother might react to the nickname Troy had crafted for her but, as usual, she never flinched.

"I'm trying to, but he's a wild one." Troy glanced at Scott and offered a sly smile.

Margaret, turning to Scott, raised an eyebrow. "Is he, now…"

"Don't listen to him!" Scott barked.

Margaret returned her attention to Troy. "No money for a haircut?"

Scott snickered, watching Troy finger the long, wild hair almost touching his shoulders. "He's going for that David Beckham look. Or is it George Harrison? Hard to say." Pointing at Troy, he added, "He doesn't know who George Harrison was."

"Well, with school starting, maybe it's time for a trim," Margaret said dryly.

Terrence ambled towards them and shook hands first with Scott, then Troy. "You boys ready to do some heavy lifting?"

"Our roommates will be back shortly to help us out," Troy volunteered. "They're picking up some more cleaning supplies."

"But we can start with the lighter stuff." Scott palmed the key his father held out to him, then tapped Troy on the arm and headed for the street. He twisted the key in the silver lock, yanked down, and unhooked it. Grunting, he pulled on the heavy door and pushed until it slammed up against the side of the U-Haul trailer. That was when he saw his mother whispering to his father as she pointed at the two-storey, red-brick house on Borden Street. The look she flashed him, and the suspicion knotted in her face, had one message: I don't like this at all.

"You haven't even seen the inside," Scott said before his mother could speak.

"Do you see that?" Margaret glared at the pink-haired woman seated on the steps of the house next door and rolling a joint. She looked at Terrence, panic wide in her eyes. "I bet they call this Junkie Row."

"It's not a bad neighbourhood," Troy said, carrying two floor lamps up the walk. "And the rent is cheap."

"I bet it is," Margaret agreed.

Scott caught his mother shaking her head as she assessed the house. The large window on the first level had a crack near the bottom that meandered halfway up the glass pane, and that the previous tenant or landlord had patched with duct tape. The blue paint was chipped and peeling. Several boards on the porch steps had been replaced, but it still sagged steeply to the right. Admittedly, it needed some work.

The house had imperfections, blending in with the other dilapidated homes on the street, but Scott didn't mind. When Troy sent him pictures of the place, he had immediately seen himself in the house. It fitted perfectly with his lifestyle, somewhat imbalanced and fragmented, with holes that needed filling and rough patches sanding. But it held promise, and more importantly, offered him another chance at the freedom residence life had failed to deliver: to *feel* like he was part of something larger, part of a community.

Besides Troy, he hadn't connected with the other students in residence. Even participating in more of the residence activities didn't change their perception of him. There remained a wall — and an awkwardness that flared with a simple, "Hello," as he passed someone in the corridor — that couldn't be bridged. Like they existed on completely different planes. And except for Anthony, it was the same with the off-campus students he'd met through Troy. According to one of the guys at Evan Lorde's party, where Scott had met Anthony, he was 'Mr. Goody Two-Shoes' because he sidestepped the joint being passed around the room, wouldn't even handle it.

Scott and Troy had just come back outside when the banged up beige Ford Taurus pulled up in front of Terrence's vehicle. He grinned when Anthony emerged from the car, wanting to run to him and kiss him, but checked the urge. That would have to wait. And following behind Anthony was the muscular red-haired beauty named Evan Lorde. Scott saw the way Evan looked at Troy, the crushing desire, and was never sure why Troy and Evan had become friends but never lovers.

"Just in time," Troy said, greeting the men with a fist bump. Giving first names only, and leaving out their associations, Troy introduced Evan and Anthony to the Davenports.

"I understand that the four of you will be living here," Margaret said, her eyes darting between Scott and the U-Haul. "That's a lot of testosterone under one roof."

"Party central." Troy grinned, then grabbed a box from the trailer.

"Now wait just a minute." Margaret blocked the path between the boys and the house. "I know a little about Stretch."

"She means Troy," Scott said.

Margaret pointed first at Evan, then Anthony. "But I don't know anything about either of you. How you met, where you're from, what you're studying, if you go to church."

"Jeez, Mom, this isn't Twenty/Twenty."

"We were in the same English class," Evan said. "I'm from Vancouver and I'm agnostic."

Anthony glanced at Scott before adding, "I was raised Catholic, but now I'm more of an atheist."

"They're teasing, Mama." Scott shot Anthony a knowing look. "We're all good, young Christian men. Most of the time." He rushed to the trailer, grabbed the laundry basket filled with small kitchen appliances and charged ahead of the others towards the house.

"Once you get everything inside," Margaret called out, "we'll chat about God and all the good things He can do for you."

It didn't take long for Scott and the others to unload the trailer, respectfully taking direction from Terrence and Margaret to "Be careful" or "Take a break." Within two hours, everything was in the apartment. Much faster than the day before, when they'd hauled Evan's and Anthony's belongings into the apartment located on the second level. Their numerous beer breaks had undoubtedly slowed them down.

"I don't know about this," Margaret said, entering the apartment for the first time, her eyes trained on Scott.

The *look* was back, and Scott knew that she wasn't impressed by the fire engine red walls of the living room, or the dark stains in one corner of the ceiling. The hardwood floors had lost their shine and were covered with scratches and scuff marks. He moved to intercept but she quickly slipped into the tiny, grimy kitchen and gasped. Two of the four upper cupboard doors were missing, and of the two remaining one looked like it would fall off at any moment. He'd told her the landlord promised to replace the doors, and paint the walls white, but that look said she didn't believe him. He returned to the living room while his parents inspected the rest of the flat.

"This is barely liveable," Margaret said as she came back into the living room. "You expect your father and I to pay for this?"

Scott, discreetly holding hands with Anthony, bounced off the sofa. "It needs a little TLC. And I'm going to get a job."

"We'll talk about that later," was Margaret's sharp reply.

Evan, standing across the room next to the window, pointed at his watch. "We need to get going."

"You're not coming out to dinner?" Terrence asked. "We're taking Scott and Stretch, er, Troy out to celebrate their new home."

"We'd love to." Anthony glanced at Scott. "But we have an ultimate game. A win tonight and we make the playoffs."

Terrence rubbed his chin. "Ultimate?"

"Frisbee." Scott sniggered. "I don't get it either."

"We'll walk you out," Troy said.

"Hold on a minute…" Margaret turned around slowly. "There's four of you, but there's only three bedrooms."

Evan raised a hand. "I drew the shortest straw. I'm going to convert the dining room into a bedroom."

"Really?" Margaret eyed him suspiciously. "That hardly —"

"It makes it cheap, Mom," Scott cut in.

"Well, I never —"

"Mom, please…" Scott's tone was odd, a mix of frustration and restraint. "Evan and Anthony gotta go."

After a round of handshakes, the four friends raced down the stairs and out of the house. Standing in front of the driver's side door to block the view, Scott reached for Anthony's hand and squeezed it.

"See you later, cutie," Anthony said, smiled, and hustled into the vehicle. The engine, after a brief struggle, flipped over, and the car rolled down the street.

Scott and Troy headed inside and found Terrence and Margaret seated on the sofa. Boxes were lined and stacked against the wall behind them, and there was one on the coffee table with its lid open. Margaret, shifting her gaze to Scott, caught a glimpse of the condom packages and stiffened. She took the flowery throw pillow that separated her from Terrence and placed it on top of the box. Occasionally disrupting the awkward silence was the sound of a car whizzing down the street, or a loud thumping sound coming through the floor from the apartment below.

"It's not so bad," Troy said, sitting down on the window ledge. "Our own little frat house."

"Frat house?" Margaret sounded distressed, her gaze latched onto Scott. "I don't like this."

"Just imagine the parties going all night." Troy winked at Terrence.

"Oh, dear Lord," Margaret moaned, lifting her hand to her chest.

"Don't listen to him, Mom," Scott said askance.

"I'm kidding, Momma D." Troy curled his lips into a mischievous smile. "We'll be good. Most of the time."

"The Lord never gives me more than I can bear." Margaret dropped her head, like she was praying. "Lord, I believe. Help my unbelief."

"Troy!" Scott barked.

Terrence chuckled. "That boy sure does crack me up."

"He thinks he's the next John Ritter." Scott sucked his teeth.

"Doesn't resemble him much." Terrence turned to Margaret, who looked up. "You know, this place reminds me of my first apartment. Do you remember that dive on Hannah Street where you and I first —"

"Terrence!" Margaret turned her attention to Scott. "I don't know why you couldn't have stayed in residence," she said in her disciplinary teacher's tone.

"The walls were too thin," Troy said. He had slipped into the kitchen to grab two Coors Light but was back, handing one of the beers to Terrence. "You could hear everyone having…"

He caught Scott's glare and bit his tongue. "Oh, you know, it made it hard to concentrate."

"And I know you're not considering opening that," Margaret said to Terrence, who shrugged.

"Would you like one, Momma D?" Troy asked ruefully. "Or Scott has some white wine that we put in the freezer, but it may not be cold yet."

Margaret glared at Scott. "One year away from home and you're drinking now?" Disappointment settled into her round face. "The devil has a mighty grip on you."

"Come on, Stretch." Terrence placed his unopened beer on the coffee table and stood. "Let's get you some real beer." At the door, he cupped his hand to Troy's shoulder. "We might make a man out of you yet."

"Terrence Davenport, I'm not very pleased with you right now," Margaret said as Terrence hustled to leave.

"I know, Margie, but you love me anyway." Terrence blew her a kiss and rushed through the door after Troy.

At the thud of the front door closing, Scott took up Troy's earlier position on the window ledge. He folded his arms and looked warily at his mother. "Don't confuse me with grandma," he said with an edge. "I'm not her. I sometimes have a glass of wine with dinner, or a beer when I'm hanging out with friends. I don't put scotch in my morning coffee, or tell everyone that it's flat ginger ale."

"Don't use that tone of voice with me." Margaret adjusted herself on the sofa, sitting with her knees pressed together and her hands resting on her thighs. "I know these are challenging times, and that there's so much pressure to be this and do that but … you've never been one to follow the crowd."

"I'm not following the crowd."

"What did I tell you about your tone?" Margaret pointed at Scott with her index finger. "You may not be your grandmother, but you saw what drinking did to her life. I would think that that would be enough of a discouragement."

"Not everybody who drinks becomes an alcoholic." He could see his mother about to speak and raised his hands in defeat. Maybe his tone was different because being away from home, on his own, had changed him. He'd become almost a man. But he had to be careful. Being away from home didn't give him license to speak to her in a way he could tell she disliked. She was his mother, not some flake he could get away with flipping the bird. "I don't plan on ending up like grandma."

"Nobody plans on becoming an alcoholic, yet look at your Uncle Randy. Toothless, penniless and homeless. All because drink got the better of him. It's like ... it's in the blood. Do you want to end up like that?"

"Mama —"

"Don't Mama me." There was a silence. "Oh, Schnookums, I'm only concerned about you."

"I'm growing up. You need to let me do that."

"I know, but it's hard." Margaret brushed away angry tears. "It's hard to watch my baby become a man." She reached for her red purse that was on the floor and pulled out a tissue to dry her eyes. "Now tell me what's really going on here."

"What do you mean?"

"I mean..." Margaret, clutching her purse, drew in a deep breath and pushed it out slowly through her nose. "I want the truth about the living arrangements. I've never seen you get close to anyone the way you have with Stretch. Are you sleeping with him? Sharing a bed?" She was stunned by the questions as much as Scott was. "Oh, I'm sorry, baby. I just..."

"No, I'm not sleeping with Troy." Scott moved off the window ledge and dropped onto the opposite end of the sofa. "Troy is my friend. Maybe he's a bit more than that." At his mother's wide-eyed look of horror, he added quickly, "He's my best friend. The big brother I —"

Margaret's hand flew in the air, her index finger again pointed at Scott. "You *have* two big brothers."

"Everything between Neal and Frank and me changed after I came out," Scott said. "You know that. With Troy ... everything is easy. He gets me." He bit down on his lower lip. "There are times when I look at Troy and know he understands. I don't have to say anything, or don't even have to finish the sentence." He offered a wry smile. "Do you think that Frank and Neal would be interested in me talking to them about what it feels like when another man —"

"Oh, dear Lord." Margaret held her hand to her chest. "Okay. I didn't mean to pry. And sometimes I think you say things just to shock, and that isn't very nice."

"This is who I am, Mama. I like guys."

"Have you tried it with a girl, baby?" There was a certain desperation in Margaret's voice. "Maybe if you tried it and —"

"I have a boyfriend," Scott blurted out and looked down.

"A boyfriend? But you said you and Stretch are just —"

"It's not Troy."

"Let me understand this." Margaret sat up straight. "You have a boyfriend. It's not Stretch. So, how long have you had this 'boyfriend?'"

"About ten months."

"Ten months? And I'm just hearing about him now?"

"I wasn't sure you'd want to know."

"Oh, baby…" Margaret reached for Scott's hand. "I just want you to be happy. I don't get this gay thing, and I know at times it seems like I'm against it but I don't know how to deal with it all. You're my first gay son, and it's not like I have a manual I can flip open to consult." She took in a deep breath. "What's his name?"

Scott lifted his gaze. "Anthony Power."

"You mean?" Margaret released Scott's hand. "That scrawny little white boy who is living here, too?"

"Yes."

"You and he… One bedroom or?"

"One."

"Well, I…" Margaret blinked magnificently. "I don't know what to say. Wait. Yes, I do. I didn't like him at all."

Scott leaned back, cupped his hands to his head and dragged them downward until they rested on his lap. "Look, I know —"

"Aren't there any decent young black men you could date?"

"There's a lot of squeaking in these stairs," Terrence said, concerned, as he entered the apartment. "You better get your landlord to check them out."

Scott left the sofa so his father could sit. "We will."

"Where's Stretch?" Margaret asked.

"Right here," Troy said, out of breath, as he came into view. He set the two cases of Heineken down on the floor just inside the door and leaned against the wall.

"Don't tell me you bought both of those cases of beer, Terrence Davenport." Margaret folded her arms. "Let me tell you now that if you did, I'll be begging the good Lord for forgiveness for a mighty long time for the beating I'll be putting on you when we get back to the hotel."

Terrence dropped onto the sofa and pulled his wife into him. "Oh, baby, talk dirty to me."

"Ew," Scott and Troy said in unison.

Margaret pushed Terrence away. "Your son has a boyfriend."

Troy dropped his gaze.

Terrence smirked. "I know."

"You know?" Margaret said with a bit of attitude.

"Any fool can see that Troy and Scott keep playing at not being a couple." Terrence looked at Scott. "Every black man goes through his white phase. I had mine before I met your mother. Troy can be an honorary black man if that makes it easier for you, Margie."

"Your son is not dating Troy," Margaret said, panicked. "He's dating that Anthony Power."

"Oh…" Terrence hung on to the 'Oh' until it tapered off. "You mean —"

"Yes, that skinny white thing we met earlier," Margaret said, disapproval raging in her voice. "And they're living here together. Sharing a bed!"

"He seemed okay." Terrence pushed his pursed lips from side to side. "Now, he didn't seem as cool as Stretch." He pointed first at Scott, then at Troy. "Why aren't you two dating each other?"

Margaret hit Terrence on the arm. "Terrence!"

"If Scott and Stretch were together," Terrence said, looking at Margaret, "that'd make sense."

Margaret fell backwards into the sofa. "Give me strength, Lord. Give … me … strength…"

Scott, seated again on the window ledge, ran his hand over his face. "So, this is what hell is like."

Margaret placed her hand on Terrence's shoulder and pulled herself forward. "And do you hear the language your son is using now? I told you that we should never have let him leave Ottawa."

"Oh, Margie," Terrence said somewhat harshly, "stop being so dramatic." He touched his hand to Margaret's thigh when she stiffened at his tone. "He's not a child. He's got to do his own thing, make his own choices. That's the only way he'll learn. We can't hold his hand for his entire life."

Troy, uncomfortable by the discussion, started to retreat from the room.

"Not so fast, Stretch," Margaret called out. "I want to know what you think of this Anthony Power."

"He's a decent guy," Troy said, avoiding eye contact with Scott, "and he does seem to care a lot about Scott."

"I have a funny feeling about this Anthony Power and his shifty eyes." Margaret glanced at her watch, reached for her purse and stood. "Come on, Terrence. We have to return the U-Haul, and I want to go back to the hotel and freshen up before supper." She approached Scott and held her hand briefly to the side of his face. "I want us to sit down, you, Anthony, your father and me, so we can properly meet him before we head home. No excuses. I'll reserve judgment of him until then."

"Yes, Mama," Scott said.

"What about you, Stretch?" Terrence asked as he stood. "Does Margie have to put her seal of approval on your boyfriend?"

Troy gave a nervous laugh. "I don't have one."

"Then we'll have to set you up," Terrence said.

"Terrence!" Margaret grabbed him by the arm and dragged him towards the door. "Really. The things you say sometimes." She started down the stairs. "We'll pick you up at seven."

When the downstairs door closed behind Terrence, Scott shut the door to the apartment and turned over the deadbolt. He and Troy locked gazes, held in an awkward silence. Then they broke out laughing.

Scott picked up a box from off the floor and carried it into the kitchen. "Why are you single?" he asked when Troy appeared.

"I keep falling for guys who are already taken," Troy said, sulking.

"What about Evan?"

"He's not my type," Troy answered flippantly, watching as Scott emptied the dishes from the box onto the counter.

"Are you going to stand there and watch me or are you going to help?"

"Right..." Troy drawled and backed out of the kitchen. "I'll go see if I can remove the mildew from the shower tiles. I'm not stepping barefoot into that as it is." Then he was gone.

There were times when something Troy said caught Scott off guard. This was, again, one of those times. *Troy's fallen for a guy who's already taken?* he wondered. *God, who is it?*

Figuring out who the mystery guy was wouldn't be easy. So many guys liked that frat boy type and, with Troy fitting the bill, they threw themselves at him. And Troy gobbled up the attention. Did Scott really care why Troy was single? No. With Anthony in his life, he was too busy testing out many of his secret fantasies.

It was the ride of his life, and nothing could bring him down off the high.

And he was right. Anthony had changed his life ... just not in the way he'd imagined.

Let's Pretend

TROY STOOD IN FRONT OF THE DOOR, HIS KEYS in his hand, but didn't move. The voices and laughter coming from the other side had his insides burning. He'd never expected things to end up like this — Anthony, not him, lying down next to Scott each night. But he'd waited too long to say anything, make a move. Too afraid to be, in the most profound way, honest. At the second outburst of laughter, he jammed the key in the lock and opened the door.

Inside, his eyes immediately travelled to the living room and latched onto Scott leaning in to kiss Anthony on the cheek. Gritting his teeth, he closed the door and dropped his knapsack to the floor by the hall closet.

"Pizza just arrived," Evan said and bit off a piece of crust.

Troy didn't speak as he kicked off his shoes, eying Scott who'd yet to acknowledge his presence. Had he forgotten to deactivate his cloaking device? But Evan could see him, so he wasn't invisible. He hung up his jacket, then turned back towards the living room and waited. Nothing. Completely ignored as Scott stroked Anthony's hair. His jaw tightened, and when Scott rested his head against Anthony's, it was all he could do to corral the metallic-tasting saliva in his mouth and not swallow it. He bolted for the bathroom, bent over the sink and spat, wiping the drool from his lips with the back of his hand. After splashing water on his face, he remained hunched over, his elbows holding him up, his breathing deep and strained.

Calm down, he encouraged himself. It took a few minutes, but when his pulse was normal again he dried his face and shuffled to the kitchen. He grabbed a beer from the fridge before joining the others.

"How'd the exam go?" Evan asked.

"Fine," Troy said dryly, slumping into the blue and white striped chair Scott's parents had bought for the apartment. "And it was a quiz."

Evan yanked apart a slice of pizza, flopped it onto a plate and handed it to Troy. "Bet you aced it."

"Thanks." Troy took the plate, but he didn't have much of an appetite watching Scott fuss over Anthony. "Maybe the lovebirds should go to their room."

Scott sat up. "Hey, Troy. How long have you been there?"

Anthony released Scott's hand and picked up his beer. "You coming out with us tonight?"

Troy folded his pizza slice in half, bit off a huge section and chewed thoughtfully, staring into his plate. When had this place stopped being home? The moment he realized Scott would never be his, not in the way he wanted.

"Troy," Scott said cautiously. "Anthony asked you a question."

Troy finished chewing, raised his head and trained his gaze at Scott. "No."

"You okay?" Scott asked.

"I'm fine." Troy rose. "And unlike the rest of you, I have class tomorrow."

"Not until tomorrow afternoon," Scott corrected. "You could come out for a bit."

Troy wolfed down the remainder of his pizza. "Got a paper to write. And, really, don't feel like it. But have fun." He started down the hall.

"Let him be," Anthony said. "He's been in a mood all week."

Troy froze. *Damn right, I'm in a mood. You don't know how lucky you are.* He almost turned around, tempted to rush Anthony and terrorize him. But no matter how angry, he wouldn't do that, wouldn't impersonate the schoolyard bully who used to rough him up. There were other ways to prove which one of them really deserved Scott's love. Instead, he tossed the plate in the kitchen sink, returned to the front hall to pick up his knapsack, then stormed to his room. He closed the door with a bang, collapsed onto his bed and listened. For a time, everything was silent. Then that heart-breaking laughter seeped under the door. He dug out his portable CD player from his bag, jammed the earbuds into his ears and pressed 'Play.'

That was one way, the only way, to beat back — temporarily, and never as long as he liked — the disappointment invading his heart.

***

THE NEXT EVENING, SCOTT, WEDGED INTO THE corner of the sofa, snapped his head back. His focus fixed on the page, the words of Thomas Paine's *The Age of Reason* blurred, flowed into each other. The moment his consciousness became aware of the unreasonable task at hand. No possible way, in his present condition, to reason meaning out of the sentences he kept rereading. His blinking slowed at the weight on his eyelids, which eventually closed. Gravity worked next on the book, slipping to the side as his grip loosened and finally crashing to the floor. His head fell forward, his mouth agape. Gone.

"Scott..."

He heard the somewhat strained voice, thought it was part of his dream, and didn't react. Then came the pressure on his shoulder and, as his body began swaying gently, he opened his eyes. "Jesus!" He pushed himself up, his breathing erratic. "What time is it?"

"Almost ten," Troy said, making himself comfortable in the wing chair. "Late night?"

"Kinda." Scott yawned. "Should've known better."

He hadn't planned on staying out until four in the morning. They were meeting up with a few guys from Evan and Anthony's ultimate league for drinks at Striker. He should have stayed home and worked on his political theory paper. They all should have. Evan and Anthony both had projects due next week. But they told him that one night out during the week, which was truly exceptional for him, wouldn't hurt. That may have been true until he found himself and the others hustling to Millennium and dancing the night away. Scott and Evan danced. Anthony, like always, remained on the sideline chatting with his friends. Then afterwards, they schlepped across the street to Hayley's, the twenty-four-hour diner with every table occupied at two thirty in the morning. He'd said to his mother that they were all 'young Christian men' most of the time. Good thing he'd emphasized *most*.

"What did it take this time?" Troy asked. "Two or three Mike's Hard Lemonade to get you drunk?"

"Three." Scott swung his feet to the floor, leaned forward, and held his thumping head in his hands. And he wasn't drunk. He was hungover, still resenting how Evan and Anthony strutted into the living room around noon acting normal. No headache. No roiling stomach. No buzzing in the ears. Ready to take on the world. "I should've stopped at two."

"Really…" Troy drawled. "You say that every time."

Scott raised his head and glared at Troy. "Bite me!"

They laughed.

"How's all that political theory going?" Troy stretched out his legs and crossed them. "Still happy you switched majors?"

"I am." Scott sat back slowly. "It feels good. And I think there'll be more job opportunities out there for me."

"You actually think you're going to become a policy analyst or an advisor of some sort?" Troy sucked his teeth. "You and I both know what you're going to do."

"I'm not going into politics straight out of school," Scott spat. "It doesn't work like that."

"Right timing, right place, right party…"

Scott reached for Paine's book that was on the floor and fanned the pages. "You said it was crazy."

"It is." Troy slouched down in the chair. "You're too nice of a guy to be subjected to that kind of bullshit. And if you believe you and Anthony are going to be together a long time, you better make sure he doesn't have any secrets. Oh, wait … he's still in the closet."

"Troy —"

"What does Momma D think? Oh, wait, let me guess. You haven't told her yet."

Scott scrunched his eyebrows. "What's wrong with you? Why are you being like this?"

"Like what?"

"Like, I don't know. But you've been in a mood all week. I was supposed to be the wallflower. You getting laid?"

Troy sat up and slid to the edge of the chair. "I'm your friend, Scott, and you can tell me anything."

"All right," Scott said nervously. "Is there something you think I should be telling you?"

"If you're not happy we can rejig the sleeping arrangements. It'd be easy to create a bedroom out of the dining room like we told your mom."

"What the fuck are you talking about? I am happy. In fact, I've never been happier."

"You don't really have much to compare to, do you? I mean, Edward doesn't really count."

Scott didn't know how to respond, or why, all of a sudden, Troy questioned his choices. There was something macabre about the way others tried to peer into someone else's life and dissect it. It disarmed his own sensibilities, had him second guessing if, in this moment, he was happy. But he and Anthony were strong. Unbreakable.

They looked searchingly at each other while the silence grew more stringent and fragile. There was still a sense of anticipation of something being owed. Scott saw it in Troy's eyes, but this time he wasn't taking the bait. They'd pretend nothing had changed between them when he knew — they both did — that Anthony had changed everything.

The tension eased at the key jiggling in the lock, only to rachet up a notch when Anthony appeared.

"How did it go?" Scott asked, pushing his books out of the way to make space for Anthony.

"It went," Anthony said, falling onto the sofa. "Group projects suck when you have dead weight. Only three of us came prepared. Now we're meeting again on Sunday. Written portion is due Wednesday, and if the other turds don't do their part, we're screwed."

Scott wrapped his arm around Anthony's shoulder, then kissed the side of his head.

Troy sprang from the chair and stomped into the hall.

"Evan asked me to remind you about tomorrow," Anthony called out after Troy. "Everyone's meeting at Striker around six for a pre-game drink."

The only answer was the soft thud of a door closing a few moments later.

Anthony swung his head in Scott's direction. "Do you know what's going on with him?"

"No, not really," Scott lied.

He knew but, for a few of the right reasons and more of the wrong, he was willing to ignore it. So, the best thing to do now was pretend ... pretend like everything was all right.

Moving abruptly, he straddled Anthony's lap and leaned forward until their mouths met. The kiss generous, in a way savagely wild, gave him freedom to imagine the world as he so long desired.

This Is It

SEATED ON THE SOFA WITH HIS JEANS AND underwear bunched at his feet, Troy scrambled for the remote at the sound of the key in the lock. Trembling, he dropped it, then fumbled to pull on his jeans and do them up. As the door to the apartment swung open, he had the remote in his hand again and pointed it at the TV. He tried to stop the video but all he managed to do was hit the 'Pause' button as Scott came into view. "What are you doing here?" he asked, breathless. He tucked his shirt into his jeans and made another attempt to pull up his zipper, this time succeeding.

"I live here, remember?" Scott kicked off his shoes before vanishing.

"I know that." Troy turned off the TV, then repeatedly tapped the remote against his thigh. "Weren't you and Anthony going to Striker? I thought I had the place to myself. Otherwise, I would have cleaned up the kitchen."

"Sure you would have." Scott reappeared in the living room, carrying two beers, and raised an eyebrow at the lube bottle on the coffee table. He handed Troy a can before crumbling onto the other end of the sofa. "Wasn't into it. Maybe I'm becoming an old fart, but I couldn't take the thumping music. I also need to finish my Modern Literature paper tomorrow, so staying out to three in the morning wasn't going to help."

Troy opened his beer and took a gulp. "You left Anthony there alone? God, you're trusting."

"He wasn't alone. Evan was there, too. Besides, Anthony and I don't have to do everything together." There was a silence. "What?"

"Nothing." Troy lifted his beer to his mouth.

"No, no." Scott wedged himself deep into the corner of the sofa. "You have something to say. Say it."

Troy spoke into his lap. "I don't get what you see in him. You're the one always showing affection. A swat on the butt or a kiss on the cheek. He barely looks at you when he comes into a room. I've never seen *him* kiss you. You've been together almost two years and you've never been to Barrie to meet his parents."

"I've met his sister, Claire," Scott countered. "And what do you care if Anthony's affectionate with me or not? We bring different things to the relationship."

"It just seems odd."

"Maybe you could try getting to know him better," Scott said with an edge. "Lately, every time he comes into a room, you walk out. What's up with that?"

Before Troy could answer, the apartment door flew open and Evan appeared.

Scott looked at his watch, then at Evan. "Where's Anthony?"

"Hanging out with some of the guys from the ultimate team," Evan said, avoiding eye contact with Scott. "I need a break from the bar scene. Jesus, guys are pigs."

They laughed.

"Grab a beer," Troy said to Evan.

"Would love to, but gotta be at work by nine." Evan started down the hall. "Night."

A few seconds later, a door banged shut.

Troy had caught the slight twitch of panic when Scott checked the time, and although he wanted to prod a little more, decided to take a softer approach. "Look, your relationship with Anthony is none of my business. Sometimes I forget that." He studied Scott, who graciously sipped his drink. And imagining those full, reddish-brown lips pressed against his own instead of the can had him hard. "You just deserve to be happy."

"Did Anthony do something to piss you off?"

Yes, Troy thought. *He wiggled his way into your life before I had a chance to ask you out.* "We see the world differently. That's all."

"Then you'll be happy to know that Anthony and I have decided to get our own place," Scott said flippantly.

Troy sat there with his long fingers wrapped around his beer can and his gaze trained at Scott. *This has got to be a joke*, he thought. But he knew how heady in love Scott was with Anthony, how blinded he was. *Why can't he see Anthony for what he is? A fraud!* There wasn't much Troy kept from Scott, except how much he disliked Anthony. It wasn't necessarily Anthony's shifty eyes, although there was that. There was something deeper. He wasn't Gary Spivey, but he sensed Anthony was holding back on Scott, that he wasn't truly committed to them. And still something else, something dark inside himself that he couldn't shake, couldn't squash. "When?"

"For the beginning of the school year," Scott said, as if it should have been obvious. "That'll give us time to figure out what to do with this place."

"Was this your idea?"

"No, actually. Anthony suggested it."

"Do you love him?" Troy asked, his tone imperious.

Scott bristled. "What type of question is that?"

"A straightforward one." Troy clumsily raised his beer can to his mouth, liquid running down his chin, and used the back of his hand to dry his face. "Has he told you that he loves you?"

"We freakin' share a bed. We've done so for that past nine months."

"That doesn't answer the question!"

"What the fuck?" Evan, sporting only his Mickey Mouse boxers, stood in the hall outside the living room and rubbed his eyes.

"Sorry," Scott said and moved to the window, keeping his back to them.

Troy eyed Evan. "Did you know?"

"Know what?" Evan snapped.

"That Scott and Anthony plan to get their own place!" Troy barked.

"Yeah, I knew." Evan folded his arms. "It's not a big deal. We'll find another roommate. But could you keep it down. I'm trying to sleep." He shuffled down the hall.

"Why are you just telling me now?" Troy asked when he was alone with Scott.

Scott spun around. "Because…"

"I saw the look on your face when Evan came home alone." Troy gulped the last mouthful of beer and set the can on the coffee table. "You think he's —"

"Why are you being so mean?"

"I want you to be certain about this. Absolutely certain."

"I … am."

"Are you?" Troy glared at Scott. "You don't sound certain."

"I thought you'd be happy for me," Scott said, his voice unsteady. "This just makes sense for us right now."

Troy's eyes widened. "Does it? What does it say about a guy who stays at the bar after his boyfriend, who he lives with, goes home?" He shook his head. "Remind me again how long you've been dating? Right. You still haven't even met his parents, yet this is the guy you want to live with?"

"I moved in with you without meeting your parents."

"Don't be an ass."

"He's not out," Scott spat. "And *you* know what it's like having a family that doesn't approve."

"That's a low blow." Troy stood. "How do you know he isn't…" He censored himself at Scott's wild look. "If this is what you want, you don't need my approval." He took a couple of steps towards the hall.

"You're my best friend, my brother. I want you to be happy for me."

Troy, when he reached the entryway, turned around and hunched his shoulders. "Anthony's your boyfriend, not mine. Look, Scott… What you do and who you do it with is none of my business. But for the record, I'll tell you this. You can do better than Anthony. Again, that's not my call."

"For Christ's sake!" Scott shouted. "You're supposed to be my best friend, and you're just telling me this now? Thanks a fucking lot!"

"I told you," Troy protested, "in a myriad of ways. And just like you said, mostly by leaving every time Anthony came into a room. But you didn't seem to get the message." A stony silence immured them as they stared critically at each other. Scott turned his back on him, and that was when Troy started down the hall.

In his bedroom, Troy collapsed onto his bed. His head was spinning and his stomach doing somersaults. He could taste his dinner edging its way up his throat. This was it. The moment he knew was coming but that he dreaded. His friendship with the most important person in his life — and his world — was coming apart at the seams. Was there anything he could do to stop the implosion?

Maybe. If he could find a way to cleanse himself, wash away a desire that was wrong. Was it wrong?

He had to *do* something, or he risked becoming an accidental man.

***

"DIDN'T CATCH YOUR NAME," ANTHONY SAID.

"Thought it wasn't necessary," was the surly reply.

"Guess it's not." Anthony sat on the edge of the bed and next to him, with less than a foot between them, was the nameless guy he'd picked up at Striker. Or was it the other way around? It didn't matter. He knew that, pushing to the side his wet bangs and then pulling on his socks.

"It was fun." The guy stepped into his grey boxer briefs. "But it's late."

"Right..." Anthony drawled, dressed quickly, and was then escorted to the front door by his bare-chested host. After slinking into the corridor, he spun around, but before he could utter a word the door closed in his face.

Had he expected more from his surprise lover? The sound of the deadbolt turning over made him stagger, then he couldn't move. Just stared blankly for a time at the brass-plated '1407' on the door until it blurred. His vibrating phone slowly brought him back to reality, and he pulled it out and read the message on the screen: *Where are you?* He shoved it back into his back pocket without responding and started for the elevator, with each step swallowing regret. Regret, not guilt. That disturbed him somewhat when it should have frightened him.

Be yourself. A mantra Scott repeated whenever they talked about their dreams and what they wanted to be. Advice Anthony wanted to heed, but the world he lived in had consequences for 'wrong' decisions. Be yourself? He couldn't risk it if he wanted to hold his life together, stay in a world he knew how to navigate. The labyrinth, as much as it took away his power, also gave him life.

That meant he had to do something. But was hooking up with a stranger, when he wasn't single, the answer? Maybe all it proved was that he wasn't willing to invite Scott into his labyrinth. After all, this wasn't his first indiscretion. Five days ago, on a night when he and Scott were considerably drunk and they had the apartment to themselves, he'd slurred, "We could be this noisy every night if we had our own place," in the middle of the sex act. He wanted to call it back, pretend like he'd never said it, but Scott instantly agreed. Since then, Scott was on the hunt for an apartment.

He and Scott may have been sharing a bed, but having Evan and Troy around made it more like four friends just hanging out together. Nothing serious or complicated. Getting a place alone with Scott was too big of a move, and he wasn't ready. He should have gone home with Scott, but ever since their talk about moving he'd been unsettled. Was that why he'd also reactivated his account on Man Seeker? Twice he'd logged in, browsing the profiles, but when the messages exchanged became explicit and there was an offer to meet, he couldn't resist. And then he ended up with the guy from the bar. Was he willingly trying to sabotage his relationship with Scott?

They were twenty and barely men. What did either of them know about love? There were other issues to consider. His parents paid his rent, gave him a generous weekly allowance, but didn't know he — or the guys he lived with — were gay. They'd been vocal about their opposition to that lifestyle. And him moving in with just Scott would be a red flag.

It was almost three in the morning when Anthony entered the silent dwelling, tiptoeing down the hall and into their bedroom. He quietly undressed and contemplated the still mound in the centre of the bed. *Fuck, what am I doing?* Anthony climbed in and wrapped his arms around Scott's warm, slender body. It was wrong, for a myriad of reasons, but when Scott rolled over and kissed him, he gave himself over to the man who loved him in a way he wasn't capable of reciprocating.

As Scott tugged at his underwear, he could see his world — with its comforts and security — falling down around him. That had him buckling, questioning everything, yet he couldn't see his next move.

God, this is fucked up!

***

"I FOUND IT," SCOTT SAID, THE EXCITEMENT brimming in his voice.

Anthony, naked and stretched out on the bed, sat up. "Found what?"

"Come see." Scott, seated at the desk that wobbled with each keystroke, scrolled to the top of the page on the monitor. Then he turned back towards the bed, his gaze locked on Anthony, who hadn't moved. "You've got to see this."

"Why don't you just come back to bed and show me later."

Anthony flashed that seductive smile that Scott couldn't resist and he heeded the call, rising to join him. And just before they kissed, the warm hand gripping his slightly painful erection almost made him explode right then. Anthony's deep groan made his back arch. This was good. Too good? Not just the sex. Them. The way they moved together, navigating through life like they knew they'd be together forever. Solid. Determined. Unbreakable. Maybe they were young. And, yes, they had their whole lives ahead of them. But the power of their love was real. Scott was certain of that and one other thing: he'd found his soul mate.

Breathless, they lay there holding each other, unable to look away, exchanging shy smiles as if this had been their first time together. Silly. Giddy. Happy. This was a moment Scott would never forget, when everything in his world was right and orderly. Anthony sliding into bed and enveloping him had eased his doubts, erased his fears. This Sunday morning was his beginning, the beginning of him being a part of something greater than himself.

Scott ran the back of his fingers over Anthony's smooth face. "I love you, you know."

"I know." Anthony took Scott's fingers and kissed each one. "That makes you crazy, you know."

"Maybe." Scott, his heart pounding, waited. Would Anthony say 'I love you' back? He wanted to hear it. Badly.

"You're pretty fantastic, too."

Scott tried to smile but wasn't sure he succeeded as his lips remained tightly pursed. That wasn't 'I love you,' but for someone as cagey as Anthony, maybe that was the best he was going to get at the moment. It was more than the 'ditto' usually offered. As much as things were 'perfect' between them, and for as long as they'd been together, why hadn't Anthony ever used the word 'love?' Scott didn't want to believe it, but maybe Troy was right. It *was* odd that he'd only met Anthony's sister. So many times they'd talked about spending a weekend in Barrie, where Anthony's parents lived, but their plans always fell through. Anthony was sick, his parents were out of town, or there were already other guests visiting the familial home and there'd be no place for them to stay. Was Scott the only one thinking about how perfect they were together?

The silence lingered, and now Anthony's hands on him resurrected old feelings of doubt and suspicion. *I have a funny feeling about this Anthony Power and his shifty eyes*, he remembered his mother saying. Was she right? No, she couldn't be. It was just her being overprotective. Nothing new there. Yet the absence of a declaration of love — when he thought he'd given his all — had him second-guessing everything. Maybe he was the fool for believing that there was no one else in the world like Anthony, whom he trusted implicitly, who had seen deep into his core.

"I should get started on my paper." Scott rolled away from Anthony and moved off the bed. With only the use of the small stream of light from the sides of the blind, he scavenged the dresser and closet for something to wear. He'd shower later. Right now, he had to escape. Dressing hurriedly, he grunted when he realized he'd pulled the T-shirt on backwards, then heard a tear as he struggled to readjust it. "Fuck," he mumbled, his eyes skimming the room but circumventing Anthony. He could not look at him, the disappointment ravaging his insides set to unleash an explosion of tears.

"What did you want me to look at earlier?" Anthony asked.

"Don't worry about it. It can wait." Scott, securing his belt, heard the squeak of the bed, then the soft shuffle of feet against the floor. And when Anthony's hairy arms wrapped around his body, it was like he'd collapsed inwards, held in a state of grace. Something had come over him, a sort of stoical consolation: a feeling he didn't quite understand but, at that moment, breathed new life into him and his dreams.

"Show me."

The hot breath in his ear had his lips twisting into a smile and he gently pulled out of Anthony's hold and stepped to the desk. He clicked the mouse, the computer humming as it came back to life, and pointed at the screen. "It's a two-bedroom on Gerrard Street, just east of Yonge. It's not exactly close to the university, but it's easy to get to with the TTC. And the rent is pretty reasonable."

Anthony slid past him, eased onto the rickety wooden chair and studied the screen. Scott's eyes roamed the naked body that he wanted to pull against him. His mind wandered, almost feeling his hands glide over that hairy slender belly and then reaching for the beefy ass. If he gave himself over to his thoughts, and the other 'bad' ideas surfacing, he'd never finish the paper.

"Looks pretty good to me," Anthony said, business-like.

"We can go see it tomorrow."

"Tomorrow's not great. I have that ultimate tournament in London. Evan and I won't be back until Tuesday evening."

"Right..." Scott moved his eyes off Anthony and into the darkness of the space behind.

Anthony stood and wrapped his arms around Scott's neck. "You go see it. And if you think we'll be happy there, take it."

"I think it's something we should do together."

"I know. But if we wait, someone else could snap it up." Anthony leaned in and pressed his lips briefly to Scott's. "I don't want you to be disappointed."

Scott placed his hands on Anthony's butt, squeezing the hairy cheeks, and smiled. "You're right. It looks like a gem. I don't want to miss out on it."

They kissed again, and when Anthony's tongue slipped over his lip, tasted him, the excitement ramping up peeled away what seemed like a long season of doubt.

Anthony broke the kiss and rested his forehead against Scott's. "Stay a little longer."

"I can't." Scott reluctantly took a step back. "Finals are less than two weeks away, and I'm not even halfway through my paper. I don't know why I wanted to take courses in the spring session. They're killing me."

"Yes, you do. You're a nerd."

"Ha-ha."

"If you need a break, come back to bed."

Scott kissed Anthony again, intentionally missing his mouth and making it more like a peck on the cheek. Then he left the bedroom, not turning around to see that delectable booty calling to him. He wouldn't let himself be baited.

Settled in at the kitchen table covered with the books he'd checked out from the library, he tapped the point of his pen against his notebook while staring blindly at the blank page. Everything around him was spinning, and he couldn't stop it. He had a man. They had a plan to move in together. He was happy.

Maybe that meant he no longer had to try to figure things out, where he fitted in. Maybe by being with Anthony — and looking to the future they'd build together — he had it all worked out.

The Betrayal

THE SHRILL OF THE PHONE CUT THROUGH THE dead silence, but Scott didn't flinch. He sat there, in the living room of his new apartment on Gerrard Street East, sipping his fourth Harvey Wallbanger. The dim light from the candles, casting a blackness over the room, kept the spiralling reality at bay. Drink was his only consolation from the betrayal that had left him broken. He rested his head against the back of the sofa, waiting to black out, waiting for a reprieve from the chaos stuck to him like a bad private investigator.

Desperate, he was, to clear his mind. Desperate to expel all memories of Anthony Power that lingered and pricked at his heart. Memories he wanted to bundle up, along with the accompanying hurt, into a neatly wrapped parcel that he could send far away. No need to include a return address because he didn't want the package back if it were undeliverable. He breathed deeply, hoping to drive out the great weight that, with each breath, clogged his airway like the plum seed he had accidently swallowed as a child.

The phone rang again, and again. He didn't budge, not until his cell phone buzzed. Then silence. Until…

Tap, tap, tap.

"Open the door!" was the order shouted from the other side of the door.

"Go away!" Scott hollered back.

"Scott, this isn't like you."

"Don't pretend to know —"

"We're not going away. Either let us in or we're going to make enough noise that your neighbours call the police."

Scott rose slowly and staggered to the door, which he yanked open. "Your being here doesn't change anything," he grunted. "How did you get in anyway?"

"The concierge let us in," Troy said, charging into the apartment ahead of Evan, "after I said you might be suicidal."

"Fuck off." Scott closed the door, returned to the living room and picked up his drink. "I'm not in the mood for visitors."

"You haven't been in the mood for much lately." Troy moved cautiously in the darkness. "Christ, what's this? A séance?"

"Lay off him," Evan spat.

Troy turned on the lamps on both end tables, blowing out candles as he navigated the room, then pointed at Scott's glass. "How many of those have you had?"

"Not enough."

"Maybe too many." Troy took a step forward, snatched the glass away and handed it to Evan. "Get rid of this."

Evan took the glass, stuck his nose in it, sniffed, then drained it.

Scott thought he might put up a fight but didn't. The owner of the Quik Mart where he bought his lottery tickets, the building's concierge, and his favourite barista all told him, daily, how tired he looked. The barista, a university student with spiked blue hair and a nose ring, was especially cutthroat in his assessment the day before: "Such wretchedness in your eyes today, Mr. Scott." Was that wretchedness still there? And could Troy and Evan see it? Scott lowered himself onto the sofa. "God, I'm such a fool."

"You're not a fool," Evan said, settling into the blue and white striped wing chair. "You're upset, and you have every right to be."

"He's right." Troy plonked down onto the sofa next to Scott and spoke calmly. "What Anthony did was cruel and unforgivable, but you've never let something stick to you like this before."

Scott rubbed his eye. "Isn't that what makes me a fool?"

Sticking to Scott, the way his grandmother's golden caramels stuck to his teeth, was Anthony's betrayal. More than a betrayal. An act so callous it had blindsided Scott, devastated him. Everything was set for their move — the lease signed, the security deposit handed over, the movers scheduled for the last Saturday in August. The day before the move, Scott was up early to finish packing the last of his belongings. He planned to help Anthony, who'd been slower at getting organized. At ten, Anthony left the apartment to get more boxes. "Be back in a bit," he'd said, sidestepping Scott's attempt to kiss him. 'A bit' stretched into an hour, and when Scott tried to call, there was no answer. The hours slipped by, and all of Scott's calls and text messages went unanswered. Finally, at ten minutes past seven, his phone rang. It was Anthony.

"Where are you?" Scott barked into the line. "Is everything okay? We're going to be up all night packing up your shit."

"I can't do it," echoed through the phone and stretched into a long silence.

"Can't do what?" Scott asked reluctantly.

"Scott, you're a nice guy, and it's not that I don't... My parents found out about me, about us. Maybe Claire said something. I don't know. And that doesn't matter now. They've threatened to cut me off financially if I don't..." Anthony sighed into the phone. "I've never really tried it like I should with a girl, so maybe —"

"I don't really understand what this is about. The money? The pressure to be straight and someone you're not?"

"I'm not like you," Anthony shot back. "I don't have scholarships —"

"Then it's about trying to please your parents and not be *you*. And then where does that leave me? Did you ever love me or was I just a good fuck?"

The new silence that set in had Scott plummeting into an abyss, a point of no return where he'd lose consciousness, where light would never reign. He couldn't think, put one goddamn word in front of another to form a sentence. It took four words — *I can't do it* — to completely unmake him.

"Scott, I —"

"Don't you fucking dare..." No matter how hard he tried, Scott couldn't stop the tears from streaking down his cheeks. "You could have said something before I signed the lease. Yet you said nothing. Nothing! I mean, you kept letting me fuck you all the while... I thought we were happy. I thought you were happy. And to do this now, and over the phone... You're a coward. A ... fucking ... coward!"

"Scott —"

Scott hung up. Something tightened around his neck, had him gasping for air — sucked him back into that dark abyss. And inside of him, a void that would never be filled again. He grabbed the hardcover thesaurus on the bed and hurled it at his bedroom door. Five seconds later, the door flew open and he turned away. He couldn't face Troy, didn't want to show the defeat knotted in his face. Why had he ignored all the signs that Troy said were suspect? Like Anthony's name absent from the lease. Anthony not offering up half of the security deposit. Anthony's muted enthusiasm for the move, for the idea of them starting a life together.

"Did he back out?" Troy asked, leaning against the doorframe.

Scott dried his face with the back of his hand before turning around. "Say, 'I told you so,' if you want. You've earned it." He dropped onto the edge of the bed, his eyes moist again and fixed on the long scratch in the floor.

"Look, Scott, despite my doubts…" Troy pushed off the doorframe and crossed to the bed. Seated, he wrapped his arm loosely around Scott's shoulders and gently shook him. "What can I do?"

"Don't say anything to anyone," Scott pleaded.

"I won't."

"I'll tell people … after the move tomorrow."

"Sure."

A loud bang, like a car backfiring, made Scott's body go rigid. Then he leaned forward, his head between his knees, and thought he'd be sick as Troy rubbed the centre of his back.

"Scott…"

"Moving in together was his idea." Scott sat up straight. "That's why I thought we meant something to each other. Why else would he have agreed to move in with me?"

"He never really agreed," Troy said, matter-of-fact, and fell backwards into the sofa as Scott stood. "If Anthony had really wanted to move in with you —"

"It always felt like everyone was against us, Anthony and me." Scott briefly cupped his hands to the back of his head. "Maybe I just wanted to prove everyone wrong."

"You're better off without him," Evan said ruefully. "Anthony and I were friends since the ninth grade when my family moved to Barrie. But in the last year he proved just how much of an asshole he can be."

"I loved him," Scott said emphatically.

"He didn't deserve your love." Evan bounced his knee up and down. "He cheated on you."

"You're lying!" Scott shouted.

Troy looked at Scott. "Why would Evan lie?"

"We were best friends," Evan said, meeting Scott's eye. "I thought I was supposed to be loyal to him no matter what. I should have said something before you signed the lease for this place, but I —"

"You knew?" Scott stepped towards Evan. "How could you not say anything? For fuck's sake, I can't afford this place on my own, and if I'd known that Anthony was..." He couldn't stop shaking. "You really need to leave."

Evan rose slowly. "Scott, I —"

"Get the fuck out!" Scott kicked sideways, his foot ramming one of the coffee table's legs and bending it slightly.

Troy scrambled to get in front of Scott and mouthed to Evan, "Just go."

After the door closed, Scott made a groaning sound as he crossed to the bookshelf in the corner. "Did you know, too? That Anthony was cheating on me?"

"No," Troy said firmly. "I would have punched his teeth in if I'd have known." After a short silence, he added, "You owe Evan an apology. You know that, right?"

"Whatever." Scott fingered the small, silver-plated lynx statue that Anthony had given him. "I posted a roommate wanted sign at the Student Services Centre. It's not that I mind having a roommate, I just feel desperate, like I'm going to have to settle for anybody. My luck, I'll end up with a big-time partier or coke addict."

"What about your parents? Can't they help you out a bit?"

Scott moaned and spun around. "I haven't told them."

"You haven't told them?" Troy took a step forward, his eyes wild. "Why not?"

"You have to ask?" Scott returned to the sofa. "It's one thing to hear you say, 'I told you so,' but I don't want to hear that from my mother."

"Momma D, gloat?" Troy flicked his eyebrows. "Don't be ridiculous."

They laughed.

Troy approached the sofa and cupped his hand to Scott's shoulder. "It's good to hear you laugh again."

"I know I'm not the first person to get dumped but…" Scott couldn't help tearing up. "It's just how he did it and the why. Or maybe the 'why' is a lie."

"You have to let it go, Scott."

"I know." Scott drew in a deep breath. "Why couldn't I see it?"

"You didn't want to. Pride —"

"Finish that sentence, and I swear, I'll —"

Troy waved Scott off. "What if we…" He sat down, shifted his body slightly and shot Scott a knowing look. "What about us being roommates?"

"You just can't move out," Scott said dismissively. "Evan will be pissed. And what about Janice?" Janice Muller had been the first person to answer the 'Room for Rent' ad he'd placed once he signed the lease for the Gerrard Street East apartment. Evan liked her, but she and Troy hit it off after discovering they were both aiming for med school. "I know it's only been a couple of weeks, but I thought things were going well."

"They are." Troy let out a nervous laugh. "Her boyfriend is there all the time. Tom's a nice guy. He's, er, vocal."

"Vocal?"

"When he and Janice are having sex."

"Oh," Scott said, but it sounded more like, "Ew."

"Tom's been having roommate issues for months and he's looking for a place." Troy picked up his cell phone and flipped it open. "Let me text Janice and see what she thinks."

"Troy…"

"It's not like you don't know what type of roommate I'd be."

"Intolerable," Scott mumbled.

"Ha-ha." Troy pushed the buttons on his cell phone and pressed the 'Send' button. Thirty seconds later, there was a beep. "Janice thinks it's a great idea. And Evan won't give a fuck."

"You don't see it."

Troy scratched his head just above his ear. "See what?"

"Evan … he *likes* you."

Troy sucked his teeth. "He's not my type. Anyway, are we roommates?"

"I'll think about it."

"You'll think about it?" Troy swiped playfully at Scott's arm. "I'm pretty certain that I'm homeless."

Scott tucked his legs underneath his body and yawned. "It's getting late."

"Nah-uh." Troy pointed back and forth between himself and Scott. "*We're* going out. You've had your time to mourn. Now you're going to rejoin the world and have a life. So, get your wallet and keys and let's skedaddle."

Scott's eyebrow arched. "Where do you come up with these words?"

"It's the Scot in me ... on my mother's side."

"And 'nah-uh?' Don't let my mother hear you talk like that."

They laughed.

Scott was slow to move, but eventually stood. He retrieved his wallet and keys from the drawer of the oak occasional table in the hall. Joining Troy at the door, he said, "One o'clock is my limit."

"Sure." Troy winked.

Scott turned off the hall light and followed Troy into the corridor. He held his gaze to the back of Troy's head and let out a huge exhalation of breath. There was, at that moment, again proof of his and Troy's connectivity — their bond, real and deep. Besides his mother, Troy had had the courage to be honest with him about the whole Anthony Power kerfuffle. That was another one of Troy's words. Sometimes Scott tried to probe the nature of their connectedness, how it had manifested and why it had staying power. A chance meeting on their first day in residence had changed their lives, and them along with it. What was strange, to both of them, was that it didn't seem like they had much in common beyond being gay and a love of scotch. What was the something deeper, metaphysical?

Inside the elevator, Scott elbowed Troy in his side. "You're my best friend."

"Yeah," Troy murmured, almost inaudible.

They smiled, and in the comforting silence an understanding that they were the type of friends who would hang on to each other forever. No matter what happened in their lives, no matter where their paths took them. They would always be important to each other, part of each other's fabric. And the debacle with Anthony proved just that.

"I feel like dancing," Scott said as they exited the apartment building.

"Millennium?" Troy blinked rapidly. "Fuck, no. I can't stand that place."

"It'll be fun."

"For you, maybe. You can dance."

"Your white man's shuffle isn't totally embarrassing." Scott chuckled. "But, please, just don't dance too close to me."

"Fuck off!"

Scott grabbed Troy by the arm. "Thank you."

"For what?"

"For always being honest with me." Scott let his hand fall away. "You've been like a brother to me. I'm glad that my parents 'adopted' you."

"I guess I'm not a bad big brother for a tall, lanky white guy." Troy grinned. "And Stretch … of all the possible nicknames…"

"Mama only gives nicknames to people she loves," Scott said, moving towards the street.

"What's yours?"

"I don't have one."

"That good, eh?" When Troy caught up to Scott, he gave him a good-natured jab in the side. "I'll ask Momma D."

"Don't you dare." Scott flagged down the approaching cab that shuttled them a few blocks south to Millennium for what he hoped would be a much-needed reprieve from a world turning in on itself.

**

TEN MINUTES LATER, WHEN THEY ENTERED Millennium, Troy made a beeline for the bar, eager to wash down his own demons. When did love become a demon? When it failed to blossom, failed to take hold, failed to freely present itself. And for that love to shine, Troy had to be courageous, and now there was no better moment since Anthony was gone from Scott's life. But was it too soon? Desperate to be more than a friend, more than a 'brother,' he couldn't risk losing Scott or their friendship. He certainly didn't want to look like a fool, either.

With his beer in hand, Troy edged his way through the crowd to the upper level. He stood near the half wall and surveyed the people grooving to "If I Could Turn Back Time." His gaze quickly locked on Scott. There it was, Scott's broad smile that unlocked that special space inside him. There was something about that smile that not only lit up the world but also blocked it out when life sucked. And he could see that when Scott danced nothing else mattered. He wanted to be like that. When Scott waved to him, he finished off his beer and joined his friend.

Under the strobe lights and, for a time, without a care in the world, they both danced away their blues.

***

THE LIGHTS CAME ON AND THE MUSIC STOPPED. Three o'clock, and well past Scott's self-imposed curfew. They guzzled back their drinks and then, crossing the dance floor on the way to the exit, Scott froze. Anthony Power stood about four feet away groping a thin, bearded brunette. There was the proof: Anthony had lied to him. Had everything about him — *them* — been a sham? Scott's stomach knotted tighter than it had during his last bout of constipation when Anthony pulled out of the kiss and their eyes met.

"Don't," Troy said, putting himself between Scott and Anthony. "It's not worth it."

Scott shoved Troy out of the way, but all he saw was the thin brunette popping a blue pill into his mouth. Anthony was gone. Scott spun around in circles, desperately searching the thinning crowd for a glimpse of the man who'd betrayed him. Panicked, he cupped his hands to the top of his head and wanted to scream. Then he saw the easily recognizable blond textured bangs emerge from the washroom and charged in that direction. He had Anthony cornered, his eyes boring into him, his fingers curling into fists. He opened his mouth to speak, but no words came.

Anthony sneered, almost mockingly, as if to prove that Scott was a naïve waif and easily duped. "What?"

"I can't believe I loved you," Scott said with control.

"I never said I wanted to get married and settle down," Anthony countered.

"You never said anything!" Scott took in a deep breath, tried to stay calm. "You're hopeless."

Anthony folded his arms. "I'm hopeless? Do you really think this country will ever elect a black *and* gay prime minister? Good luck with that."

Then it happened. Scott heard something snap as his fist crashed into the side of Anthony's meaty nose. The next thing he felt was the burly bouncer's rough hands on his shoulders and shoving him towards the exit. He turned back once to see Anthony, with his hand cupped to his nose, being picked up off the floor.

"Christ," Troy said once they were outside. "Why did you do that?"

"He deserved it," Scott fired back, unapologetic.

"It doesn't change what happened."

"Maybe not. But it felt good."

Scott picked up his pace, the distance growing between him and Troy. He was sliding back towards the abyss, choking on the void that was tightening the muscles within the arteries of his heart. He couldn't cope, couldn't let it go.

Nearing his apartment building, his hand began to throb. He examined it, saw the swelling, and thought about going to the emergency room, but he just needed to be alone.

Then he found himself re-enacting his showdown with Anthony and couldn't help but smile through the pain.

The Talk

"I WAS DOWN AND IN DESPAIR, CARRYING BURdens too much to bear," Margaret Davenport sang as she vigorously kneaded the mound of dough on the flour-dusted counter. That Scott had written a song for her fiftieth birthday still gave her goosebumps five years after the fact. At first, it was just a poem. Then, with the help of the church organist, he'd set it to music. And when he sang it that Sunday morning in church, his voice cornering on a dime and seemingly reaching up to heaven, she and the rest of the congregation were on their feet and clapping to the beat. She could see God using him as His instrument, but would it last, be permanent — help him steer his life? She hoped it would. *But whatever Your will for him*, she'd prayed, *I will trust and accept.* That proved to be more difficult than she'd thought.

She placed the dough in a greased bowl and covered it with a damp cloth. She heard the faint patter of feet coming from above and glanced at the clock. Two minutes past eight. *What's he waiting for?* she wondered. She knew he'd been up for a while. He wasn't like his father, who'd sleep in until noon if she'd let him. Scott had gotten that early morning gene from her, and when he was younger it was always their special time together. She missed that and their talks. *Maybe he's avoiding me.* She saw the shame in his eyes when he and Troy arrived home last night, but there wasn't a good moment for her to corner him. It gave her more reason to worry, which she did every day, about him being alone in such a big city and seemingly cut off. Well, not completely. He had Stretch. Still, she worried that he'd never tried to *believe*. Worried that

Anthony Power was a fraud and would break her baby's heart. Worried that her baby didn't need her anymore.

Rinsing the dish cloth in the sink, Margaret stared out the window at the dust of snow covering the ground. Just four days to Christmas, and the slightest warm-up would reveal the brown grass underneath. She was happy to have Scott home again, and to soon have the entire family together. She missed the days when loud voices ricocheted off the walls as the boys roughhoused with each other and she'd call Terrence to intervene. Some days, with the boys living on their own, the house seemed so empty.

She wrung out the dish cloth and just when she'd finished wiping down the countertop, Scott came into the kitchen. "Morning, Schnookums."

Scott yawned. "Morning."

"What would you like for breakfast?" she asked, pulling out the pan she used for scrambled eggs.

Scott poured himself a cup of coffee. "This is breakfast."

"That's not enough." Margaret marched to the fridge and pulled out the egg carton. "How about an omelette?"

"Mama, really, I'm not hungry," he said with a hint of annoyance.

"Let's stop this nonsense right now." Margaret took out a bowl and started cracking eggs into it. "You're going to have more than coffee for breakfast."

"Whatever."

"You didn't just whatever me." Margaret looked coolly at Scott. "I don't like your attitude."

Scott, his shoulders stooped, dropped his gaze. "Sorry."

"I don't think I quite heard you."

"I'm sorry, Mama."

"Oh, Schnookums," Margaret said when Scott looked up and, seeing the tears pooling in his eyes, rushed to hug him. "What's wrong?"

Scott pulled out of the embrace and wiped his face. "Anthony and I, well…"

"I knew it." Margaret stomped her foot. "I knew he was no good."

"Everybody knew it but me." Scott took a seat at the kitchen table, his gaze held to his coffee. "He never moved in. He chickened out the day before the move."

"And you're just telling me this now?" She lowered herself onto the chair next to him, touched her hand to his chin and lifted his head until their eyes met. "Why didn't you tell me? Do you need money? For your rent?"

"I'm managing —"

"Scott!" Margaret held his hand. "Do you need help?"

"Troy moved in," he said. "I didn't tell you because I wanted to show you that I could take care of myself. Like Dad said... I had to make my own choices. And live with them. Even the bad ones."

At the silence creeping in, Margaret squeezed Scott's hand to get his attention.

"Ouch," he groaned and gently pulled his hand away.

"What else is wrong?" she asked, one more time seeing the shame in his eyes.

"Nothing."

Troy entered the kitchen. "Good morning."

"Good morning, Stretch." Margaret's voice was strained as she held Scott's wrist and examined it.

"Lucky he didn't break anything." Troy poured himself a coffee.

"Shut up, Troy," Scott said with clenched teeth.

"Just a sprain," Troy volunteered.

Margaret let go of Scott's wrist. "A sprain? How?"

"When he punched Anthony." Troy slurped his coffee. "Caught him square in the face. Doctor said Scott almost needed surgery."

"Surgery?" Margaret gasped. "Are you sure you're okay?"

"I'm fine, Mama." Scott shot Troy a cool look. "The doctor said I sprained my thumb and index finger, and that maybe I should learn to box."

Margaret frowned. "That's not funny."

"It is a little," Scott said. "Fine. But it's healing. It all happened so quickly and —"

Margaret placed two of her fingers to Scott's lips. "I told you that boy had shifty eyes, and while I certainly don't condone violence..." She stood. "I hope you knocked his crooked teeth down his throat."

"Broke his nose," Troy boasted.

"Good." Margaret studied her son a moment longer, the lost look on his face caused her a deep pain. *He keeps hold-*

*ing things back from me and I don't know why. Doesn't he
know that I'll always be there for him, no matter what?* She
turned to Troy and said, "Be a dear and go tell Terrence that
breakfast will be ready in twenty minutes. It won't be, but if I
don't give him a deadline he'll be out there tinkling with that
car forever." That car was a 1970 Plymouth Road Runner he'd
started rebuilding when he retired.

"Sure thing." Troy disappeared out the back door.

"What else is bothering you?" Margaret asked when she
was alone again with Scott.

Scott traced his index finger around the rim of his mug.
"Nothing."

"Nothing." She took out her frustration on the eggs, whisk-
ing them violently. "Is that the only word you know today?"

"I don't know what I'm supposed to do."

"What do you mean?"

"After I graduate. What the fu..." Scott bit down on his
lower lip, his eyes roaming the kitchen. "I mean, Troy's going into medicine, so his path is clear. He has real choices.
Christ ... what choices, real choices, do I have? Oh, I'm sorry,
but don't look at me like that."

"I don't know where you learned to talk like that, but let me
tell you this..." Margaret pointed the whisk at Scott. "Twenty-
two years old or not, if I hear you take the Lord, my God's
name in vain one more time I'll wash your mouth out with
soap." Then she continued encouragingly, "What about going
on to do a master's? You'd be the first in this family to have a
graduate degree." She ground black pepper into the egg mix-
ture. "Besides, there are lots of things you can do with your
degree. Proofread, edit or teach. Write, even. What did you
do with all that stuff you wrote while sitting up in that tree?"

Scott's eyes widened. "You know about that?"

The tall maple tree in the backyard near the far edge of
the property was where Scott had, as a teenager, holed himself up writing. He thought it was his secret hiding place, but
she knew all about it. She could always see him, although he
thought she couldn't, balanced on the large branch and scrib-
bling in a notebook. Curious, too, about what he wrote, she
had once tried to find his notebooks. That was the one secret
he did manage to keep. She worried, and still did, that he spent

too much time dreaming of another world instead of fully inhabiting the present.

"Schnookums, there isn't much a mother doesn't know." *Whether we want to know it or not,* she thought, offering an encouraging smile to the son she admired most. "Don't compare yourself to Stretch or anyone else. You have to follow your own path. You'll know what to do when the moment comes."

"Do you mean that? That I should follow my own path?"

"Of course I mean it," Margaret said, indignant. "If you don't do what you love, you end up miserable ... and so does everyone around you. Your Uncle Randy didn't end up toothless, penniless and homeless just because he drank. He wanted to be an actor, but back in the day everyone told him a black man couldn't succeed in film. Instead of trying, he worked in a bank. First black branch manager, yet he hated it. And the only way for him to tolerate it was to drink. And, Lordy, did he drink until he couldn't 'function' without it. Cost him everything. His job. His family. His home."

"Then there's something you should know."

"What's that?"

"I changed majors."

Margaret held Scott's gaze. "Come again?"

"I still have my scholarship," Scott said with emphasis, "but the English program ... it bored me. Yet when I was in my political science class, something in me just came alive. I felt like it was the path that would let me *do* something, be a vehicle of change. Now, I'm majoring in —"

"Don't say it," Margaret pleaded.

"Political science."

"He said it, Lord." Margaret looked at the ceiling, as if waiting for help. "Why, Lord? Why? Why? Why?"

"I'm not saying I'm going to get into politics," he said quickly. "I think it'd be cool to be the expert everyone turns to to explain certain phenomena, or an election result. Or maybe I want to set policy, or —"

"Stop!" Margaret dropped her head, drew in two deep breaths, then levelled her gaze at Scott. "As much as I'd like to, I can't choose for you the road you should travel. I know you see how nasty the world of politics is today, and I hope you'll think long and hard before going that route. But whatever you choose to do, your father and I will support you."

"Thanks, Mom."

She contemplated the sadness gleaming in his eyes that quickly eclipsed the excitement in his voice. There was still a pain that she couldn't console. "I'm sorry about you and Anthony. I know you … sometimes love hurts and disappoints. We've all experienced that. With time we find a way to move on."

"Maybe I'll become a monk."

"You know, Schnookums…" Margaret placed her hands on her curvy hips. "I may not understand the whole gay thing, but to borrow your father's expression, any fool can see that there's someone who cares an awful lot for you."

"Mothers are supposed to love their children."

"You need to check that attitude," she said sternly. "Who do you think you're talking to?"

"Sorry."

"I'm talking about Stretch," she said bluntly.

"Troy? Pfft." Scott curbed his urge to laugh. "He has guys coming in and out of his pants faster than he can change his underwear."

"Oh!" Margaret, taking the butter out of the fridge, swallowed her shock. "Well, I hope that's not the case with you."

"Troy's interested in pretty little white boys with the tight jeans that make their asses disappear."

"This is my last warning about your language, young man." *Lord, You certainly are testing me this morning.* "Well, I think he's interested in you."

"He's white, you know." Scott raised an eyebrow. "You said you wanted me to date black men."

"That's not what I said. And that's beside the point. I mean, how many times did you bring Anthony home?" A silence. "That's my point. When you come to visit, Troy's right there nipping at your heels. He's like a part of the family now."

"Like a brother," Scott said.

"Well, go see what's keeping your father and your 'brother.' Next thing you know, they'll both have grease up to their elbows."

Scott smirked, polished off his coffee and left.

When the back door banged shut, Margaret stood very still and closed her eyes. She drew in long, deep breaths, hoping to instill a calm. She was doing her best to be supportive, to love unconditionally, and maybe Scott sensed her effort. She was, when he told her that he was gay, devastated. The news shocked, made her doubt herself as a mother and, worst of all, shook her faith. There was a period when whenever she looked at him she'd cry and rush out of the room. And she didn't have the strength to protest when Terrence proposed, on Scott's behalf, that he spend a couple of weeks with Norman.

Norman Clarke was Margaret's older brother and had been more like a father to his younger sister. She was eight when their father died and Norman, the eldest of the children still living at home, eagerly stepped into the protector role. When it came to Scott and the homosexual question, Norman had sought purposely to intervene. Norman's middle child, Tyler, was gay, and the news — only four months after he buried his wife — was a bombshell. Norman, paralyzed by grief, threw Tyler out of the house, declaring boldly, "My son is dead." When the shock cleared, Norman was filled with guilt and remorse. Before he could apologize, Tyler had packed what he could into a duffel bag and left the house. Years went by without Norman having any direct contact with his son, only receiving news second-hand from his two daughters. When Tyler returned to Ottawa for his godfather's funeral, Norman made an attempt at reconciliation. The reunion was not joyous but they managed to, on some level, strike up a fragile and temperamental relationship. Margaret knew her brother wanted better for her and Scott. They deserved more than strained, five-minute phone calls on birthdays and Christmas.

Margaret, schooled in the old-fashioned ways, could not comprehend the homosexual question. She prayed daily for understanding, for the Lord, her God, to give her the strength and courage to understand. More than her belief in God, it was how she anchored herself in the Holy Scriptures that had moulded her opinions. That was the paradox because she loved her son, who secretly had always been her favourite. So, she continued to pray and asked for God's direction. That was because deep down, when she had had time to *seriously* think about it, she knew that Scott had always been somehow different from Neal and Frank.

Unlike his brothers, Scott spent much of his spare time with his nose in a book. She caught him, when he was eight, reading James Baldwin's *Giovanni's Room*. That should have been a sign, right? He showed little interest in TV and sports. Frank and Neal played soccer and baseball in their youth, and always looked forward to the annual father and sons trip to Montréal or Toronto to see an NHL game. Scott went because he had to. He often wore earplugs to block out the noise and read through the game. To please his father, Scott played little league baseball for two years, but he always struck out. Frank and Neal, as soon as they hit puberty, were dating girls and coming home with hickeys on their necks. Scott didn't show any interests in the opposite sex and was thought to be a late bloomer. Maybe that was a good thing since he didn't end up like Frank and a father at nineteen. But Scott saying the words, "I'm gay," stunned, sent her spinning.

Three weeks after Scott moved in with his Uncle Norman, Margaret sent Terrence to collect their son. The shock had worn off, the tears had stopped. When Scott walked through the door, she rushed to him — almost tackled him like a linebacker. "I love you, I love you. You know that, right? Oh, Schnookums, I love you." She saw the way he looked at her, searchingly, reluctant to believe that she could accept him as he was. Even if she didn't understand or accept the situation, she knew that with Scott back at home she could monitor his comings and goings. She worried that Norman had let Scott do as he pleased — that that would have been her brother's way of doing right by Scott where he had failed his own son.

But Margaret did more than monitor Scott's comings and goings. She had — unintentionally or perhaps willingly, it was hard to say — treated him like an inmate serving out a sentence at Millhaven Institution. She rolled back his weekend curfew to ten from midnight. Before she knew he was gay, she'd liked Edward Doyle, Scott's best friend during high school. That changed one Sunday morning at church when she saw the way Scott and Edward looked at each other. She understood the true nature of their 'friendship' and ordered Scott to sever all contact with Edward. Conversations didn't come easily to them like they used to, and at Terrence's prompting they made an appointment to see a therapist. It might have worked, but Margaret sobbed all the way through the sessions and knew

Scott resented the fact that they were seeing a Christian psychologist. And Margaret insisted, stood her ground, that Scott would attend church faithfully on Sunday mornings.

At the sound of footsteps on the back veranda, Margaret opened her eyes. *I can't change the past, but I can try to do better now.* She still wanted to protect Scott, and she couldn't shake the feeling that he was headed down a dangerous road. He wasn't in physical danger, but spiritual. She sensed that Anthony Power's duplicity had closed his heart to love. That pained her because she didn't want her son to lead a solitary life. She wanted him to prosper, to be of good courage, to dare to be a man hoping to change the world. Even if it was wrong for her to say, she didn't want Scott to end up like his brothers, to disappoint. Not that managing the Midtown Grocery wasn't decent work for Frank, who had three kids and never went to university. And she was 'proud' of Neal, who'd been named Toyota's 'Top Regional Salesperson' for the past three years running. But call it mother's intuition, Margaret believed that Scott could — and would — do great things.

She turned on the gas burner under the frying pan and smiled when Scott came into view. *Guide Scott, oh my great Jehovah*, was her silent prayer. *Speak to his heart. Let him do Your will.*

Part II

April 2001 – June 2003

Moody Blues

ABOUT TO KNOCK ON THE OPEN DOOR, TROY stopped himself at the last moment. Instead, he leaned up against the doorframe and studied Scott, who was hunched over the desk and writing furiously. And then it happened, almost instantly, the sudden bulge in his pants that he tried to discreetly adjust. This wasn't good. He knew that, but he didn't know what to do. Watching Scott sit there, his attention seemingly unbreakable, had Troy trying to push down that long-simmering ache. He wanted to cross to the desk, place his hands on Scott's shoulders and massage them. Then he'd slide his hands down Scott's chest to his waist and yank on the belt buckle. God, he was hard and ready and … naïve.

There was a brief moment when Scott's hand froze, and that was when Troy finally tapped on the door. "What are you working on?"

"Nothing," Scott said and flipped closed the notebook.

"It didn't look like nothing." Troy advanced into the room. "I've been standing at the door for almost ten minutes and you never looked up, never noticed me."

"That's kind of creepy." Scott rose from the desk and made for the door.

Troy manoeuvred to block Scott's path. "Why won't you tell me what you're working on?"

"Because it's nothing important." Scott stepped around Troy and left the room.

Troy followed Scott into the kitchen. They didn't say anything, moving about on autopilot. Troy never liked it when Scott went silent and ignored him. Ever since the debacle with Anthony, Scott held back on him. *He can trust me. Doesn't he know that?* Troy accepted the Corona Scott held out to him, and the touch of their fingers had his manhood stirring again.

"Did I do something wrong?" Troy asked, then took a couple of gulps of beer.

"No, Troy, you haven't..." Scott let out a nervous laugh. "I guess I've been a bit of a grouch lately. Sorry about that."

Troy pulled out a chair and sat down at the kitchen table. "I told you before that you can tell me anything. I won't judge."

Scott raised an eyebrow. "That's not really true, is it."

"Fine." Troy smirked. "I'll try not to judge if you promise to stop being a Gloomy Gus."

"Deal."

They laughed, but then a silence hung in the air, their eyes roving the room while they sipped their beers. What would Troy have to say to get Scott to talk to him?

"Can I ask you something?" Troy asked, unable to catch Scott's eye.

"'You can tell me anything' and 'Can I ask you something?' are never great conversation starters for us," Scott said somewhat cheekily.

"Only because I care about you. When you cut yourself off from the world, go back to having that love affair with the library, I just wonder —"

"Wonder ... what?"

Troy tapped his fingers against his bottle. "Have you gotten over Anthony?"

"Oh, for fuck's sake, Troy." Scott sank onto the chair across from Troy. "It's been almost a year and a half. You don't think I'm over him?"

"I don't know. You don't confide in me like you used to, like you're always holding something back. I mean, I tell you everything."

"I don't think you tell me *everything*."

The silence returned, this time a little more awkward. Troy's heart raced as he watched Scott take a swig of beer. Those full, reddish-brown kissable lips pressed to the bottle. The rise of his Adam's apple with each swallow. Then the quiet placement of the bottle to the table. Graceful movements, each perfectly choreographed, that had Troy imagining the elegance of Scott's lovemaking — the tenderness of his touch, his endurance, his passion.

"All I'm saying is that not all guys are like Anthony," Troy said, matter-of-fact.

Scott chuckled. "I know that, Troy."

"And maybe there's someone out there who'll actually love you the way you deserve."

"Someone…"

Me! Troy screamed to himself. *Me, can't you see it's me?*

"Maybe you're right," Scott said ruefully. "I have kind of become that wallflower again. But it's not because of Anthony. Well, maybe a little. I mean, I remember what you said … about it being dangerous to move so fast with a guy. I haven't been wanting to get close to anyone. Don't want to fall that hard again."

"Fair enough. But you should get out there and live a little."

"I'm not there yet." Scott's voice trembled. "Again, not because of Anthony. I'm trying to figure out what I want to do, who I want to be. Breaking up with Anthony … it got me thinking about my future. I don't want to be the guy at forty-five who's still searching for his 'why' to life, or the guy who's been too afraid to chase after it."

Troy held Scott's gaze. "I don't follow."

"You said it's crazy for me to go into politics. Maybe you're right. I know my mother agrees with you. And what I went through with Anthony…" Scott bit his lip. "Trying to sort it all out got me writing again. First, I was just journaling about how much of a prick Anthony was, and that I didn't know if I'd ever love again or if I wanted to. Next thing I knew, I was writing a story that seems to have morphed into a book."

Troy sat up straight and grinned. "You're writing a book? That's what you didn't want to tell me earlier?"

"Thought you'd tell me I was crazy again."

"I think it's fantastic," Troy cheered. "What's it about?"

"Not sure yet. I'm still working it all out. First draft and all. I think it's too soon to talk about it. And I'll probably never try to get it published."

"When you're ready, I'd love to read it."

"Great. A critique from the aspiring doctor who got a C in English."

"It was a C plus," Troy corrected.

They laughed.

"Is that what you were planning on doing tonight? Lock yourself in your room and write?"

Scott shifted on his chair. "I should try studying for my Comparative Politics final. I tried earlier but I just couldn't get into it."

Troy chuckled. "And my virology exam's next week too, but maybe we deserve a break?"

"I'm not going clubbing," Scott said and lifted his beer to his mouth.

"I was thinking we could watch a movie." Troy kicked at Scott's foot under the table when there was no reaction. "There's got to be something on the movie channel." He saw how Scott tried to discreetly sidle his eyes to the microwave clock. It wasn't even eight thirty. "I'm not taking no for an answer." He stood, grabbed Scott by the arm and dragged him off his chair.

They moseyed into the living room and settled into the cosy sofa. Troy picked up the remote and started searching for a movie. He occasionally glanced over at Scott, who seemed almost lifeless, like there was no wind in his sails. Anthony had done that, took away his power. Troy wanted to cheer up his friend, hear that contagious boisterous laugh, revel in that coy smile. He selected *Sister Act*, one of Scott's favourite movies and sure to make him laugh. And there it was, from the moment Whoopi Goldberg appeared on the screen, that seductive smile that had Troy hard as steel.

As the movie played, they shifted into various positions and couldn't help but touch each other, which had Troy fighting back that ache. He knew Scott was oblivious to how much being that close drove him crazy. The night rolled on, and instead of going to bed when the movie ended, Scott didn't protest when Troy suggested watching the sequel. But Troy could tell that Scott struggled with the lateness of the hour. Sometimes, trying to sneak a sidelong glance of Scott, he'd catch him with his eyes closed. Then it happened. The weight of Scott's head pressing down on his shoulder as if it were a pillow. Troy didn't move, didn't dare to breathe. He stayed still. Absolutely still.

In that moment, his world was perfect. He was whole and didn't want the night — or the feeling of complete rightness — to end.

He closed his eyes and smiled.

Here it was. His little bit of heaven.

***

ONE WEEK LATER. TROY CHECKED HIS WATCH under the lit candle in the centre of the table. Two minutes to midnight. The rowdy conversations and loud music came at him with the speed of an assassin set to take out his mark. He had no defense, no skill to protect himself. He sighed, leaned back and rested his head against the high wall of the dark wood panelled booth. "Let's just order."

"Give him a couple more minutes," Janice said, running her hand through her shoulder-length brown hair.

Troy flipped open one of the menus on the table. "He's not coming."

"What did he say he was doing tonight?" Evan asked, and plunged his lips into the foam head of his Guinness.

"He wasn't doing anything," Troy said, annoyed.

"Then I'm with Troy." Evan reached for a menu. "Let's order."

Heads bowed, and they fell silent, swallowed by the chatter rising and falling at Rouge, an eatery popular with students for its three-dollar pints on Wednesdays. But it was Thursday, the restaurant packed with U2 fans who had flooded onto Yonge Street after the concert. Nothing seemed to break their concentration, even the server rushing back and forth in front of their booth and who occasionally stopped to see if they were ready to order. But no one looked up.

Troy glared at the menu so long the words blurred. He blinked a couple of times, the words coming back into focus. There was still so much that was fuzzy, and just when he thought there was clarity the fog rolled back in, hampering visibility. He hadn't stopped thinking about that night, just a week ago, when Scott had used his shoulder as a pillow. Neither of them had budged, and that had driven Troy crazy as Scott cuddled his side. With each breath Troy inhaled the sweet scent drifting off Scott. He couldn't believe what was happening, its breathtaking beauty. Then, as the film credits rolled, Scott woke up suddenly and sat up straight. Troy saw the 'shock' in Scott's eyes, the embarrassment as if something physical had just happened. He recoiled at the unexpectedly terse, "Goodnight!" Scott barked at him before rushing out of the room. And since that night, Scott barely looked at him and avoided him as if he couldn't stand to be in the same room.

Where was Scott? Troy had no idea. Scott had left the apartment before he stumbled out of bed. And with the tension lingering between them, Scott didn't voluntarily share his plans. Troy slumped down on the bench. Their final exams finished, in a few short weeks they'd walk across the stage to receive their diplomas. They had succeeded, they had survived — by supporting each other and because of each other. They had reason to celebrate, the concert and dinner that followed a well-deserved treat for what they had achieved. *He should be here*, Troy thought.

"Troy…" When there was no response, Janice reached out and snapped her fingers. "Troy!"

Troy levelled his eyes at her, unmoved by the harsh glare she threw at him. "What?"

Janice pointed at the green-haired server standing in front of the table.

"Do you need a few more minutes?" the guy asked.

"I'll be ready by the time everyone else orders," Troy snapped.

"We already ordered," Evan said coolly.

Troy closed the menu and handed it to the stone-faced server. "The salmon burger with fries."

Janice drained her gin and tonic, signalled for another before the waiter walked off, then looked at Troy. "What's wrong with you?"

"I don't know." Troy raised his glass of water to his lips and drained it slowly. "Have you noticed anything different about Scott?"

"Not really," Janice said. "But he and I aren't that close."

"Well, I have." Troy picked up the plastic water pitcher and refilled his glass. "He's been different ever since Anthony bailed on him. He says he's over him, but it seems more like he's, I don't know … almost broken."

Janice reached across the table and placed her hand on Troy's. "What Anthony did was shitty, but it's been a freakin' long time. Maybe he's over Anthony, maybe he's not. And so what if he's keeping to himself a bit. Doesn't mean he's unhappy or broken. And good for him for not rushing into another relationship or dropping his pants for every guy who winks at him."

Troy stared blankly at the candle flame. "I just want him to be happy."

"Oh, we know," Evan said drily.

"Just let him be," Janice counselled. "Even better, just be his friend."

"You're not his boyfriend," Evan spat. "Why do you care if he's 'broken' anyway?"

"Because I *am* his friend." Troy's voice was on the rise. "I live with him. I see him go to class, come home and mope around the apartment. To me, that's not normal."

Evan sneered. "Maybe you should live your own life instead of worrying about Scott's all the time. Wait, I know. Scott *is* your life. Always has been."

"You've never liked him anyway." Troy met Evan's gaze and held it. "It's not like you care."

"He's never liked me, either." Evan ran his hand through his longish red curls. "I was Anthony's friend. That made me complicit by —"

"You were complicit," Troy interrupted. "You knew and didn't say anything."

Janice winked at the server, who'd discreetly set her drink on the table, then trained her gaze at Troy. "Have you tried talking to him?"

Troy tilted his head, the smile on his face restrained. "He's not really in a sharing mood these days … about anything. Maybe I'm the one making a big deal out of nothing."

"Ya think?" Evan tied his face in knots. "Christ, tell him that you're in love with him already."

"I can't!" The force in Troy's voice thundered through the restaurant, drawing the attention of the group at the table across from them. Barely able to control himself, he looked down, his fists clenched under the table. "I can't," he repeated calmly.

"All right. Calm down." Janice pointed at Evan. "Leave him alone." Her focus was back on Troy. "You either need to tell him or let it go. And I'll be honest. I've never understood why you and Scott *haven't* dated. Like my grandmother would say, you're joined at the hip."

"And no one even dares to ask either of you out," Evan hissed. "Everyone thinks you and Scott *are* dating."

"Thinks who's dating?"

Heads swung in the direction of the deep, commanding voice that made everyone sit up straight.

Troy's eyes landed on Scott. "Where have you been?"

"Sorry I'm late. I fell asleep." Scott took a seat next to Janice. "Who meets up for dinner at midnight? And trying to get in this place... Yonge Street's a zoo."

"We didn't have time to eat before the concert," Evan said, his gaze briefly fixed on Scott, who ignored him.

Janice touched her hand to Scott's arm. "You missed a great show."

"Never been a U2 fan," Scott admitted apprehensively.

"What are you a fan of?" Evan asked, still unable to catch Scott's eye.

"Wouldn't you like to know," Scott said without looking at Evan.

Evan turned to Troy. "That, right there, is why I don't like him. His attitude."

"Thank the Good Lord," Janice said as the green-haired server distributed their meals.

Scott ordered a glass of wine before the man left.

"Help yourself," Janice said to Scott, pointing at the mountain of fries on her plate.

Scott raised his hand. "I'm good, thanks."

Janice popped a fry into her mouth and looked at Troy. "When do you two leave?"

"Not sure." Troy eyeballed Scott. "Have you decided if you're coming?"

"Still trying to convince my mother," Scott said.

Evan's eyes bulged. "Go where?"

"Europe," Janice said quickly. "Six weeks travelling around —"

"Jesus Henry Christ!" Evan sat back, his head hitting the wall of the booth with a thud. "Why don't you two just get married already?"

"Evan..." Janice, her harsh tone a warning immediately understood, held Evan's gaze until he started shovelling food into his mouth.

Scott reached for the wineglass the server had just put down in front of him. "What's your problem?"

"*My* problem?" Evan asked as he chewed. "Are you fucking kidding me?"

"Guys!" Troy's elevated voice again drew attention, heads from a couple of tables swinging in his direction. "Not tonight."

"I have a problem?" Evan shrieked.

Scott nodded. "Apparently."

"My problem is that you're blind," Evan spat. "You don't see —"

"Hey!" Troy slammed his fist down on the table. The questioning looks being thrown at their table made him feel like a silly-ass drunk who'd passed his limit but didn't care. He had their attention. That's what mattered. "Can we, please, just try to enjoy ourselves?"

The rowdiness of the other tables propelled them back into an awkward silence. That shouldn't have been a surprise. Evan and Scott were never close, but Anthony's betrayal deepened the wedge between them. But Scott, Janice, Evan ... these were his friends, each with different associations but still connected to each other. Connections he hoped would last a long time because they were all important to him. They were his family. And despite whatever doubts they had about each other, he was desperate to hang on to all of them.

Looking around the table, a renewed sense of calm seized him. Finally, he understood. Some families had secrets, others had misunderstandings always simmering near the surface. But when in need, Troy had to believe — like Momma D had said — that this family would be there for him.

Homecoming

AFTER THE THIRD RING, JUST BEFORE THE VOICE-mail message played, Troy pulled the phone away from his ear. His heart sank as he studied his brother's number and groaned. Had he dialled the wrong number? Or was his call purposely being avoided? He hit the redial button and listened nervously, but there was still no answer. He folded the white card, with its elegant, slanted script, in two and shoved it into his pants pocket. The tear running down his cheek surprised him. Or maybe not. He wasn't sure what to think anymore, wasn't sure who he was.

"Hey!"

Troy turned his head towards the contralto voice and smiled faintly. "Hey."

"Everything okay?" Scott asked and cupped his hand to Troy's shoulder when he was close enough.

"Yeah, of course." Troy rubbed his right eye. "Needed some air."

Scott balanced himself on the arm of the Muskoka chair next to Troy, who looked pained. "You're a horrible liar."

Troy dropped his gaze. *He sees right through me every time. Psychic or soul mate? Neither, because he doesn't believe in either.* "I'm a little tired."

"Is that the story you plan on sticking with?" Silence. "Fine. But, look, people are starting to arrive."

"Give me a moment."

Scott stood, again placed his hand on Troy's shoulder, and then strutted into the house.

Troy could still feel the weight of Scott's hand on his shoulder, its warmth, the slight pressure before it slipped away. In a world of loose associations, Scott was his only real connection, the only person he trusted enough to confide his deepest fears. Flunking out of med school. How cats gave him the heebie-jeebies. Ending up alone. And here he was, a university graduate, celebrating with Scott and the family that had 'adopted' him. Proof of their bond, proof of their brotherhood, proof that he was holding on to grudges that held him back. Would he ever be able to reach out to his own family? Share his successes with them? And would they care?

The laughter seeping outside set him on edge. A happy occasion, or it was supposed to be, but he was dead inside. Numb like his mouth after his dentist injected the Lidocaine into his gums before extracting the baby tooth that had never fallen out. Terrence and Margaret included him so that he knew this was his home too, tried to make this his day as much as it was Scott's. But this wasn't his home, and he wasn't blood. He rose, fingered the card in his pocket, then headed for the house.

Inside, the voices rushed at him, new faces dissecting him in a way that left him feeling naked and exposed. He caught Margaret's look — part encouragement, part displeasure — as if she understood his struggle. Still dodging the curious looks being thrown at him, he made a beeline for Scott in the living room.

"Uncle Norman," Scott said, pointing at Troy, "you remember —"

"How could I forget Troy." Norman stretched out his hand. "He's as tall as Big Ben."

A ripple of laughter tore across the room.

"I'm not that tall," Troy said at the release of the handshake.

Norman scratched the side of his large, sturdy nose. "Never had the chance to tell you I was sorry to hear about what Anthony put you through. But that was a long time ago. You seeing anyone now?"

"Norman!" Margaret, eavesdropping from the kitchen, shook her head to discourage her brother's line of questioning.

Troy dropped his head.

"Thanks, Uncle Norman," Scott said, his voice cracking. "Wasn't meant to be. And, no, I'm happily single."

Norman pointed at Troy. "You ever think of giving him a test drive?"

"Norman!" Margaret snapped.

"Well, Margie, I never got to see for myself those shifty eyes you complained about so much." Norman chuckled. "At least Troy doesn't have shifty eyes."

"Amen," Margaret cheered.

Troy tasted the fried eggs he'd eaten for breakfast edging back up his throat.

"Maybe that'd be a little weird," Norman said to Scott. "But I know you young people sure do recover quickly, hopping from one bed to the next. Kinda surprised that no one's snatched you up. We Clarke men are irresistible."

"He's a Davenport," Terrence emphasized from the leather wing chair.

"But he gets his good looks from his mother," Norman countered.

Another wave of laughter swept the room.

"Stretch and Scott are 'just' friends," Terrence added.

Troy wouldn't look up, worried that everyone would see the disappointment contorting his face.

"Oh, well." Norman laughed grandly as he eyed Troy. "Stretch! I like that. Margie, did you come up with that? Tall. Lanky. White."

Troy raised his head and crossed his arms. "I'm not lanky."

"Lanky," Scott and Norman said, and high-fived each other.

Troy listened as Norman interrogated Scott about their trip to Europe. He caught the brief twitch of surprise in Norman's face the third time Scott started his response with 'we.' Clearly, Norman understood that 'we' meant Scott *and* Troy. It was his idea to tour around Europe for part of the summer, which he billed as a way to celebrate their academic success. Yet his silent hope was that the time away would help Scott be open to letting someone new into his life.

"What about you, Stretch?" Norman asked. When there was no response, he snapped his fingers in front of Troy's face. "Anyone home?"

"Sorry." Troy unfolded his arms and shoved his hands in his pockets. "Med school."

"We'll have our own doctor in the family," Terrence said as he stood. "No more two-hour waits at the clinic."

Norman scrunched his eyebrows. "But you said ... Scott and Stretch aren't ... I'm confused."

"Oh, Norman." Margaret laughed. "A figure of speech. Stretch is part of the family."

"Well, I'm proud of you both." Norman's face lit up with pride as if he were singly responsible for their success. "You're doing something with your lives, following your own paths." His voice fell an octave. "We don't all have the courage to do that."

Troy looked down. *I don't have the courage to go after what I really want.* He lifted his head when Scott elbowed him in the side.

"You told me once," Scott said, "that we do the best we can with the knowledge we have at the time."

"Yes, I did, didn't I. Well, then, I guess that's true." Norman's thick lips arched into a self-congratulating smile as he made for the kitchen.

"What's wrong with you?" Scott asked through gritted teeth.

"Nothing." Troy avoided eye contact with Scott.

"I told you already. You're a horrible liar."

Knowing that Scott was waiting for an explanation, Troy turned slightly to be out of his line of sight. Then Scott walked away and Troy, when he thought no one was watching, disappeared outside through the front door. He plunked down on the porch steps, hid his face in his hands and breathed slowly. Alone, displaced, shipwrecked, he didn't know how to live in a world where he couldn't express his love for Scott. What held him back? What would happen if he just said, "Scott, I love you?" At the squeaking sound, he uncovered his face and cranked his head in the direction of the front door. Margaret stood there, her hands on her hips and shooting him a knowing look.

"I was just getting some air," Troy said.

"Don't lie to me." Margaret shooed Troy over and settled in next to him. "Is this about your family? I know you say you're not close, but I bet they'd be proud of you. The way I'm proud of you."

"Maybe." Troy bit the inside of his cheek. "I don't think they'd care, though."

"Then what is it about?" Silence. "Am I talking into thin air?"

"I'm ... it's just ... you see..."

"I see the way you look at Scott." Margaret took Troy's hand in hers and squeezed it. "Tell him."

"I can't."

"Why not?"

Troy let the tear streak down his face. "Because I'll lose him forever."

***

EARLY THE NEXT EVENING, TROY AND SCOTT were at the Ottawa Macdonald-Cartier International Airport handing off their large knapsacks to the check-in agent.

"Too heavy," the plump, unsmiling woman said.

"We'll just pay the fee," Scott insisted.

"Five dollars a pound." The woman motioned with her head for him to step to the side. "Go take some things out."

"We'll just pay the fee," Scott repeated.

The woman adjusted her black-framed glasses on the bridge of her narrow nose. "You could just —"

"Pay the fee," Margaret said, gently pushing Troy and Scott aside. "Is that going to be a problem?"

Scott couldn't conceal his smirk. His mother's mildly impertinent tone said it all: she was about to break into the stern voice she'd employed to warn her rambunctious students when they tested her limits. The formidable woman that she was, it didn't take long for students to cower. He thought he could see the woman, with her bird nest's hairdo, convulse.

"Well, er, of course not." The woman held her gaze to the monitor as her fingers danced across the keyboard.

"My babies are going to spend six weeks travelling across Europe." Margaret spoke in a conciliatory tone, leaning forward to read the small letters on the woman's nametag. Angie. "I just want to make sure that they have everything they need. Any mother would surely understand that, right, Angie?"

Angie forced a smile and, barely moving her lips, said, "Of course." The amount owing for the overweight bags that was on the screen dropped to zero. Angie tagged the backpacks and held down a button that moved them along the conveyor belt. "Have a great trip."

"Really," Margaret said, exasperated, to Terrence as they walked with Troy and Scott down the bright corridor. "Five dollars a pound. Highway robbery. What's next? Paying to use the lavatory on the plane?"

Everyone laughed.

They stopped a few feet away from the escalator that led to the security screening area on the lower level and exchanged curious looks, as if this were the end of something, a final goodbye. Troy moved abruptly, advancing to hug Margaret, and then he shook hands with Terrence.

Margaret rushed towards Scott and drew him in for her famous crushing embrace. She pushed back, but cupped her hands to his broad shoulders. "I want you to call me once you arrive. No buts. You call to let me know that you've arrived safely. And then I want to hear from you every two days."

"Mama," Scott said somewhat coolly, "I'm not a baby. I'll call you once a week."

"And you, Stretch," Margaret said as she removed her hands from Scott's shoulders, "you better take care of my Schnookums."

"Schnookums?" Troy howled.

Scott, embarrassed by his mother's pet name for him, ran his hand over his face.

"Don't talk to strangers," Margaret warned.

"That's going to be difficult, Mama." Scott's voice bristled with sarcasm. "We're going to have to eat."

"You know what I mean," Margaret said in her disciplining tone that always cut through Scott. "And be careful. Why do you have to go for so long?"

"Six weeks isn't a lifetime." Scott adjusted the strap of his carry-on satchel. "We've got to go."

"All right." Margaret hugged them one more time. "Remember, as soon as your feet hit the ground in London I want to hear from you."

"That would be like..." Troy counted on his fingers. "That's four thirty in the morning."

"Oh, you can wait and call us later in the day," Terrence said.

"Terrence!" Margaret looked harshly at him. "Four thirty or two o'clock in the morning, I don't care. You call me."

Terrence moved behind his wife and, waving his hands in the air, mouthed, "Later. Call later." He stepped forward and shook his son's hand. "Have a blast!"

Scott and Troy stepped onto the escalator, and as it carried them to the level below, they turned and waved to Margaret and Terrence. They heard Margaret say, "Why do you have to encourage them? You know the devil is running rampant in this world, and you tell them to have a blast?" They laughed.

On the lower level, they joined the long and slow-moving line leading to the security screening area. They had their boarding cards in their hands, and occasionally stole sidelong glances of each other.

While they were best friends, Scott was unsure what this trip would do to their friendship. Would it cement their bond or tear them apart? He also wasn't sure why he was concerned about this. As roommates over the past three years, they seemed perfectly matched. They didn't get in the other's way, didn't hover and led, for the most part, separate lives. But this trip changed all of that. They would be holed up together in tiny hotel rooms, inseparable in a new way that would allow them to *see* inside each other, inside themselves. Was he prepared for that? Was Troy?

One of the security officers flagged them in, and they turned and looked in the direction of the escalator. Terrence and Margaret were still there, on the upper level, leaning against the railing and surveying the scene. They waved. Rattled by a sudden rush of anxiousness, the other passengers around him swam before his eyes. *Do they love me or do I still disappoint?* He breathed deeply and followed Troy into the large room, trying to imagine the ways this trip would, hopefully, transform his life.

Lead Me Not into Temptation

"YOU WANT TO TELL ME WHAT'S WRONG?" Scott asked, tossing his knapsack onto the bed.

Troy, his back to Scott, fingered the corner of the white card sticking out from his bag. "Nothing's wrong."

But everything was wrong. Had been since Amsterdam. Unlike their stops in London, Brussels, Frankfurt and Geneva, Troy expected them to be arrested by the allure of Amsterdam's eccentric Red Light District. He wanted the city's salaciousness to, in a way, inspire, feed his curiosity, let him — with Scott as his co-conspirator — explore the limits of his sexuality. But on their first day in Amsterdam, the city became a game-changer that threw him a curveball named Mason Devereaux. The rugged, brown-haired American staying across the hall had done what Troy had failed to do: charm Scott into bed. And during their four-day stay, Scott and Mason were inseparable.

Troy disliked everything about Mason — his 'fake' southern twang and excessive hand gestures, his opinion on everything despite an overt ignorance of world affairs, his enduring high school jock looks. Such a pure Americanness, to boldly go after what he wanted, in this case Scott, and to get it. And, perhaps knowingly, sidelining Troy and his ambitions.

Then, out of nowhere, Troy was on the bed — Scott on top of him like a strongside linebacker tackling the running back. He twisted and turned, freeing his arm trapped under his body, and Scott somehow matching his movements. The scrimmage continued, Troy unable to find a rhythm to outmanoeuvre Scott. When his nose pressed into Scott's neck and filled with the scent of basil and sage, even a hint of spice, something happened. Maybe it was the panic running roughshod over his body, Scott's hot breath in his ear, a grunt. Something had him tapping into a spirit and energy he'd lacked earlier. He flung his arm wide, knocking Scott off him and, giving no time to react, rolled on top of him. Grabbing both of Scott's wrists and straddling his waist, he pinned him down.

He locked onto the dark brown eyes that, without even knowing it, demanded submission — and he was ready to comply. But he couldn't move, couldn't think of anything to say. And for a time, as their heavy breathing eased, life seemed perfect. Until it happened. Scott had realized it before him. It wasn't anger in his eyes as much as it was part curiosity, part surprise. Then utter confusion.

Troy's steel cock pressed into Scott's stomach. When it hit him — that this might be the beginning of his greatest fantasy coming to life — he released Scott. Trembling, he bounced off the bed and trained his gaze at the small crack in the wall next to the window.

"I know something's wrong, Troy," Scott said, his voice pitching high, and slid to the foot of the bed. "You can't bullshit me."

Troy, running his hand through his longish hair in desperate need of a trim, collapsed onto the desk chair. Still thinking about the awesome feeling of having Scott's full weight on him, he wanted to hide his boner. He studied the white duvet, unwilling to look at Scott because he couldn't stand that kind of probing. Deep, hard and long. Didn't want to be held to account. *Why am I always waiting? Really, what am I so fucking scared of?* And now here they were at the end of their European tour, and nothing had changed. Not the way he'd hoped. If anything, he worried their friendship was in jeopardy, like a couple in the process of becoming estranged from each other and unsure if their love was worth salvaging.

"We can forget Paris and just go home," Scott said askance. "Or maybe you'd like to tell me what's on that piece of paper you keep fawning over?"

Troy shot out of the chair and stood in front of the window, the Eifel Tower a beacon against the night sky. He had so many expectations for this trip, so many hopes, all of which had so far gone unfulfilled. He hadn't bridged that space between him and Scott that would have allowed him to love openly, go beyond himself. That required courage he didn't have — to call checkmate, to conquer Scott. Did that make him a fool? Maybe. Nobody wanted to be conquered, and he knew that. He swallowed hard and turned around. "Is it the city of lights or love?"

"Both. Troy —"

"I'm hungry." Troy glanced at his watch. "We should think about getting something to eat."

"Jesus Henry effing Christ. What the fuck is wrong with you?" Scott sat up. "I'm sorry. But, frig, Troy … we're best friends. We tell each other everything, so I know when something's wrong."

Troy rubbed his left eye before the tear could roll down his cheek, then moved to retrieve the paper from his knapsack and handed it to Scott.

"A wedding invitation," Scott drawled. "What's the big deal?"

"Did you read it?" Troy watched as Scott scanned the card again.

"Your brother's getting married." Scott handed the partially crumpled invitation back to Troy. "Again, what's the big deal?"

Troy, sitting back down, slammed the invitation down on the desk. "He didn't even call to tell me. He sends me an invitation in the mail like I'm some third cousin once removed that he's obligated to invite."

Scott bit down on his lower lip. "It's not just Patrick's fault, though, is it? Maybe you could have tried reaching out to him."

Troy sucked his teeth. "I tried. Multiple times before we left. He never answered my calls."

"How many times did you try calling him over the past three or four years?"

"No fucking way! You don't get to be the righteous one here. I mean, let's be honest … you'd hardly win brother-of-the-year." When Scott stood, Troy reached out and grabbed his arm. "That's not what I meant."

"Sure it is." Scott jerked his arm away. "I'm going to shower. Then we can go eat." He rummaged through his bag for a change of clothes and then disappeared into the bathroom.

The bathroom door banged shut and Troy stiffened. "Damn it!" He gripped his hair in both hands and then smoothed it out as a new, crippling distress swelled inside of him. There, in the shower ... gliding the bar of soap over Scott's back in broad, gentle strokes, then pulling Scott into him and kissing the nape of his neck. Yet another one of his silly dreams, the type of fantasy that tormented, summoned the demons eager to torture the mind. Buttoned tightly around Troy's body was the slip coat of fear that he couldn't peel off.

Tears banked in his eyes, the way they did a lot lately, but he wouldn't let himself cry. The wedding invitation, which had arrived five days before he and Scott left on their trip, became the icing on the Mason-shaped cake. Fully briefed on his family history, Scott should have known that the invitation would have opened old wounds of regret and displacement. Or so Troy believed. It was a reminder of the discord that permeated through Troy's family, and revived the sense of homelessness and uncertainty of his own identity. He didn't have strong family ties like Scott, and that despite Scott's fragile relationship with his brothers. Troy had nothing to moor himself to. Worse, he'd been cut loose and set adrift.

The cutting loose had been his parent's divorce when he and Patrick were students at Manor Park College, a private all-boys school in Edmonton. Even now Troy could smell the dampness of his father's clothes that clung to him when he arrived unannounced at the school. It was a Wednesday afternoon, late October, at the beginning of the fourth period, when the principal collected him and Patrick from their French class. When the principal told them their father was there, Troy thought that his nanna had died. Not the case. His father, a rather stern and unaffected man, patted at his wet hair and said, "Your mother and I are getting divorced. Do you know what that means? Good. That doesn't change how we feel about you." His father didn't offer any type of explanation. Instead, he spent about ten minutes asking them about their studies and friends, and then he was gone. Only several years later did Troy learn that his father's visit, perhaps simply convenient, corresponded with the interview that led to his job as a deputy minister.

Troy mistakenly took his father's, "That doesn't change how we feel about you," for, "Of course, nothing changes."

But everything did change because the news devastated him, made him wonder if he had done something wrong. He had so many questions but no answers. What happened during the four years he and Patrick were at Manor Park? How come he hadn't noticed the shift between his parents when he was at home during the holidays? Did his father have a mistress? Where would he spend Christmas?

A tear strayed from Troy's eye, and he wiped it away when Scott was back in the room. He always wanted to be more like Patrick who, from the moment they learned of their parents' divorce, threw himself into his extracurricular activities. Patrick was strong, disciplined, centred. The word their father used? Manly. Patrick became the college's star quarterback, Troy the school's ghost. Never heard and barely seen. He poured all of his energies into his studies, and was either number one or number two at the top of the honour roll. While Patrick was popular for his football skills, Troy's popularity came at the expense of his terrible case of acne. Everyone called him Pepperoni Face. His father repeatedly told him to be more like Patrick, to be a man. The problem was that his parents' divorce stripped him of his identity, as if his entire life had become a lie. Added to that was his realization, at fourteen, that he *liked* guys — especially his young English teacher. No wonder it seemed like his whole world was crumbling down around him.

Troy studied Scott, who fiddled with the items in his knapsack and pretended like he was alone in the room. It seemed silly that they'd argue now, at the end of their trip, and let it stick to them, create a wedge. Amsterdam had been the only 'hiccup.' In every other city they seemed to really enjoy travelling together, quite effortlessly agreeing on their daily schedules. Now, he couldn't let his bitterness towards his family — or his rage at Mason Devereaux outsmarting him — to mar the entire trip, and broke the silence. "I'm sorry, Scott. I was out of line."

Scott turned to look at him. "Thanks, but, no, you weren't. And let's not get into all that again."

Troy stood, picked up his wallet and key from off the desk and shoved them in his pockets. "Do you think I should go?"

"Go where?" Scott bounced off the bed and stabbed his feet into his shoes.

Troy rocked on his heels. "To Patrick's wedding."

"Yes, I do." Scott dropped onto the bed, tied his laces, then looked up at Troy. "Don't you?"

"No," Troy said, slightly raising his voice, like a two-year-old who finally understood the meaning of the word. "It'll be awkward."

"Maybe at first." Scott rose and clasped his hands behind his back. "It could also go well, you and Patrick ending up tight again. You're right, though. I'd never win brother-of-the-year, but you could if you took a chance."

"I wouldn't know what to say to him."

"Start with, 'Hello.'"

"Don't be an ass."

They laughed.

"All right." Scott started for the door. "I'll go with you. I know you can handle it on your own, but I'll be there for moral support. And just so we're clear, you're buying my ticket."

"Buy your own ticket."

"Pfft!" Scott grabbed the doorknob. "When is it, anyway?"

"Second weekend in August." Troy headed towards Scott, and when he was close enough, tapped his arm. "I'd like to eat somewhere on the *Champs Elysées*."

"Let's," Scott said buoyantly, hoping to lighten the sombre mood enveloping them. "We'll toast life under the starry Paris sky."

"I've always loved your idealism." Troy cupped his hand to Scott's shoulder. "You *are* my best friend, you know."

"That's because I'm the only one who'll put up with you." Scott cranked the doorknob.

Troy placed his hand on the door, preventing Scott from opening it.

Scott glared at him. "What? Oh ... well, of course."

"Can't you say it?"

"Why do I have to say it?" Scott tried to pull the door open, but Troy held it firmly closed. "I'm here, aren't I?" He sounded exasperated. "Otherwise, I wouldn't have spent the last six weeks sharing hotel rooms and suffering through your stinky farts and coma-inducing morning breath."

"I need to hear it," Troy said with emphasis.

"Fine. Yes, you are."

"I'm what?"

"My ... best ... friend."

Troy released the door. "Was that so difficult?"

They made their way down to the lobby and outside under the warm Paris sky. They ambled towards the *Champs Elysées*, swept up in the majesty of this old-world city that had the power to, still, move the hearts of men. Was it the city of love or the city of lights? For Troy, stealing sidelong glances of Scott, it was the city of love. He could not imagine being in Paris with anyone but Scott. When he saw a young couple leaning in to kiss each other as they strolled past them, he had to curb his desire to pull Scott into a crushing embrace. It was a terrible demon, this love he had for Scott and his inability to confess it. If only he could be daring and bold, summon the courage to say what he felt. How long would it be before another Mason came along and stole Scott's heart? That would be unbearable, and he would once again be sidelined. He tried to steal another sidelong glance of Scott, who caught him and smiled. *I love his smile,* Troy thought, the excitement immediately bulging in his pants. Then he purposely bumped into Scott, and it was a gesture of friendship, a mark of their connectedness. Right then, walking aimlessly down the *Champs Elysées*, he imagined that this was what happiness looked like, and maybe the closest he'd get to it during his terrestrial sojourn.

Family Matters

"I'M NOT AVOIDING HIM," TROY SPAT, THEN turned away and chugged his beer.

"It looks like you are," Scott said.

"I'm not. I just —"

"I told you…" Scott grabbed Troy by the wrist, preventing him from taking another swig of beer. "Start with, 'Hello.' And let things go from there. Better yet, congratulate him on his wedding."

"I'm nervous," Troy admitted and looked down.

"Hey…" Scott cupped his hands to Troy's shoulders. "Don't be. You and Patrick just drifted apart. It happens. But to me it's pretty clear you both want each other in your lives. Otherwise, he wouldn't have invited you and you wouldn't have come." He shook Troy gently and waited until he raised his head before continuing. "You've got this."

"Maybe you're right."

"Maybe?" Scott's hands fell to his side. "Look around you, Troy. Everyone's having a good time while you're off sulking in a corner."

"I'm not sulking," Troy protested, then gulped his beer.

"Right." Scott took a step forward, placed his hand in the square of Troy's back and whispered, "When you stop doing whatever it is you think you're not doing and talk to your brother, explain one thing to him for me."

Troy scrunched his eyebrows. "What?"

"That I'm *not* your boyfriend." Scott walked off, immediately swallowed up by the crowd.

Troy spun around and searched the multitude for a glimpse of Scott, who'd already vanished. He guzzled back the remainder of his beer, and that seemed to take the edge off. He listened. The energetic voices, the laughter and music all swirling about and clashing in the air under the black night sky. He was, in a way, immune to it. He checked the time. Three minutes past eleven. The air was still warm yet he shivered and staggered back a step. Too much drink? Maybe. Alcohol slowly freed him from the anxiousness pinning him down. And maybe, too, Scott was right. He *was* avoiding Patrick. No surprise there. They hadn't spoken in over three years. What was Troy supposed to say to him?

Despite the festivities, Troy wasn't in the mood to celebrate. Almost two months since he and Scott had returned from Europe, the legacy of that trip left him disappointed. No, more that than. Crushed. Nothing had changed between them, not in the way he wanted. Left chasing some foolish fairy tale that, now more than ever, he was convinced wouldn't come true. There had been one moment, just before they left Paris, when he almost heard himself say, "Scott, I'm in love with you." But the ding of Scott's phone, and then watching those kissable lips curl into a smile while reading aloud a message from Mason… That took away his words.

What am I doing here? he wondered, edging his way to the bar. *And why did I drag Scott along?* He knew the answer to the first question. To, on some level, reconnect with his brother, create his own sense of family. The years of silence, unintentional or not, made fashioning a connection again — one that was real and deep — seem impossible. Would he try? Slurping his beer and aimlessly roaming the grounds, he thought about why he'd wanted Scott to come. Simple. He wanted one more chance to make his move, make Scott see just how perfect they could be together. This time, could he summon up the courage and declare his love? He lifted the can to his wet mouth and that was when Patrick came into view. They stared at each other, the way they had at the church as Patrick and his new bride walked down the aisle. Troy lowered the beer can without taking a sip and dropped his head. It reminded him of Frankfurt, when the store clerks spoke German to him. Foreign and incomprehensible. In that moment, he knew that this wasn't home. Even more devastating, that he didn't belong. A hand pressed down on his shoulder and he looked up to see Patrick offering a thin smile. Their eyes locked and, after a time, they fell into a clumsy embrace.

"I'm so glad you came," Patrick said as they pushed apart. He tapped Troy lightly on the arm and led him away from the gathering to the pond area that was less populated. When they reached a stone bench, shaped like a crescent moon, he sat down while Troy remained standing. He patted the seat of the bench twice and waited for Troy to sit. "Your date seems nice."

"His name is Scott," Troy said pointedly. "And he's not my date."

"Oh…" Patrick's eyebrows arched. "Who is he then?"

"He's a friend." Troy took a swig of his beer. "My best friend."

Patrick touched his hand to Troy's arm, then pointed towards the Manor. "Scott sure can dance."

Troy swung his head around and focused his gaze on the dance floor underneath the marquee. Watching Scott bust a groove with Jennifer, Patrick's now wife, a gargantuan pang of jealousy made him quietly snarl. "He's good at everything," he said with an edge and shifted to face the pond.

There was a long silence during which Troy, holding his beer can between his legs, kicked at the grass with his foot. He could feel his brother's eyes on him, but words still failed him. He couldn't even bring himself to look directly at Patrick. *What does he think of me?* he wondered, suddenly angry with himself for wanting to cry. *Am I that weak?*

"Tell me what you're doing with your life," Patrick said, breaking the silence.

Troy repeatedly flicked his middle finger against his beer can. "I start med school in September."

"Where?"

"U of T." Troy's eyes met Patrick's. "Where else?"

"Well, there's a good medical school here in Calgary."

"The one at U of T is better." Troy sounded petulant. "Plus, I got a scholarship."

"Still a nerd," Patrick teased.

"Ha-ha. Don't think my first-year English prof would agree. His class was the morning after poker night, and I slept through it. Managed to get a C plus." Troy bit his lip. "What about you?"

"Like my little brother, I'm going to med school, but apparently to a substandard one. Should have studied hard like you. Broke my wrist the summer after first-year and had no choice but to give up football and my scholarship. Now the student loans are piling up." Patrick playfully shoved Troy. "I want to specialize in psychiatry."

"Good. Maybe you can fix me."

"Why do you need to be fixed?"

"No reason." Troy forced a laugh. "Just trying to be funny. Scott tells me I'm no John Ritter."

They laughed.

"Have you thought about your specialty?" Patrick asked.

"Emergency medicine."

There was another brief silence.

"What happened to us?" Patrick shifted his focus to the people wandering the grounds on the other side of the pond.

Troy scratched the back of his full mane. "I don't know. I … I couldn't come back to Calgary after high school. I mean, after Mom and Dad's divorce it never felt like home. I know we tried to keep in touch in the beginning, but I was building a life in a new city, busy with school and making new friends." He gulped the last mouthful of his beer. "I don't think it matters who stopped calling, but after the days of not calling turned into weeks, and then months … it was easier not to call."

"I know," Patrick said ruefully. "I should have tried harder to keep in touch but, like you said, life got busy." He levelled his gaze at Troy. "I know the divorce hit you hard, but I didn't know how to deal with it then, either. I'm sorry I let you down. I'm your big brother, and I should have been there for you."

"A lousy one minute and fifty-two seconds, and luck of the draw," Troy said mockingly. Their mother had had a Caesarean section.

"But I'm still older."

"Well, big brother, you didn't let me down," Troy said. "Mom and Dad did. They just paid for boarding school and sent money once a month. And neither of them came to our high school graduation, too busy with their new families. We didn't matter anymore, didn't exist. That's what I can't let go of."

"Find a way to let go," Patrick counselled, as if he were already practicing the psychiatric profession. "I mean, I hope we won't let another three or four years pass by without seeing each other."

"Me, too." Troy bounced his knee up and down. "How did you track me down?"

"Really? You can't guess?"

"No, not really."

Patrick grinned. "Keren."

"Who's Keren?"

"Cousin Keren. Remember how we always made fun of her because of how nosy she was? Oh, come on. Don't you remember that Christmas when Keren asked Uncle Ben why he was playing doctor with her Aunt Emma, her mother's sister?"

"Right. But I haven't talked to Keren in years."

"She had your address. She's like our family's own Mossad." Patrick nudged Troy. "Nanna didn't like Aunt Leah much."

"Nanna didn't like anything that wasn't white and protestant." Troy clasped his hands together, letting them dangle between his knees. "Jennifer's beautiful, and she seems nice."

"She's amazing." Patrick flashed his teeth. "And she actually likes her siblings. Well, it's just her and her sister, but they're very close."

"Since you brought it up, and since Kent and Lisa are here, does that mean you're speaking?"

"Hardly. I've tried, but we… Mom and Dad insisted that I invite them, pretend to be one big happy family. The thing is…" Patrick paused. "I can't even remember why we're not talking."

"Nanna's will," Troy reminded his brother. "She left all her grand kids one thousand dollars, except —"

"Right!" Patrick slapped his knee. "She left you and me three thousand each, because twins were special. That seems silly now. Kent's a self-made millionaire and Lisa married one."

"Isn't money the root of all evil and misunderstandings?"

Patrick tied his face up in knots. "No. It's our limiting beliefs about money that screw us over."

"Go on, Dr. Phil!" Troy sniffled, then rubbed his nose. "I never wanted us to slip away from each other. There was so much chaos after the divorce, being away at boarding school and feeling completely isolated. Me coming out, you being the popular kid at school…" He pushed down the tears fighting for freedom. "I didn't feel like I was a part of something. Do you get what I mean?"

Patrick wrapped his arm around Troy's shoulders. "You know, I never cared about the gay thing. As long as you're happy, that's all that matters. Maybe I should have said that at the time." Patrick ran his hand through Troy's dark mane, messing it up the way he used to when they were kids. "Tell me about *him*?"

Troy looked at Patrick. "Who?"

"Your date."

"He's … not … my … date." Troy pursed his lips tightly and rolled them. "He's my best friend. We met at university."

"You look at him the way I look at Jennifer," Patrick said, matter-of-fact, "like your heart's on fire."

"I can talk to Scott, and it doesn't feel like he's judging me or wishing that I'd be someone else. It's weird because there are times when I'm certain that he looks beyond my faults and sees my needs. He's there for me, no matter what."

Patrick slid to his left a bit and swung his right leg over the bench, which he was now straddling. "Are you in love with Scott?"

"Oh, I don't know," Troy said, irritated. "Maybe. I've never been connected to someone the way I am with him."

"Have you told him how you feel?"

"Scott sees me like a brother." Troy rubbed his right eye. "Momma D knows how I feel. She's called me on it."

"Momma D?" Patrick chuckled. "Who's that?"

"Margaret Davenport, Scott's mother," Troy stammered. "Ever since I met Scott, I've spent every major holiday with his family. I call her Momma D, she calls me Stretch because, according to her, I'm a tall, lanky white boy. She's been like a mother to me."

"You spend every holiday with Scott and his family, and you don't think he feels more for you, more than friendship?" Patrick sounded surprised. "Best friends hang out, go to movies, get away for a guys' weekend, confide in one another. You make it sound like the two of you are a couple."

Troy stared blankly at his empty beer can. *We're not a couple. I wish Scott did love me, and not like a brother. And why am I so afraid to tell him how I feel?* It was time for him to change the subject. "Jennifer's not pregnant, is she?"

Patrick looked curiously at Troy. "Why would you think she's pregnant?"

"Wouldn't it have made sense to wait until after you finished med school to get married?"

"I met Jennifer during my second year," Patrick said thoughtfully. "Sure, we could have waited until after she's done law school or I finish med school, but why?" He cupped his hand to Troy's shoulder. "She's the one for me." Pointing at his heart with his other hand, he added, "I know that here." He clasped his hands together and took in the sadness gleaming in Troy's eyes. "We need to see each other more. You should come and spend Thanksgiving with us."

"You could come to Toronto," Troy countered and stood. "I need another drink."

"I think you need to slow down," Scott said as he approached the bench. "I can't carry your heavy ass back to the hotel tonight."

Patrick stifled his laugh as Troy and Scott looked warily at each other.

"I need another drink," Troy repeated dryly, then pushed past Scott and headed for the bar.

Patrick lifted himself up off the bench and stepped towards Scott. "Troy has always been a bit temperamental."

"Is that what you think?" Scott asked, his voice rife with surprise. "There are just days when he doesn't know his limits, and today's one of them. But for some reason or other, we love him anyway."

"Speaking of love…" Patrick wrapped his arm around Scott's shoulders the way he had done a short time ago with Troy. "There's something I want to talk to you about…"

A New Beginning?

"I DON'T GET IT," TROY SAID, BOTH DISPLEASURE
and distrust rumbling in his voice. "You've accepted a job as
a proof-reader?"

"Yes," Scott confirmed.

"Why?"

"Troy..."

In the two years that had passed, Scott had — finally —
found his joy. His graduate studies, and his research on lib-
eralism and the threat to Canada's sovereignty, lit a spark in
him. More than that, it gave him a calling. And it was a big
dream: to become a political theorist. But that meant he didn't
have to slug it out in the political arena, hoping to corner op-
ponents into untenable positions. No being on the hustings.
No slick TV ads. No beholding to influential donors. His
weapon would be his pen, constructing and evaluating political theory. A modern-day James Locke or Immanuel Kant. He
imagined himself leading roundtables at annual conferences
of the Canadian Political Science Association, penning articles for international journals, and interpreting election results
and sparring with Peter Mansbridge on *The National*. He had
direction, a path, a destination.

But he needed a break. His dream job had a major require-
ment: a doctorate degree. With five and half years of learning
already completed, the idea of launching into another four-
year cycle was unthinkable. One year to clear his mind, to do
a sort of reset, would suffice. Besides, he was ready to stop
living off his parents, who'd already used a good chunk of
their retirement savings to fund his education. Time for him
to hold his own.

So, what didn't Troy get? That Scott's compass was no longer broken. He knew who he wanted to become and where he hoped to go. No more waiting around for life to happen *to* him.

That was the good news. There had been no evolution on the love front. Not that he had tried dating, because he hadn't. He stuck to quick, anonymous meet-ups that kept him and his heart closed off. Even if he'd sensed a 'connection,' he never dared to take it farther. All he needed, all he wanted, was good, clean sex. No fuss. No mess. No strings. But that eventually bored him, and he deleted his profiles off all the dating sites. And the few fleeting weekends he'd had with Mason, the American he'd met in Amsterdam, left him … unsatisfied. For similar reasons, they weren't interested in pursuing a relationship. Absent in love and love absent in him, it was perhaps odd — but no longer disturbing — that masturbation had become a more satisfying way to quench his sexual thirst.

"But Junction?" Troy said, exasperated. "Why not Oakville or Burlington?"

"I need a job, a real job." Scott refilled his coffee. "I'm not made to be a barista my entire life. And I need to do something."

In conference in the kitchen of their Gerrard Street East apartment, they talked in hushed voices, like two soldiers trapped behind enemy lines planning their escape. Scott didn't want the movers overhearing in case they sensed his last-minute panic. Not that they could hear much with their work boots clamouring against the hardwood floor.

Waiting to defend his thesis, he'd been hired as an assistant to Allister Crosby, his MPP. He'd passed the oral comprehensive exam in November, graduated in May, and now it was mid-June. In addition to working for Mr. Crosby, he spent forty to fifty hours a week making lattes and cappuccinos at Second Cup. Anything, in his year to recharge, not to return to Ottawa. But he realized that some people found it easy to make small talk with customers about the weather, learn their drink order and have it ready for them when they reached the cash. It showed they cared about the goings-on in a stranger's life. He wasn't one of those people. Even though this was just a time-out before embarking on his doctoral studies, he still wanted to do something meaningful with his life.

For the last three months, he'd been serving soymilk lattes with a fake smile. No, he couldn't stay. Not without becoming one of those bitter people who stayed too long in a job they hated and made their colleagues' lives even more miserable than their own.

"Something would've come along here if —"

"I'm struggling, Troy. I can barely pay my bills. I'm surviving on Mr. Noodles and Hungry-Man meals. I owe you for part of this month's rent." Scott paused to calm down, but he could hear himself mimicking his mother's lecturing tone. "I have you telling me to wait and see what comes up here. My mother's telling me God has it all under control. I'm tired of being broke all the time. I've got a year, well, maybe a little more than that, to live without a care in the world. I don't want to spend that time stressing how I'm going to pay next month's rent. Going to Junction will be an adventure. And there weren't any other job offers. So, I took it. *Point final.*"

"Christ, don't bite my head off. And I never said you owed me anything." Troy set his mug down on the counter and folded his arms. "You may not be a barista, but you're not an office man, either. You'll be bored. I don't want you to become the guy who shoots up his office because he's unhappy."

"I'd shoot myself first."

"Or maybe just quit." Troy offered a courteous smile. "It seems like a big move for just a year. My Aunt Chloe said she was going to be a flight attendant for a summer. Thirty-five years later —"

"I have a plan," Scott cut in. He gulped the last mouthful of his lukewarm coffee, then placed the mug in the sink. "Or maybe you'd like me to stay so you can take care of me? Troy Muir, my sugar daddy."

"Fuck off."

They laughed.

"Are you going to drive me to Junction looking like that?" Scott studied Troy who, when the movers arrived, emerged from his bedroom barefoot, his bed hair a jumbled mess, and wearing torn blue jeans and a wrinkled black Metallica T-shirt. "Joan Rivers would have a field day."

"Ha-ha." Troy topped up his coffee and left the kitchen.

After Scott heard the bathroom door bang shut, he made his way into the living room, sidestepping the movers rushing in and out of the apartment, and stepped onto the long and narrow balcony. He shivered, watching as his cloud of breath disappeared into the air. Troy's exasperated tone cornered him. *But Junction?* Why not Junction? He leaned out a little over the railing to see part of the CN Tower. Something had to give because he was tired of eating frozen dinners, tired of rummaging daily through the sofa cushions for the loose change that 'slipped' out of Troy's pockets. The job poster for the proof-reader at Martin Boswell, an international accounting firm, had intrigued him. He often read over Troy's term papers, got a little high from correcting them. And he'd finished the novel he'd started after breaking up with Anthony. It may not have been his dream job or in his dream location, but it would give him stability. So, he applied. And like all the other jobs he'd applied to, once he hit the 'Submit' button, he waited.

The waiting … torturous, unbearable, terrifying. But his current diet of Pizza Pops or the no name Kraft Dinner wannabe were surely signs that homelessness was his next stop. One way to stave off that homelessness would be to become a prost … prosti … prostitute. He couldn't imagine being any good or dedicated to *that.* More than anything, not finding work would force him back to Ottawa, and being branded a failure would be the ultimate disgrace.

The morning sun beaming into his eyes made his lips curl. He would never be homeless. His mother would never let that happen. But that didn't, at the time, quell his fear. And he knew fear had power, could alter any sane man's perception. Fear could drive a man mad.

Hope arrived on the Friday of the May Two-Four weekend. Scott, wrapped up neatly in despair, returned home from work feeling weak and pathetic and hapless. He grabbed one of Troy's beers from the fridge and fell onto the sofa. Staring blankly into the room, he sipped his drink and wondered if he'd ever pull himself out of the downward spiralling slump. Writing had helped to heal his broken heart. Would it do good now, bring him back from the edge of some type of breakdown? Maybe. But he wasn't sure he was ready for another round of rejection letters, wasn't sure he could survive that. Yet every now and then he'd pull out the manuscript from the drawer of his nightstand and flip through it. *Nope,* was his standard assessment. *I'm done with that kind of writing.* And back in the drawer it went.

Catching a glimpse of the flashing red light on the phone, Scott hesitated, but eventually left the sofa to listen to the message. After the fifth playback, he held his beer can against his forehead for a moment, and then started jumping around the room. No concern for the beer spilling over top of the can and onto him, the furniture and the floor. The message was from Jacob Hoyt, the HR manager at Martin Boswell, inviting him for an interview. Approaching midnight, Scott didn't care about the lateness of the hour and dialled Jacob's number to confirm the date and time of the interview.

On the day of the interview, Scott made the two-and-a-half-hour trip to Junction by bus. Wearing his best black wool suit, his only suit actually, and sporting his generous smile, he was ready. Determined. He hoped that all the time he'd spent preparing and rehearsing his answers to roughly fifty interview questions he had found on the internet would pay off. The meeting with Jacob and the senior editor, who was also the unit supervisor, lasted close to ninety minutes. While Scott believed the interview went well, he didn't come away feeling like he had wowed them. By the time he returned home, repeatedly replaying the exchanges in his mind and second-guessing his answers, he was less confident about his performance. Then a week passed without him hearing anything about the job. *I blew it*, was his initial thought. But then the phone rang, and he was both shocked and relieved to be invited back for another interview.

During his second visit to Martin Boswell's offices, he met with one of the associate partners. Much less formal than the first, it was more of a meet-and-greet. Jacob was present but in the role of an emissary who was only there to intervene in case of conflict. When Scott and Jacob were alone again, they acted like two friends catching up after a long absence, laughter constantly erupting between them. If he didn't get the job, he at least believed that he may have made a friend. That was silly but, on some level, he and Jacob had a connection. Not in a romantic sense, although he thought there was a slight attraction, but more that Jacob understood him. Jacob reminded him a little of Troy — confident, articulate, ambitious — without the excessive use of expletives and outward neediness.

"I don't come across very many applicants who've read Sartre," Jacob said as they headed back to the reception area.

"I've just always liked the idea of being responsible for my actions, of who I can become," Scott affirmed. "Thought it might be useful in my studies on political theory. My thesis director didn't quite agree." He took a deep breath. "I've never been a fan of those who believe in fate."

"You must act," Jacob said, "to live the life you imagine."

With a parting handshake, Scott couldn't get the metallic taste out of his mouth as he headed towards the bus station. In an instant, Jacob had joined his rather private club and became, along side Troy, someone he really believed he could trust. That made him suspicious when most people still seemed to run away from him. *Maybe I'm imagining it ... a connection that isn't really there because I'm desperate to feel like I'm part of something.* But when the job offer came three days later, Scott accepted it without hesitation.

"Mr. Davenport..."

Scott spun around to see the rugged-looking man standing at the patio doors. His gaze, as it did when the guy first walked into the apartment, fell on the large matrix-style tattoo running the length of the muscled right arm. "Are you done already?"

"The other guys are loading the last load onto the truck now."

This is happening way too fast. When their eyes met, Scott offered an appreciative smile.

Scott hadn't expected much from a moving company called Bad Attitude Moving, except to have his furniture banged about. He was wrong. When he looked past the guy's tattoo and scruffiness, he saw a kind and professional man who took pride in his work. That was what he loved about the city. He loved its richness, walking through the streets as English, French, Cantonese, Arabic and so many other languages collided. The concerts in Dundas Square and the summer festivals that took over the streets. When he wasn't broke, his daily visits to Rosa's Café for a blueberry muffin and a latte. That he could, in so many ways, be nameless and faceless. But now there was nothing, and no one, important holding him here.

And as much as he loved Toronto, things had changed after Anthony Power. The city had taken on a new staleness, like a straitjacket tightening with each attempt to break loose and squeezing life out of him. He was, in a very real way, homeless. Living with Troy was the one constant in his life, and it had also shifted. During their undergraduate studies, they had more associations in common, ended up at the same events. But once he started his master's program and Troy med school, they — involuntarily or not — carved out their own circle of friends. Well, Troy did. Scott became even more of a loner. Sometimes they walked to the university together in the morning, and occasionally met up for a coffee or beer in between classes. They were still 'close' and confided in each other, but their life paths were leading them away from each other.

Even if the job at Martin Boswell turned out to be a disaster, Scott wouldn't return to Toronto. A city that had overwhelmed him when he first arrived, his time in Toronto had moulded him into a confident, strong-willed man. But in some way, it'd lost its allure. Sure, he was a loner, loved to be lost in the city, yet he still had a powerful desire to be connected to something. Feel at home, be a part of a community. That want gone unfulfilled, Toronto became his past. Unlike Troy, he didn't draw people to him, and for the few who'd shown an interest he held back, wouldn't let them in. What made Troy the exception? Scott didn't have a MySpace page, wasn't partying every weekend or shooting off text messages every five minutes. For all these reasons, and a few more he wasn't ready to admit, Junction held the promise of his present and future. He would make it work, would not be defeated.

"Let me take one last look around to make sure you haven't missed anything," Scott said and jetted inside. He roamed about the apartment, examining each room with a critical eye, and was taken unawares by the sudden urge to cry. The movers had removed every trace of him, wiped out his imprint. *It's too late to change your mind*, he thought, returning to the living room. "All right. See you in Junction shortly."

Troy appeared in the living room just as the rugged-looking man disappeared. "I'm ready."

"Me, too," Scott said, his voice cracking. He pulled out his keys, slipped the one to the apartment off his key ring and handed it to Troy. "This makes it real."

"I guess." Troy pocketed the key.

Scott, with his lips pursed, surveyed the apartment one last time. He stood in the doorway of his old bedroom and stared into the empty room. When he realized he was leaving behind a part of himself, his stomach flipped. Maybe he was wrong. Maybe this *was* home? And if it were home, Troy was a big part of what made it so. What did that mean? He slid his hands in his pockets and made for the door.

In the corridor, Scott watched as Troy pulled the door closed, locked it and then rushed him. He accepted the clumsy embrace, tightening his grip around Troy's lanky body. It was just the moment he needed to catch his breath, and reassurance that he was on the right path. Yes, this was his next right thing to do. Even more so, it was assurance that they'd find a way to stay connected. He pulled away first, rubbing his eye as Troy stepped ahead of him to push the elevator call button. When their eyes locked, Troy gave his trademark soul-searching stare and Scott had no doubt. Their bond was necessary, real, and unbreakable. He was stronger because of Troy.

What Scott had once believed was an end was in fact a beginning, and somewhere in that beginning he would find himself, grow into who he really was.

The elevator bell dinged, the doors slid open and, still holding Troy's gaze, Scott's legs shook.

Oh ... my ... God...

***

"HOW DID YOU FIND THIS PLACE?" TROY ASKED as he made his way cautiously up the walk. The duplex, with the paint nearly all peeled off the front of the house and the sagging roofline, sent chills down his spine. He pictured it as the perfect place to film a low-budget porn flick. Or a meeting place for unscrupulous people who didn't want to be seen.

"Kind of like our first place on Borden Street," Scott said and jammed the key into the lock.

"If only that good," Troy whispered and followed Scott inside. The house was spacious and, sizing up his surroundings, he knew it had been lived in. The walls, painted white, carried the faint flowery design of the wallpaper that had never been stripped. The staircase had a visible, and troubling, slope to it. The smell of stale cigarette smoke, maybe even cannabis, lingered. He looked up, saw the hallway chandelier carved out of wood and in the shape of moose antlers, and howled. "Are you kidding me?"

"It's a little dated." Scott took the two knapsacks he had brought into the house and stored them in the far corner of the living room, next to the boarded-up fireplace. "But the rent is cheap."

Troy glanced at his watch. "Will you be okay alone until the movers get here?"

"You're leaving? Let me buy you lunch at least."

"Aren't you broke?"

"My parents gave me a little cushion in my bank account," Scott said, "to help me through the transition."

"Momma D wouldn't be happy if she knew you were spending her cushion on dinners out."

"Who's going to tell her? Besides, I was thinking McDonald's. Or Harvey's. You choose."

"Oh, fuck you."

They laughed, their eyes roaming the room and unsettled by the stony silence they feared would dominate them. Troy didn't want to stay, didn't want to be alone with Scott and the fantasy that kept poking at him. He limped into the living room and sunk onto the wide ledge of the large rectangular window. Scott took a seat next to him a few seconds later. Troy caught the faint sage scent of Scott's cologne and his head began to spin. In no time he was naked and stretched out on the caramel-coloured hardwood floor, a devilish grin on his thin pink lips as he watched Scott tear open the condom package. Lost in the fantasy that came to him daily, his heart pumping, he didn't hear the honking horn until Scott jabbed him in the side. He turned partially around, saw the white moving truck edging backwards towards the house and thought he'd be sick.

Scott stood. "Where'd you go?"

"Nowhere." Troy looked down. "I'm a little tired."

"You can't lie to save your life." Scott sucked his teeth and scooted to the front door.

Troy levelled his eyes at Scott's ass, the torment of that long-burning ache made him tremble. When Scott rounded the corner and disappeared, he leaned back and rested his head against the window, his gaze falling on the foot-long black smudge on the far wall. It seemed like he was losing his best friend, especially when the rugged mover with the matrix tattoo appeared and positioned protective mats on the floor. Back in Toronto, he didn't like how the guy eyeballed Scott, stripping him down almost, lusting. Then he noticed the gold band on the guy's wedding finger, but what did that mean these days? Childish, he knew, to think that Scott was being hit on by every guy who passed through his life. But he couldn't help himself, not when he lacked their courage. When the other movers started herding furniture and boxes into the house, he slipped into the kitchen and out the back door. Seated on the top rung of the wobbly veranda stairs, he stared blindly into the long and narrow backyard, which was shaded by the large red oaks that ran down the middle of the property. A tall divider offered privacy from the neighbours, but Troy could hear someone dragging on a cigarette on the other side. Then he heard a chair scraping across the veranda floor. He closed his eyes, trying to shut out everything around him and hear himself think.

"Moving day, eh?" the voice cracked.

Troy opened his eyes and his gaze found the grey-haired, hawk-eyed woman who peered at him. His focus shifted to the cigarette being held between her chapped lips. "Yes," he said with no emotion.

"You ain't livin' here, too, are ya?" The woman dragged on her cigarette and removed it from her lips. "Scott said he'd be livin' here alone, and Lord knows I don't need no tenants like the last group of hoodlums. Last time I done call the police I kicked 'em out."

"I just drove Scott up from Toronto," Troy confirmed, although he'd wanted to say, "Yes, I'm living here, too."

"You don't look like trouble." She pointed the cigarette at Troy, but focused on Scott, who'd just appeared on the veranda. "He ain't livin' here, right?"

Scott chuckled. "No, Mrs. Boyle."

"Good. And it's Leila." She took another drag on her cigarette, shifting her gaze between Troy and Scott as if trying to uncover some secret agenda. "Well, if you need me, I next door." She slinked off, coughing roughly several times, followed by the sound of her corralling the phlegm lodged in her throat. A short time later, a door banged shut.

"Movers are gone," Scott said.

"Already?" Troy lifted himself up and slid his hands in his pockets. "I should get on the road then."

"I'm buying you lunch, remember?" Scott crossed his arms. "Why are you in such a fucking hurry to leave? That desperate to get rid of me? Turn the apartment into the long-anticipated love den?"

I want to hang on to you. You have no idea.

"After lunch you can help me unpack the kitchen. Or we can unpack the kitchen and then go to lunch. The choice is yours." Scott opened the back door. "I don't know why you're looking at me like that. It's Thursday, and you don't have class tomorrow. I told you to bring some clothes and stay the weekend."

Troy rolled his shoulders. "I thought you'd want to be alone the first night in your new home."

"It seems so foreign and weird." Scott waved his arms, gesturing Troy to go inside. "It would be great to have some company —"

"To help with the unpacking?"

"And my initial trip to the grocery store. Your car will come in handy for that."

They headed inside, Scott leading the way to the living room.

"I don't have any clothes with me, as you pointed out," Troy said somewhat cheekily.

Scott pointed at the two knapsacks in the corner. "The blue one. When I did laundry yesterday, I threw some of your clothes in it. Should get you through until Sunday, but you might have to buy some toiletries."

"Unbelievable." Troy thought he'd paint the walls brown with the coffee he drank during the drive. "All right. Let's go for lunch first. Then we'll do groceries and after that we'll try to bring order to this place. But I'm going to need some beer."

Troy, directed to lock the back door, did that and then stole into the bathroom. The idea of being alone with Scott tackled him, had him back to the fantasy of them naked together. Standing in front of the toilet bowl, he shoved his jeans down and violently stroked his slender cock to the thought of Scott pounding his smooth, tight ass. He came, breathless, and wasn't so nervous anymore.

"Finally," Scott said when Troy appeared outside.

"You can't rush nature." Troy shoved his hand in his pocket, discreetly adjusted himself, and headed towards his beige Corolla parked on the street. He looked back at the house and, as his best friend approached the car, hoped that spending the next few days together would see him through his doubts and fears.

The Wait is Over

A CRACKLING SOUND. A FLASH. OUTSIDE THE window, the dark night sky lit up. Then darkness again. Rumbling, trailing off slowly, lingered at the door like a spurned lover hoping to be called back. Silence. The lights flickered. Tap, tap against the window. Water pooling on the window sill. Tap, tap, from *andante* to *allegro*. The lights flickered again. Darkness.

"Candles?" Troy said, sitting up on the sofa.

"Somewhere," was Scott's dry reply. "Let's see how long the outage lasts."

Troy leaned forward and gently moved his hand across the coffee table until he found his cell phone. He unlocked the screen and held it out to Scott. A small stream of light cut through the blackness. "Not much of a torch, but it'll help if you want to look —"

"We know what each other looks like." Scott didn't move. "Our eyes will adjust."

Troy closed his mobile, the room falling back into darkness. More lightning blazed in the sky. Rain pelted the windowpane with such force that he sometimes thought it would crack. He sat still, his legs tucked under his body, his eyes fixed on Scott, whose face lit up each time the lightning flashed.

Saturday night, a few minutes before ten, and since their arrival in Junction two days ago, all the furniture had been arranged and the boxes unpacked. Time flew by, filled with the laughter and warmth of two people sure of their unbreakable bond. Yet they were unaware of the intense change occurring and set to transform them. A change so swift that had them, for the very first time, really seeing inside themselves.

Troy stretched out his left leg and with his foot tapped Scott's thigh. "Truth or dare?"

"I'm not playing one of your silly drinking games," Scott said, shoving Troy's foot away.

"Then what?"

"Sit here and enjoy the quiet." Scott gave a contented sigh.

But it wasn't quiet. Not for Troy. It wasn't the rain or the earth-rattling thunder, but the clamour of his thoughts that caused him pain. Real pain, not imagined, pulsing behind his right eye, making the socket vibrate. He lifted his hand to his throbbing eye, applying a little pressure, and that briefly dulled the pain. When he pulled his hand away the pain had ebbed, but not completely. By this time, when his right eye came back into focus, both eyes had adjusted to the darkness. He could see Scott clearly, staring into the room while balancing his wineglass on the arm of the sofa. Scott present and absent, and Troy uncertain as to how to reconnect. The pain in his eye was back.

Again, Troy tapped his foot, this time more forcefully, against Scott's leg. "You never did answer my question."

"I'm not playing —"

"Not about that." Troy kicked Scott again. "About how you found this place."

"See-it."

"Wow." The use of an online rental site surprised Troy because Scott often acted like a conspiracy theorist, convinced that secret government agents were out to get him and using the internet would give away his position. "And did you see it? Live, I mean."

"Couldn't afford to. Hoped the pictures were up-to-date. Had to do a telephone interview with Leila."

"Yet you're still not on Myspace. Imagine."

They laughed. Then a return to silence. The rain had let up, the thunder and lightning intermittent. The pain in Troy's eye less but still present.

"Do you want another beer?" Scott asked, swinging his empty wineglass.

"Not yet, thanks." Troy watched as Scott rose and left the room. His heart pumped at the surge of longing he couldn't outrun. He could not remember ever feeling this way about a man, or why he couldn't shake it when he knew the object of his affection had no such ache.

The lights came on as Scott entered the living room, and they exchanged smiles of relief. Troy ogled Scott, who was barefoot and wore a white T-shirt and grey jogging pants. He tried to recall the last time he had seen Scott so relaxed. *Maybe this move is exactly what he needs.* His gaze was again glued to Scott's ass as he passed by. There it was again, that deep yearning that consumed him. He slid to the edge of the sofa, realized this was *his* moment. Time to act.

"Scott…" Troy set his near-empty beer bottle on the end table and stood. He placed his hand on Scott's shoulder, spun him around and then took away the wineglass. Did Scott, in that moment, understand the message, the tension that needed to be released? Did he, *now*, feel it, too? Didn't they both need some type of freeing from the uncertainty that inhabited them, the uncertainty of where their paths were set to lead them?

Troy, trembling, cupped his hand to the back of Scott's shaved head. He hesitated, swallowed repeatedly, but knew that it was now or never. He had to go for it and he did. Pulled Scott forward until their lips met, his head swimming, his dick swollen and ready. No resistance, no fumbling. Just him and Scott locked in a tight embrace with their lips pressed together. Their mouths opened, and when their tongues touched the rhythm of the kiss intensified. He couldn't believe that Scott was willingly giving in, devouring him. But he was.

And Troy couldn't let go of Scott or the kiss as they, peeling off each other's clothes, shuffled to the bedroom.

Why? Why had he waited so long?

Recovering from their hectic, animal-like lovemaking, Troy lay awkwardly in Scott's arms, trying to discover the perfect fit that didn't, at that point, come naturally to them. He tried again, centring his head between Scott's nipples, and Scott seemed to purposely resist his movements. He sat up, his lips pursed tightly, and grabbed the pillow he'd placed under his stomach to prop up his ass during the lovemaking. After covering his crotch, he looked at Scott but couldn't catch his eye. The warmth of comfort, the glow, the deep longing were gone, extinguished when the sex act was done. A new disconnect. Separation.

"What's wrong, Scott?" Troy touched his hand to Scott's bare thigh and pressed gently. "Scott..."

Scott turned his head to Troy, their eyes locked. "This is."

Troy drew the pillow covering his crotch into him, holding on tight like his life depended on it. How could this be wrong? The force of the first kiss made him believe that Scott had the same desire, really ached for it. It was, after all, Troy who had surrendered his will, letting Scott take control. Use him. Dominate him. Ravage him. There, in the bed together, the intent stares, the panting, the deep caresses, Scott's hot breath in his ear willing him to obey. Their movements matched and perfectly timed, not chaotic and clumsy like first-time lovers. A natural ebb and flow to the lovemaking that belonged to lovers who'd been together a lifetime. An absolute rightness that had freed them from the uncertainty inhabiting them. Now the uncertainty was back, hovering, sending Troy spinning. "I..." He shifted his gaze to the chrome-plated lamp on the nightstand to Scott's right. "I don't understand."

Scott pushed himself up in the bed, his back against the wall, his knees drawn up to his chest along with the bed sheets. "We're best friends, Troy. Not lovers or sex buddies." He leaned forward to grab Troy's hand, squeezed it and let go. "I need you to always be my best friend."

"I just thought that maybe..." Troy saw the questioning look in Scott's eyes, the hint of reproach, borderline disgust. *It's like he had sex with his brother, and he's repulsed as it finally sinks in.* He cast off the pillow, his own gesture of revulsion, found his underwear — the only piece of his clothing that had made it from the living room — and stepped into them. He made a beeline for the door.

"Troy..."

Troy turned partially around, but kept his gaze low as tears gathered in his eyes. "It's late. I'll —"

"Are we okay?"

Troy forced a thin smile. "I'm not sure." He left the bedroom, drawing the door closed behind him, and fled downstairs. Collapsing onto the sofa, tears streamed down his face.

Just when he thought Scott had saved his life, life had been taken away.

The Shift

IN THE MORNING, EVERYTHING WAS DIFFER-
ENT. Scott knew that, felt it deep inside him. The world, *his*
world — an unsettling labyrinth of emotion — had him constantly questioning his decisions, doubting his own worth. A
jackal. That was how he saw himself now. He was a jackal. A
terribly harsh assessment perhaps, but one that seemed to fit.
He had been reckless. Sleeping with Troy had been reckless
and dangerous. But his labyrinth of disappointment — most of
all in love — gave him nothing to firmly anchor himself to in
the way he imagined. Until Troy's kiss, which had touched off
something in him, a type of longing. Not necessarily for Troy
or against him, either. For intimacy, for a certain satisfaction
of feeling desired and loved.

There was a sweetness to Troy's tenderness, a gentleness
to his touch, a *desire* to please that made Scott, after a long
dry season, almost come alive. Such closeness. Such famil-
iarity. Such joy. Then such absolute horror. Scott knew that
sex had the power to change everything, yet he yielded voluntarily to that murky world of desire. It was, for him, simply
about being cherished, for a little while, by someone familiar. A moment where hope would dance, for an hour or two,
maybe more, and lift them up. Perhaps running into several
days, they'd have a memory of something *good* because they
both needed a release from their self-made labyrinths. Could
it even be something more than that?

No, not now. Not when Scott believed his friendship with
the most important person in his life had been altered in such
an unforgivable way. Why? Because he wasn't being honest
with himself. And seeing both the hope and defeat that raged

in Troy's eyes in a span of hours didn't sway him from his position. Instead, he wished he could go back in time. But he couldn't go back, couldn't change what happened. Together, they'd have to find a way forward, if they had the will.

At the sound of the creaking staircase, Scott, seated at the square bistro table in the kitchen, got up and poured out a second mug of coffee. He turned around and there was Troy, standing in the kitchen doorway with the strap of the blue knapsack slung across his shoulder. They looked past each other. Scott pointed at the coffee mug. "That's for you. What do you feel like for breakfast?"

"I'm not hungry," Troy said in a steely voice. "I'm going to head out."

"Troy, I'm —"

"Let's forget it."

"I can't. I mean…" Scott breathed deeply. "I'm sorry. What happened last night … I shouldn't have … it's my fault. Blame me."

"We're both to blame. Me, especially, for my stupidity."

"Troy —"

"But like I said, let's forget it." Troy was silent for a moment. "Do you need to run any errands before I go?"

"No, I think I have everything, thanks."

"Then I guess —"

"Wait a minute." Scott took the silver travel mug next to the coffee maker and filled it. He screwed on the tap and handed it to Troy. "For the road."

Troy took the mug. "Thanks."

Their eyes locked, both of them trying to understand how their friendship had shifted, and them along with it. When Troy backed out of the kitchen, Scott followed him to the front door. Again, another intent look shared. Then, without a word, Troy abruptly opened the door and left.

Scott, slow to exit the house, stopped at the end of the walk. He watched as Troy, his movements rigid and calculated, placed the travel mug in the cup holder between the two front seats and then tossed the knapsack onto the back seat. *I've lost him*, he thought, pained.

Troy rested his arms on top of the car doorframe. "You should think about getting a car."

"With what? Monopoly money?" Scott stepped off the walk and onto the driveway, his hands clasped behind his back. "Thanks for driving me down here, and for helping me set up the place. I really do appreciate it."

"It's what friends do," Troy said tersely.

Friends ... are we still friends? Scott wasn't so sure, but he hoped so. He hugged Troy.

Troy loosely returned the embrace and quickly pulled away. "If you need anything, anything at all, just call or text me."

Genuine or false offer? Scott wondered before saying, "I will," knowing it was his own false promise.

Troy got into his car, closed the door and flipped the engine. He rolled down the window, drew the seat belt across his chest and looked up at Scott. "Are you sure about this?" flew out of his mouth.

"Don't forget about Labour Day. Mama's expecting you for the family barbecue. You'll be there, right?"

"Yes."

More false promises, more words spoken disingenuously to sustain the illusion of friendship, to broker a fragile peace.

It took only seconds for Troy's car to roll out of the driveway and, tires squealing, burn down the street.

Scott walked to the end of the driveway and stood there until Troy's car turned the corner and disappeared. His throat constricted, and he blinked rapidly to check his tears. He was, for the first time since he had gone off to university, alone in a strange city, once again starting over, hoping to put down roots. Was he sure about this? His most honest answer: mostly. He wasn't sure what to make of his new home in the district known as Malbeck, a part of the city with dilapidated housing and sketchy businesses. He cupped his hands briefly to the back of his round head and then let them drop to his sides. Cutting across the green grass, he stared at the white clouds and hoped for a sign, direction. Something, anything, to untangle the messy mix of feelings knotted in his heart. When he reached the front steps, he glimpsed Leila peeking out the window through the crack in the curtains and waved. Leila vanished, but seconds later her front door opened and she burst onto her stoop.

"He's quite the looker," Leila said and laughed, snorting.

"He's my best friend," Scott said with tenderness and, despite his earlier doubts, meant it.

"Oh!" Leila brought the cigarette she held in her fingers to her lips and lit it. "I thought he might be, well, you know … it's all right to be *that* these days. My brother's funny like that." She took a drag and coughed. "Boy, would he sure like you."

Scott's eyes narrowed and widened. He pointed at the house. "I should finish unpacking," he lied to get away and advanced towards his front door.

"Anything you need, I here," Leila called out.

"Thanks." Scott rushed into the house, closing the door behind him and locking it. He walked into the living room and collapsed onto the sofa. What was he to do? How was he supposed to begin again? Had he completely messed up his friendship with Troy? He sat there for a long time staring aimlessly into the room. Then suddenly, his nose impregnated with Troy's manly scent that lingered, he pulled his keys out of his pocket and bolted for the door.

Outside, he ran across the lawn to be out of Leila's line of vision as quickly as possible and didn't stop until he reached the corner of the street. He veered to the right and walked leisurely in the direction of the McDonald's sign that stretched high into the blue sky off in the distance. *It's insane. I don't love him. I mean, I can't. We're just friends. How could we be anything more?* No, no more love. No more giving his heart to a guy only to have it broken. Besides, he had a plan and he'd stick to it. And maybe this place could be — now, perhaps forever? — home, where he could finally be himself.

The panic that overwhelmed him earlier as Troy drove off began to subside. Yes, this was his chance to transform his life, reinvent himself.

But was he committed to the cause?

Part III

February 2004 – June 2006

No, Never Alone

A COUGH. NOT FAR AWAY. INTENTIONAL, *pianissimo* and repeated, like a dare, to draw out the assassin hiding behind a pillar. Scott, standing in front of his office window and watching the snow tumble to the ground, didn't take up the dare. The real threat was outside, and he slowly turned around.

"You're still here?" the deep voice said.

Scott, his gaze locked on the tall figure approaching his desk, dropped into his chair and leaned back. He sidled his eyes to the bottom of the computer screen and noted the time. Quarter past one, and ninety minutes after the office had closed. It was mid-February, and Junction had barely finished digging out from the two feet of snow from the storm four days ago as winter was, once again, pounding the city. Fiercely. The early morning special weather statement from Environment Canada warned of another heavy snowfall, possibly a blizzard. And on Valentine's Day! Scott was still at the office, even as the city was shutting down, because he had no place to be, no one to cradle him and his dreams. He flashed his visitor a curious look. "So are you."

"The place is deserted." Jacob Hoyt loosened his blue striped tie. "Go before the storm gets any worse."

Scott randomly shuffled the papers on his desk. "Nothing's plowed. The buses are off the road. I can't walk home in *that*." He gave a wry laugh as he pointed at the papers neatly stacked on the top tray of his in-basket. "I'll have a romantic rendez-vous with those performance evaluations your assistant keeps pestering me about."

"Valentine's Day…" Jacob drawled, his sharp tone unable to mask the simmering disgust. "I've never understood why we need a day to celebrate love."

"We never understand it when we're single."

"It's like there's a day for everything. Chocolate Covered Everything Day. Donald Duck Day. Hug Day. Skyscraper Day, for the love of God. What's next? National Arse-Wiping Day?" Jacob let out a forced laugh. "Sorry. This day just makes me so … frustrated."

"You know, there are websites for that … to help relieve the frustration."

Silence, and a few seconds later, laughter.

Jacob glanced at his watch. "Well, the evaluations can wait. You can't stay here because the building's closing at two. If you can't get home, my place is two blocks away. You're welcome to hang out there until the buses are back on the road."

"I doubt that's going to be any time soon."

"Still, you can't stay here. There's food and wine at my place. Lots of wine, actually." Jacob shoved his hands in his pants pockets and crossed back to the door. "I'll meet you downstairs in ten. Don't make me come back up here. It won't be pretty." He strutted off down the corridor.

Scott sat still, holding his breath, as he waited for that sound, which came five seconds later, of the glass door leading to the elevators latching closed. He exhaled forcefully and listened. A new silence thrust him into a sort of paralysis. He couldn't move, couldn't think, couldn't breathe. The resurgence of a familiar and disconcerting uneasiness that unearthed old wounds and bad judgments. That disquiet had a terrifying name. Desire. Scott had to put off Jacob, stay clear of him. He couldn't risk letting himself be corrupted by desire. That seedy culprit had severely maimed his friendship with Troy, created a wedge that had yet to be bridged. In the seven months he'd been in Junction, he and Jacob had established a solid, if somewhat accidental, alliance. He saw their friendship as proof that he was putting down roots, and there was no way he was going to let desire wound that friendship, make it bleed.

A loud rumble made him flinch, and he bounced out of his chair to look out the window. A snow plow slid down the street, its tires spinning, and Scott held his breath. A black

SUV coasted, in slow-moving circles, towards the large blade of the snow plow. Thud. That was all it sounded like from Scott's sixth-floor office when the two vehicles collided. He stepped back from the window, panic enveloping him. Jacob was right. He had to get out, flee far and fast. He shut down his computer, jammed file folders and his notebook into his attaché, then grabbed his coat as he darted out of his office. A few minutes later, he arrived in the building's main lobby to see Jacob pacing the area in front of the revolving doors, impatience etched in his square face.

"Finally," Jacob growled playfully, pulled up his hood and charged towards the exit.

Outside, they were nearly swept off their feet by the violent gusts of wind that twirled the snow around their heads. Once they were able to steady themselves, they began shuffling down the sidewalk. Scott walked with his head bowed but looked up occasionally to make sure he had Jacob in his sights. He grunted. The dampness of his clothes against his skin made him shiver as he struggled through the snow, which almost reached his knees. An eeriness hovered over the streets, littered with cars and trucks abandoned by their owners. Most of the shops and offices along Main Street were closed, or closing. Twelve minutes after leaving the office, they rushed into the lobby of Jacob's Broadview Street condo building, breathless, sweaty, and on the verge of collapse.

They stomped the snow off their boots, ignoring the concierge's annoyed look, peeled off their hats and gloves, and undid their jackets as they made for the elevator. Jacob pushed the call button and the doors slid open. After a quick ride to the ninth floor, they staggered down the long corridor to the corner unit. Jacob hung up their coats on the hooks just inside the door, kicked off his boots and moved further into the dark condo to turn on lights. The grey skies mimicked that moment when night was about to displace day. When Jacob returned to the front hall, Scott hadn't moved, looking about the space as if he didn't know what to do next.

"Come in," Jacob said with an unintentional edge.

Scott advanced into the living room and stood in front of the large window. He surveyed the street below, his gaze locked on the intermittent flashing red dot. The traffic light at the corner swung back and forth, the strong winds battering it, and so close it seemed to being torn off the pole. He spun around, let his eyes rove the medium-size room with a deep, four-cushioned grey tweed sofa against the wall opposite the window. Above the sofa hung five black and white photos, in black frames, of places Scott didn't recognize. There was a large square coffee table with polished chrome legs, and neatly positioned across its glass surface were a silver-plated apple, a pile of three magazines with *Details* on top, and Iris Murdoch's *Sartre: Romantic Rationalist*. Tall, dark-stained bookshelves covered the other walls, the shelves filled with books and photos. "Huh," slipped out at the realization that there wasn't a TV in the room.

He lowered himself onto the far end of the sofa and, from time to time, leaned forward to finger his pant legs that were damp and cold against his skin. He was nervous even though he had no reason to be. This was not the first time he and Jacob had been alone together. That had happened in November.

Scott remembered that day, stormy like this one, but not as bad. Most days after work, he either took off straight home or stopped in at Mo's Café where, sipping on a decaf latte, he'd read. Maybe it was the bone-chilling wind, but as soon as he stepped outside he made a beeline for Finn's, the popular Irish pub across the street. The hostess, a petite brunette, offered a faint smile when he asked for a table for one and led him to the far side of the pub, in the corner. To his surprise, he ordered a pint of Rickard's Red when the server appeared. He hadn't touched a lager since his disastrous weekend with Troy.

He had a clear view of the entrance and couldn't help but look up each time the bell chimed as the pub door opened, not that he was expecting anyone to join him. Still more of a loner, he hadn't befriended anyone at work. He pulled out a black notebook and a pen, then started writing.

Actually, the page remained blank through his first ten sips of beer. Since settling down in Junction, writing had become an occasional hobby, something he still flirted with but no longer saw as a career path. His plan hadn't changed, either. He'd already submitted applications to seven universities, hoping to be accepted into their doctoral programs. Surprisingly, and never believing he wanted to return to Toronto, U of T was his first choice. By the fall, he'd be back in the one place he excelled: academia. Maybe it was the beer, or the unexpected calm sweeping over him, but his hand started moving and the world around him collapsed, fell away. He'd forgotten that writing had that effect on him, made everyone — and every-thing — around him disappear. Was that a sign?

"Next round's on me…"

It took a moment to realize that that baritone voice was di-rected at him. He lifted his head and froze as those mysterious nickel eyes bore into him. "Sorry, I —"

"I'm sorry." Jacob stepped back from the table. "I seem to be intruding."

"No, it's okay." Scott gestured for Jacob to sit. "I was lost in another world."

Jacob hung up his jacket on the back of his chair. "Want to tell me about it?"

"Not really." Scott closed his notebook and slid it into his satchel along with the pen.

Seated, Jacob whispered, "I won't tell anyone. Promise."

Scott flicked his eyebrows.

The gangly waiter, who'd nearly spilled his drink, was back.

Jacob ordered a pitcher of beer, waited for the server to leave, then asked, "Is this where you hide out after work?"

"No." Scott fidgeted with the coaster under his empty beer stein. "Sometimes I stop at Mo's. Mostly I hide out at home. Today, well … I don't know. Felt like changing it up."

"I'm glad you did." Jacob leaned back as the scrawny, hairy hand passed in front of his face, the amber liquid sway-ing in the plastic jug as it landed in the centre of the table.

"Anything else at the moment, gentlemen?" the guy asked, setting down the other beer stein with a hard clank.

"No, we're good, thanks." Jacob reached for the pitcher and poured the beer slowly into each stein to avoid making head on them. "Cheers!"

"Cheers." Scott raised his glass and touched its rim against Jacob's, then took a sip. Then what he hoped wouldn't hap-pen did. An uncomfortable silence settled in, he and Jacob looking away every time their eyes met. What was different now? After his first interview, he'd imagined them becoming friends. Now, they were together — like friends catching up over a drink — and he didn't know what to say.

"So, what does Scott Davenport do when he's not working?" Jacob asked, hunched over his drink.

"Not much, really." Scott glanced away, his normal reaction every time someone tried to get personal with him. He hoped it would give him time to come up with a more interesting answer, but it never did.

"Do you read? Go to the movies? Play hockey?"

Scott howled. "Do I look like someone who plays hockey?"

"It's not that funny," Jacob said askance, then sipped his beer. "And I'm just trying to make conversation. You don't play hockey. Understood. You were writing when I came in. Are you a writer? Someone I should know?"

"No, I'm not a writer. I write, but..." Scott bit his lip. "I kind of 'fool around' with writing. It's something I do for a while, then stop. I like it, just not serious about it like some might be. I mean, it's not easy getting published."

"Are you trying? To get published, I mean. Are you making submissions?"

"God, no," Scott said dismissively.

"Maybe you should. Anything can happen, right?"

Scott dropped his head.

"All right. New subject." Jacob waited for Scott to meet his gaze, then continued. "Are you settling in all right? I know it's not easy. The locals are nice and friendly, but they don't easily let newcomers into their circles."

Scott looked up. "You're a local."

"Well, not a full-fledged local. I'm originally from Sarnia. Moved here right after university."

"I haven't really met anyone. It's hard enough hanging onto the friends I do have."

Jacob raised an eyebrow. "Did you have a falling out with someone?"

"Kind of. Something happened that just..." Scott's voice broke off, regret making it crack. "It cost me my best friend."

"Sorry to hear that."

"I should have known better."

"Should have known better about what?"

Scott flashed a look that he hoped conveyed the obvious, but Jacob just stared blankly at him. "Sex changes everything."

"Ah..."

It surprised Scott to be telling Jacob about him and Troy, to want to relive that pain again. Yet there was something about Jacob that reassured. Then it came to him. He wasn't being judged.

The pitcher of beer was empty. When Jacob suggested ordering another, Scott readily agreed. After all, he had nowhere else to be, no one waiting on him. His stomach rumbled, and even with the loud music and boisterous conversation, he knew Jacob had heard it.

Jacob smiled coyly. "Maybe we should order some food, too."

Over nachos, chicken fingers and potato skins, they talked long into the evening. At a time when Scott was still new to Junction and hungry for some sort of companionship, Jacob came into his life in a new way. Had they just become more than colleagues? Maybe.

A siren wailed, jolting Scott. He moved off the sofa to look out the window again. A car's alarm, the headlights flashing and the owner of the other vehicle that had T-boned it inspected the damage. *Stay calm and focused*, he counselled himself, and wilted into his earlier position on the sofa. He had to be strong. On a night like this, when desire battled for dominion, he couldn't let it win out again.

Maybe he *wanted* the sex. Something physical to remind him he was human. But the idea of committing to someone and trusting them ... no way. He'd fucked up with Troy, unwilling to imagine them as a couple. Not because he didn't love Troy. In a way, he'd always had. But he wouldn't let himself get that close to someone again. Not Troy. Not Jacob. Especially not Jacob, whose friendship meant too much to him to be derailed by a moment of weakness. No way would history be allowed to repeat itself.

"Here..." Jacob came into the living room carrying two large white mugs and handed one to Scott. "Hot chocolate. It'll warm you up." He eased onto the other end of the sofa, tucked his legs under his body, then blew on the steaming liquid. In between sips, he looked at Scott. "It's possible the office will remain closed tomorrow, depending on how long the storm lasts and how the cleanup goes."

Scott stared at his beverage. "No one's going to complain about having an extra long weekend."

"If the buses still aren't running later…" Jacob tapped the sofa. "It pulls out into a bed."

"Oh!" Scott focused on a spot on the dark wood floor. "The storm has got to let up at some point."

They shared a nervous laugh, and then an awkward, stony silence swept over them in one broad stroke. The howling wind outside instilled a calm, as if sensing each of their fears and trying to soothe their doubts. When the wind died down, the tick tock of the clock in the kitchen reminded them of the burdens they long carried and could not shake. What were they to do? What did being together now mean? A stormy night was the perfect time for a romantic interlude, especially on Valentine's Day, but that was a thought Scott worked to hold at bay. That could lead to too many unpredictable complications, unmake him in ways he knew could destroy them. Trust. It all came down to trust. Maybe their friendship could survive sex, but could he risk putting himself in a situation where he lost control of his feelings? Could he trust Jacob not to hurt him? And that had him wondering something else: could they hold their smoldering desires in check?

Jacob removed his legs from under his body, wedged himself into the corner of the sofa, and drew his knees towards his chest. "Can I ask you something?"

"Sure," Scott said when he really wanted to say, "No way."

"Is it everything you expected? The job, the move to Junction?"

"Honestly, I didn't know what to expect." Scott lifted the mug to his mouth and drained it. "I was at a point in my life when I needed a change, when I thought I would breakdown psychologically if something good didn't come my way. Maybe you've had that feeling, too. You know the one. Getting that one break you think will turn around your whole world. That's how I felt about the job, that if I got it then I'd be able to change my entire life, set me on the path —"

"Don't say to greatness," Jacob interrupted, then slurped his hot chocolate.

"Yes, greatness," Scott shot back, his gaze levelled at Jacob. "Not greatness in the sense that I'm the next big reality TV star or self-proclaimed saviour of humanity. Don't need any more of those. But I hoped that getting the job would, in a way, let me set myself up on the path to fulfilling my greatness, to heed the call of what it is I feel compelled to do."

"An idealist." Jacob took Scott's empty mug from him and stood. "I need something stronger for this conversation."

"And what are you?"

Jacob laughed as he headed for the kitchen. When he reappeared in the living room a few minutes later, he handed Scott a generous glass of red wine. "Sorry. I know you prefer white." He settled onto the sofa. "And I'm a cynic. That's why we need more idealists, especially those who haven't been corrupted by society and its crass materialism. Don't mind me. I'm this way because I've been screwed over more times than I care to count."

"That sounds —"

"Pathetic? Absolutely." Jacob took a large gulp of his wine. "Sorry. You don't need to listen to me bitch." He ran his hand across his face. "Are you happy here?"

"I'm not unhappy," Scott blurted out without taking any time to think about his response. "I mean, really, it's all still new, and I'm still settling in, trying to find myself."

"Christ, that's what we're all trying to do."

"Some more than others. Some people seem to know almost intuitively what they want to do and know how to get it. They boldly go for it, brazenly so." Scott sighed. "I'm still trying to figure out who I want to be."

"Let's start a club," Jacob said cheekily. "Or maybe a game show. 'Who Do You Want to Be?' instead of 'Who Wants to be a Millionaire?' Maybe we can get Meredith Vieira to host."

"Or maybe Oprah."

Their giddy laughter eased the subtle tension between them.

Jacob leaned back, stretched out his legs and crossed them, then lifted them in the air. He held the pose for five seconds before his legs dropped to the floor. "You don't seem like the kind of guy who's still 'figuring out' who he wants to be. That's just the sense I get."

"Maybe you're right." Scott smiled thinly. "Maybe I already know who I want to be. I just … I don't have the courage to be that man." He looked down and cringed. Not again. Not even a third of the way through his glass of wine and he was babbling and involuntarily revealing his life story. Like he did that night at Finn's. *Am I that drunk already?*

"So, let's try this again," Jacob said with a grandiose air. "Who does Scott Davenport want to be?"

"I don't want to be afraid to live life fully or chase after my dreams."

"That's how you want to live." Jacob spoke like he was conducting a job interview and backing the interviewee into a corner. "Who do you want to be?"

Scott rolled his pursed lips, a heaviness needling his heart. Jacob deserved a straight answer, not slick posturing. But the question made him doubt his worth, doubt his ability to succeed. "Look, Jacob, I haven't been honest with you," he said into his wineglass.

"What do you mean?"

"It's not that I lied per se, but that I just haven't told the whole truth."

"Here it comes," Jacob spat. "You're straight. And married. Got a kid, too?"

"No, no." Scott looked up. "Taking this job and moving to Junction has been great. You took a chance on me, a guy with little to no proof-reading experience, and I'm grateful. I said a lot of things in the interview to land the job, but I'm not in it for the long term. And I'll be leaving by September."

"L–Leaving?" Panic roared in Jacob's voice. "To go where?"

"Back to school. For my doctorate degree in political science. Application's submitted. Just waiting for a response."

"Jeez." Jacob raised his glass to his mouth. "Kind of wish you'd said you were straight and married. Maybe that way you'd have stuck around a while."

"You asked me who I want to be. It's sort of complicated. I don't want to just be and do one thing. You know, spend thirty-five years in the same job, see the same people and end up bored."

"Life doesn't have to be like that," Jacob countered. "Some people stay in a job because they love what they do. Don't fucking generalize. And remember what I told you during your second interview?"

"'You must act to live the life you imagine.' Haven't forgotten that." Scott paused, but he needed to hear himself say the words. "When you imagine being the first openly gay prime minister, a highly sought-after political commentator and maybe a novelist ... how do you do it all?"

"Hold up." Jacob set his wineglass down on the coffee table. "You want to go into politics, be on *Larry King Live* and maybe be the next Alan Hollinghurst?"

"You're making fun of me. You think I'm crazy, right?"

"I'm not making fun of you and I don't think you're crazy." Jacob leaned back into the sofa. "It kind of sounds like you don't exactly know what you want."

"I do," Scott protested. "I did. Fuck, I don't know anymore."

"Then why spend the next four years getting a degree you're not sure you want?"

"It's been my plan. I've told everyone —"

"You can change your mind, you know," Jacob interrupted. "People do every day. Besides, you have three big dreams. It doesn't matter what order you do them in."

"The longer I put off going back to school, the harder it'll be."

"That's an excuse we tell ourselves. If it's something you really want, I don't think you'd let anything stop you." Jacob picked up his glass. "And you could always go part-time, unless you're torn between school and something else."

"There was a time when all I wanted to be was a writer," Scott admitted.

"Then be a writer," Jacob said bluntly.

"A successful writer. The type who makes a living from it, even if it's rare as hell."

"Then be the example," Jacob counselled, stretched out his leg and tapped his foot lightly against Scott's thigh. "Just go for it."

"But the odds —"

"Don't think about the odds. You have to visualize the success and believe you can succeed."

"I did try. Got rejected. Guess I'm not good enough. Anyway, it's just a silly dream."

"Why can't it be more than a dream? Like *you* said ... be one of those people who boldly go for what they want."

Scott couldn't take Jacob's look — part admiration, part questioning — and shifted his focus to the window. The snow had yet to let up, and he had the sickening sense that he was going to be trapped at Jacob's place well into the evening, if not longer. That seemed dangerous. "I thought you said you were cynical?"

"Maybe I'm not that cynical." Jacob pushed the hair out of his face. "I've just never been passionate about anything, not like you. I didn't go into human resources management because I was passionate about it. It was a tactical move. At the time, there was a huge demand. I bought my first condo when I was twenty-five, and then made a shitload of money when I sold it three years later. I'm set. I can have almost anything I want, whatever new fad hits the market. I'm not trying to brag, but I'm solid financially while I know many people around me struggle. By all accounts, I'm that successful career man who everyone loves to hate. But there's still a hole —"

"It's not too late to discover what you may be passionate about," Scott cut in, his eyes meeting Jacob's.

Jacob chuckled. "I'm not interested in starting over."

"I don't think you'd have to start over. You could begin where you are. And that seems like a pretty good place from where I'm sitting."

"Christ, how did you become such an idealist?" Jacob slumped down in the sofa and stared into his wine. "I turned thirty-two last month. Another birthday that I celebrated alone."

"What?" Scott sat up straight. "How come I didn't know that?"

"I don't like to make a fuss." Jacob slowly raised his head. "And I just meant alone in the romantic sense. Now I'm asking myself different questions than I did when I was twenty. What'll happen if I get sick and I'm alone? Will the other side of the bed always be empty? Would anyone care if I didn't wake up in the morning? That probably seems silly to you. You're still young."

"I don't think that's silly," Scott said in a controlled manner to mask his annoyance. "I think that, when it comes to love, we have to be patient, let it find us." *Oh, my God. I'm becoming my mother!* "I'm not saying don't date and wait on some divine intervention. It's that … if we go out intentionally looking for love, don't we risk letting ourselves be swept off our feet by the first person who shows a little interest in us? That could be disastrous. They may not be the right person, the one, but we settle because we're afraid that no one else will love us in a way that makes us feel extraordinary." Scott's tone was becoming sharp. "And maybe they're as lonely as we are."

One of Jacob's eyebrows arched. "Are you speaking from personal experience?"

"Maybe. A little. Oh, Christ, yes." Scott sipped his wine. "Love will find you. Give it time."

"What choice do I have?" Jacob stood. "Are you hungry?"

"A little."

"I'm not a cook. I have a frozen pizza I can throw in the oven."

"Sounds good."

Jacob left the room, and Scott moved off the sofa and again stood in front of the window. The snowstorm had turned into a blizzard, and he couldn't see the buildings across the street. Calm and relaxed, the idea of being alone with Jacob made him smile. Something had just shifted and shored up their friendship. He saw Jacob's reflection in the window and turned around.

Jacob had the wine bottle, topped up their glasses, then curled up again in the corner of the sofa. "Last time we talked like this, you said you hadn't really met anyone. Friends, I mean. Has that changed?"

"No," Scott said, his voice dipping low, and took up his earlier position.

"Haven't you gone to Harry's?"

"Harry's?" Scott's eyes widened. That was the only gay bar in town and he'd yet to step foot in it. "I've thought about going, but I always chicken out."

"You're not missing much. Dating one gay man from this city is like dating them all. They'll all know your business."

"Are you talking from personal experience?"

Jacob raised his wineglass in the air, as if to propose a toast. "Touché." He took a large gulp.

"Lucky for me I'm not into dating right now."

"Well, if you ever need a discreet fuck buddy, let me know," Jacob said quickly.

Scott's body went rigid. *He's joking, right? Of course he is. Or maybe...*

A new silence had them unable to look at each other as they sipped their wine. Jacob bounced off the sofa to turn on some music. Scott had his eyes glued to the white shirt hugging Jacob's chest and revealing the lean torso. They shared a coy smile before Jacob left the room to put the pizza in the oven. *Don't panic. Nothing's going to happen. You won't let it.* He needed to hang on to this feeling of belonging. This might not have been where he thought he'd end up on Valentine's Day, but there was something heartwarming about being with Jacob on such a turbulent day. Jacob was back, but they didn't speak. It wasn't necessary. Being there, together, was enough — to not be or feel alone in the world.

When the pizza was done, they moved into the cosy dining room to eat, talking about the office and their colleagues. They avoided talk about *them*, as if Jacob's surprise offer hovered over them.

"I'll clean up," Jacob said, shooing Scott out of the kitchen.

Scott slunk into the living room, once again drawn to the window and to the chaos swirling about outside. He wasn't going to make it home tonight, and now he held his breath. *Be strong. Don't fuck up another friendship.* Could he be strong? Could he outrun temptation? He exhaled quietly when his gaze connected with Jacob's in the window's reflection, but this time he was slow to face him. He saw how Jacob's Adam's apple twitched when he swallowed. Jacob had something to say, something Scott didn't want to hear.

But no words came. Jacob lunged at him unexpectedly. Scott surrendered, closing his eyes as Jacob's velvety lips passed over his. Pinned against the window, he wrapped his arms around Jacob's lean runner's body and pulled him closer. When Jacob's tongue slipped into his mouth, he groaned, the kiss deepening and breathing life into that long-simmering ache. Without releasing the kiss, they shuffled backwards to the sofa. Scott needed — wanted — more. But...

Scott pulled away, breathless. "Jacob, you know my history."

"I'm not Troy." Jacob reached for Scott's hand, stretched out on the sofa and pulled Scott down on top of him.

Scott held his body up slightly, like he was prepared to hold the plank position. "Tomorrow, I don't —"

Jacob placed his index finger to Scott's lips. "Let's not worry about tomorrow." He brought his head forward until their lips met.

Scott collapsed, that distinct hardness pressed against his own that had him tugging on Jacob's shirt.

It was too late to stop it, and neither of them resisted as the world around them fell away.

An Ugly Truth

THE LONG COLD, DREAM-BUSTING WINTER HAD finally given way to spring, yet people still carried the feeling of being battered and bruised. Troy Muir was one of those tortured by a winter that left him caged, stuck, and no amount of salt or sand tossed in his way could get him moving again. Even though the earth had thawed and the temperatures had warmed, he remained frozen in a hinterland of doubt, grief and disappointment — cut loose not only from the world, but also from himself, his hopes and dreams.

The soft evening breeze caressed his skin as he sat alone at the corner table on the patio at Hair of the Dog, the partially latticed roof blocking out the warmth of the receding sun bouncing off the back of his neck. It was a Wednesday, mid-June, and he was exhausted from the long day he had put in at Mount Sinai Hospital as part of his surgery rotation. Sitting on a patio in the Gay Village was the last place he wanted to be, but he could no longer dodge Janice and Evan. They'd been pestering him for the past two weeks to meet up for drinks. He finally agreed, as he told Evan, just to shut them up.

Troy had yet to find a way to nurse the wound, the hotbed of suffering, marked by the end of his and Scott's friendship. Neither of them had really tried to save it, not the way they should have if they were — like Scott had said — brothers. Then a silence implanted itself and had been allowed to fester. He wasn't naïve and knew that sex between them would bring about a change. But he'd envisioned a good change. A transformative change. A kind of spiritual awakening. He had not expected, or more aptly had not been sufficiently prepared for, the change that did occur. A baleful change. A devastating change. The awakening of a spiritual malaise. It shocked him how easily he and Scott had let go of each other, of their brotherhood, like their history didn't really matter.

The charge of his medical studies had, in the beginning, shifted his focus off the loss of his friend. Neither of them really expected him to show up for the Davenports' Labour Day barbecue. But when Christmas rolled around, and there had still been no word from Scott, no contact, that was when he understood their friendship was over, irreparable, dead. For the first time since he moved to Toronto, Troy didn't spend Christmas in Ottawa with the Davenports. Instead, he'd been orphaned, discarded without having been given the chance to explain his side of things. He tried to imagine what Scott had told his parents and how truthful his version of events was. Now, as spring unfolded and lovers walked the streets holding hands and stealing kisses, the loss of his best friend was deep. Could a strong dose of morphine subdue the pain? He was tempted to get his hands on some and find out.

At the sound of a chair scraping across the cement blocks of the patio, Troy lifted his gaze from his untouched Heineken. "Hey."

"You look awful," Janice said.

"Thanks," Troy grunted.

The server appeared, as if from behind a magician's invisible wall, and Janice jumped. After catching her breath, she ordered a gin and tonic as she sat down. "What a day!"

"I can't wait for this year to be over." Troy lifted his beer stein to his mouth and took a couple of sips.

Janice leaned forward and rested her arms on the table. "What's happened to you?"

"Janice, please ... don't." There was an edge in Troy's voice. "Don't play psychiatrist with me."

"That's not what I'm doing." Janice kicked under the table with her foot until it found Troy's leg. "You just haven't been yourself for a while. I'm concerned."

"I'm fine. You understand what this year has been like. It's tough, and sometimes I wonder if I really have what it takes."

Janice reached across the table and held Troy's hand. "You have exactly what it takes." She squeezed and let go. "Tell me something. Why don't you ever talk about Scott?"

"All right. I arrived just in time for the juicy parts." Evan plopped down next to Janice. "What did I miss?"

"Fuck off," Troy said, exaggerating his annoyance.

"I asked Troy about Scott," Janice said.

"Oh, hey." Evan ogled the muscled blond delivering Janice's drink. "A rum and coke, please." When the guy disappeared, he looked at Janice. "And what did he say?"

Janice sat back in her chair. "Nothing yet."

"Fuck off," Troy growled.

Evan chuckled. "That's because he's too embarrassed to say anything. Really, it's not that big of a deal."

"Jesus Christ, I slept with Scott," Troy blurted out. "Now, can we talk about something else?"

"What?" Janice shifted her wide-eyed look between Troy and Evan. "When?"

"Last summer," Evan volunteered. "The weekend Scott moved to Junction."

"You're right." Troy held Evan's gaze. "It's not a big deal. So, let's not talk about it anymore."

"Not a ... it's a *huge* deal." Janice's eyes narrowed. "And it explains a lot. I mean, you finally slept with Scott. You'd been crushing on him for years. Did you date?"

"No," Troy said with restraint. "A one-time fling. Didn't mean a thing."

"Thanks." Evan grinned as the server handed him his drink, then looked at Janice. "'Didn't mean a thing?' Who are you kidding? You're in love with Scott, but he doesn't feel the same."

"Is that true, Troy?" Janice stared at Troy. "Does Scott know how you feel?"

"Look, we were drunk," Troy lied. "It's the past."

"Oh, Troy." Janice again reached for Troy's hand. "Be honest with yourself, be honest with Scott. Tell him how you feel."

"I haven't spoken to him since..." Troy ran the back of his hand over his wet mouth. "It doesn't matter."

"Scott can't love you if he doesn't know how you feel," Evan insisted.

Troy chugged his beer until it was gone, then stood.

"Where are you going?" Janice asked with disbelief.

Troy didn't say a word as he pulled out his wallet and tossed three ten-dollar bills on the table.

"Oh, come on..." Evan leaned forward. "Don't go. We promise not to talk about Scott."

"I just..." Troy censored himself and, clutching his wallet in his hand, slunk off towards the exit. They couldn't understand the depth of the betrayal that kept jabbing his heart, or the humiliation. Nothing could make them understand or change what had happened. He had to let it go, but could he?

The Reunion

"CHRIST!" SCOTT, BREATHING HEAVILY, BENT forward, his legs spread apart and his hands on his hips. Sweat dripped from his brow, darkening a spot on the asphalt below. He straightened himself up and used his forearms to wipe his forehead dry. Looking at Jacob, he offered a rueful smile. "It's hard today. If you want to keep going without me, that's okay."

"Some days are like that." Jacob briefly placed his hand on Scott's shoulder. "Let's just walk back."

Scott took a few more minutes to catch his breath before he and Jacob continued along the bike path. It was early Saturday morning, the beginning of the August long weekend. And, finally, after sixteen months the embers of their Valentine's Day fling extinguished. But that stormy February night had delivered them both from months of wandering endlessly in the woods, lost in the hinterland of the disappointments populating their lives. The frustration of living in a world of which they never truly felt apart. The loneliness that coddled them at night instead of the lover with whom they'd imagined spending a lifetime. Like a caterpillar spins itself a silky cocoon, their naked bodies locked together was like a protective casing that shielded them from a world of hurt. More than a metamorphosis, the lovemaking was a new transformation that changed them, changed how they saw each other.

And it came, initially, with a cost.

In the days and weeks that followed, they couldn't look at each other. In meetings, they sat as far away from each other as possible. Any questions Scott had, he sent by e-mail to Jacob's assistant. Scott wished he could have been stronger that night and not given into temptation. He had, one more time, let sex ravage a friendship. Again, not because he didn't crave it, but where it could possibly lead … if he'd let it. Would he ever be brave enough to trust again?

Two motorized wheelchairs whizzed past them, music blaring from speakers, a familiar tune that Scott couldn't place. The music had him back in the elevator in May, him and Jacob alone, eyes roving the enclosed space. He caught the moment when Jacob winced, the pain etched in the bearded face. "Are you all right?"

Jacob stood still. "Yes. I've been going to the Wednesday night running clinic at Junction Runners' Shop. Not stretching as much as I should and sometimes my leg muscles just tense up."

"Like a Charlie horse?"

"Similar yet different. I can't really explain it except to say it hurts like hell."

"Then maybe you should stretch more," Scott said, curbing his urge to laugh.

"Since you're so great at doling out advice, I better see you Saturday morning," Jacob said bitterly. The elevator doors slid open and, half limping into the lobby, he added, "We meet at the entrance to Joan Myers Park. Run starts at eight."

Just before eight o'clock on Saturday morning, Scott found Jacob huddled with a couple of people decked out in the latest runners' outfits. He tapped Jacob on the shoulder and said into his ear, "Did you stretch?" He cracked a smile when Jacob elbowed him playfully in the side.

After a few weeks of running, when Scott was more confident in his abilities, it became their custom to jog together. They usually ran on Sunday mornings along the system of bike paths that crisscrossed the city. Jacob ran effortlessly while Scott could only go for about eight minutes before he had to stop and walk.

A car horn honked twice as they crossed the street, Scott lagging behind Jacob. It was time for Scott to challenge himself, and he picked up his pace and ran past Jacob.

Running together was another transformative moment in their friendship that brought a new level of intimacy. Not in a romantic sense, but in how they spoke to each other. Scott saw Jacob differently, and admired the way he imparted advice. The way his grandmother used to — drunk and sober. Physically, Jacob's lean frame became muscular. Something else, too. More dramatic, even. Running gave Jacob confidence. He had a bit of a swagger, a determination to, now more than even, not let the valleys in life bring him down.

"How's the packing going?" Jacob asked as they slowed down to wait for the light to change where the path joined River Road.

"Not bad." Scott, his hands on his hips and stretching backwards, sounded somewhat out of breath. "I'm trying to go through everything and get rid of what I don't need or haven't used in a long time. Stuff accumulates so quickly."

It wasn't how he'd planned it, but Scott was packing up his life again, this time escaping his contingent neighbourhood for a nicer part of the city. He'd promised himself one year in Junction, then back to school for a doctorate degree. But of the seven universities he'd applied to, only five had accepted him, and U of T wasn't one of them. His alma mater had rejected him. Then he wasn't so sure what he wanted. *Then why spend four years getting a degree you're not sure you want?* That was Jacob's advice, and he was right. It was time for a new game plan, even if he wasn't sure what exactly it looked like. So, he deferred acceptance to McGill, his second choice, and remained in Junction.

Now, in dismantling his home, he hoped to pack away his fears and disappointments that lingered. He was making some big changes in his life, and deep within himself he sensed the shift. Things would finally be different. He had checked his doubts. Fear would no longer rule him.

The light changed and they crossed the street, following as the bike path veered away from the Minor River and led them to Main Street. The morning air was warm, the start of another hot and sticky day. Scott and Jacob, as they often did after a run, stopped at JavaTime for lattes. Sometimes they'd sit outside and talk about their plans for the day, but not this time. Scott was eager to get home and continue packing up his belongings. Too excited to, in two weeks, be in his new home, reinventing his life and himself.

Outside JavaTime, they stood at the edge of the sidewalk, separated by a parking meter, sipping their drinks. Scott wanted to leave, but Jacob's presence instilled a calm. He wasn't ready to let go of that feeling. When their eyes met, they smiled, ignoring the current of desire that was still live between them. And Jacob's new, close-trimmed beard didn't help. It only made him *hotter*.

Scott broke the silence first. "How are things with Bryan?"

"Dead," Jacob said bluntly. "We weren't really compatible."

"Sorry to hear that."

"Don't be." Jacob sipped his iced latte. "He's into some weird fetish shit that —"

Scott raised a hand. "Say no more."

"And you? Still wearing that chastity belt?"

"Funny." Scott glanced at his watch. "You were right. Dating one guy in this town is like dating everyone."

"I hope you're not talking about me. I mean, Christ..." Jacob's voice was elevated. "You and I didn't date, and I never told anyone about —"

"I wasn't talking about you." *Maybe he doesn't know,* Scott thought. In March, he'd met a guy whose name he wouldn't now utter even if his life depended on it. They'd met up six times, singly for sex. The day after their first encounter, Scott had dinner at Manhattan's and Dave, the bartender, knew about his date — and how voracious he was in bed. On the days after every other hookup, when Scott stopped at JavaTime for his morning Americano, the baristas giggled.

"Then who?"

"Not important."

"Now you're holding back on me."

Scott gave a thumbs-up. "Absolutely."

"I'll find out."

"Not from..." Scott's voice broke off when, looking down the street, he saw the tall, dark-haired man holding open the door to Manhattan's.

Jacob cranked his head around and turned back to Scott. "What? Is it him? What do you see?"

"A ghost," Scott barely got out. Then when his and the dark-haired man's gazes met, he thought he'd spit up his Adam's apple.

Jacob cupped his hand to Scott's shoulder. "Are you okay?"

"No. Yes. I'm fine." Scott looked at Jacob. "I have a lot of packing to do. Thanks for the coffee. My treat next time. See you on Monday." Scott walked hurriedly towards

Manhattan's, his heart thumping in his chest, hoping to catch a glimpse of that tall stranger as he passed by. *It can't be him. But if it is, what's he doing here?* He slowed his pace in front of the entrance to Manhattan's, but all he saw were the backs of heads of four tall men waiting to be seated.

Scott made his way back to his Malbeck neighbourhood home, unable to shake the image of that man who, now more than ever, he was convinced wasn't a stranger at all. No, they knew each other, in a way so many people didn't understand. And to see each other again, more than two years after their last meeting — and to not say anything — proved just how much fear still ruled him.

Would that ever change?

***

LATER THAT DAY, SCOTT, STANDING IN THE doorway to his den, surveyed the cluttered room filled with boxes of books and papers, and snippets of a life unimagined. The morning sighting of his ghost had him spinning in circles and not doing much. He couldn't *think*, couldn't move himself forward. At the shrills of laughter that seeped through the open window, instead of a much-needed breeze, he crossed the room and took in the scene below. The kids across the street were running through the yard spraying each other with water guns that were bigger than them, trying to stay cool on a hot and humid day. That made Scott smile as he thought about their innocence and envied that simplicity. To be that young and carefree again.

As he turned away from the window, he noticed a piece of paper on the floor by his desk chair. He bent over and picked it up. His heart sank. It wasn't a piece of paper but a photograph of him and Troy, taken outside of their residence building during their first year of university. Their lips stretched into broad smiles, their arms wrapped around each other, and their free hands waving the peace sign. In their eyes gleamed the joy of an enduring, shatterproof friendship. But that unbreakable bond was broken by how they'd both reacted after sleeping together. Troy wanted more and Scott was too afraid to let himself love again. Scott took the photo and slipped it into the box that was open on his desk and left the den.

He made his way downstairs to the kitchen and poured himself a glass of the open Willm Gewurztraminer Reserve. It was almost six, and the time that he usually sat down for supper, but he wasn't hungry. Finding the photo of him and Troy took away his appetite, numbed him. Nearing the end of his second summer in Junction, he choked up when he thought about how he'd let Troy slip out of his life. He had tried to hang on to Troy. Actually, he just tried to carry on as if nothing had happened. Convinced himself that he'd disconnected his emotions from the sex act, the only way to protect himself as his very being came under siege. Then he couldn't — wouldn't — open himself up to love. Even knowing, deep down, it meant ending their friendship. They tried to talk, but long pauses dominated their conversations that once danced to the rhythm of modern tap. Maybe they even convinced themselves that they acted in ordinary ways, but the frequency of their text messages and e-mails slowed, eventually stopping altogether. That was what gave birth to the silence that mushroomed. Despite the silence and the long absence, Scott couldn't fathom the idea of Troy being gone from his life in a permanent way.

He moved from the kitchen to the living room, the one room that remained, so far, unaffected by the impending move. The late-afternoon sun lit up the space like a campfire, so he drew closed the blue polyester curtains. He turned on the lamps on the end tables that sandwiched the fraying wool upholstered sofa and plunked down on it. Thinking about the upcoming move had a metallic taste swirling in his mouth. Not the move itself but what it meant. His doctoral studies were on hold. Indefinitely. Writing, politics … he didn't know what he wanted anymore. But being in a stable job and buying his first home were signs that he was putting down roots. That mattered. Proved he was growing up. His next challenge was to widen his social circle. After all this time in Junction, Jacob had become his only friend. That disappointed him. Why was it so difficult for him to connect with others?

The doorbell sounded, and it took a moment for him to react. He set his wineglass on the coffee table and moseyed to the front door, which he opened just a crack until the tall figure came into view. He eased the door open wide and stood there, frozen, unable to say or do anything. His *ghost*.

"Hey," the voice squeaked. After a moment came, "Hello," with more confidence.

"Hey, there." Scott slid his hands in his pockets, his gaze locked onto the hazel eyes staring back at him. *Is this real or am I dreaming?*

"Scott..."

"Yes?"

"May I come in?"

Scott stepped backwards, still trying to swallow his shock. He pulled his hands out of his pockets and closed the door once his guest was inside. Their eyes were locked, questioning, curious, then blank. "This morning outside Manhattan's —"

"I wasn't sure that was you." Troy briefly glanced away. "You were with some guy, both of you dressed for running."

"Jacob," Scott said abruptly. "A work colleague. We run together twice a week."

"You, run?" Troy asked, almost laughing. "Since when?"

"A lot has changed..." Scott's voice trailed off. He didn't have to explain himself, justify running to someone who'd become a stranger. "What are you doing here?"

"Honestly, I don't know." Troy ran his hands though his short hair. "I mean, seeing you this morning ... I know what happened, how I reacted..." He bit down on his lower lip. "I really miss my best friend." There was a long silence. "I think we both needed space in order to get past what happened. I never imagined that we'd let the silence go on for so long. Then this morning ... I thought about what happened between me and Patrick. I didn't want that to happen to us."

Scott stood there, his eyes glued to Troy's, unsure of what to say, unsure of what he wanted. Could they really be friends again, best friends? Could they resurrect that bond that was special, deep and real? "Do you feel like grabbing a bite to eat?"

"Sure," Troy said, his lips curling into a smile.

"Manhattan's?"

"Perfect."

"Let's cab it." Scott picked up his keys, phone and wallet from the occasional table. "In case it turns out to be one of *those* nights."

Scott dialled the number of the local cab company and, as he slipped on his shoes, repeated his address to the dispatcher.

Outside, waiting by the curb, the sun beat down on them, him and Troy arrested by a necessary silence and unable to look at each other. What did that mean for the future of their friendship? They were together one more time, but could they begin again?

Fifteen minutes later, they were seated in a quiet part of the restaurant perusing the menus the hostess had left on the table.

"Hey, Scott," came the cheerful greeting from the bearded man approaching the table. "We're out of the Wolf Blass sauvignon blanc you like. A screw-up with the order this week."

Scott gave a nervous smile. "No problem, Dave. Two Heineken, please."

Dave chuckled, but when he realized Scott was serious, cracked his knuckles. "Two Heineken it is." He lingered a moment, throwing Scott a questioning look, then left.

Troy drummed his fingers into the table. "Heineken, really?"

Scott, his lips pursed tightly, flipped open his menu. *Is this what it's going to be like? Troy questioning my every decision?* Inevitable … that they would change, grow, evolve, in the time they'd been separated from each other. Scott had changed. Had Troy? He hoped Troy couldn't see him trembling. *Don't be an ass this time.* He closed his menu.

"Two Heineken," Dave said as he set the beer steins down on the table. "Any decisions on food? Scott, the lamb burger or beef tartar?"

"The lamb burger," Scott said.

Dave turned to Troy. "And for yourself?"

"The fish and chips." Troy critically watched Dave collect the menus, then shifted his attention back to Scott. "Is this your hangout or is there something going on between you and Dave?"

"I hang out here sometimes," Scott said askance. "The Village is two blocks long, and in this city there's no such thing as anonymity. And there's nothing going on between Dave and me."

"All right." Troy leaned back in his chair. "I'm just trying to make conversation."

"We never had to 'make' it before. It used to flow freely."

"Well, at least I'm trying."

A silence. A rebuke that cut through them both, for its savageness, and that made Troy look away. The silence … a hold, brokering a peace that would, perhaps, not come easily, if at all. What had happened to them? How had they let themselves and their friendship be completely unmade?

"There's a 'For Rent' sign in your living room window," Troy said hesitantly. "Moving?"

Scott bit his lip. "In a couple of weeks."

"Back to Toronto?"

"No," was Scott's harsh reply. "You expected me to fail, for this to fail. From the beginning —"

"Fuck, Scott, what's your problem? It was just a question."

"Just making conversation."

"Maybe this is a mistake." Troy slid to the end of the bench, ready to bolt. "Maybe we're not ready for this."

"What exactly is this?"

"A truce. Reconciliation." Troy massaged the back of his neck. "I said I was sorry."

"You never actually said it."

"Neither did you." Troy's eyes widened. "Why all the attitude? Do you hate me?"

"No, I don't hate you, I just…" Scott ran his hand over his face. "I'm sorry. Maybe it's the shock of seeing you, and not really knowing what to say."

"Say *anything*," Troy pleaded with a hint of desperation, and glided across the bench until he was directly opposite Scott. "Tell me about your move, or about the guy I saw you with this morning. Are you dating him?"

Scott, after taking several swigs of his beer and trying to avoid direct eye contact, told Troy about his move and the other changes that had occurred in his life. For whatever reasons he wasn't privy to, a steady stream of departures from his unit made him the senior proof-reader at Martin Boswell. The promotion came with a significant pay raise. After a few months in the role and living frugally, he bought a car. In June, he applied for a mortgage and, to his surprise, the application was approved.

As Scott talked, Dave brought their meals, and for a brief time it seemed like he and Troy had found a rhythm. Not their original rhythm, but one that allowed them to relax in each other's company. No longer strangers, but not necessarily friends.

Troy popped his last French fry into his mouth. "What about that guy you were with this morning? Was it Jacob?"

"I'm not dating Dave, I'm not dating Jacob!" Scott scratched his eyebrow. "I really don't mean to snap." He dabbed his serviette to the corners of his mouth. "What are you doing now?"

Troy twirled his knife on the table. "Well, I —"

"Oh, for Christ's sake, Troy, spit it out."

Troy stiffened and didn't speak for about fifteen seconds. "I'm doing my residency at Junction Collegiate."

Scott, about to gulp his last mouthful of beer, locked his gaze on Troy. He returned his beer stein to the table without finishing it. A long silence followed that gave way to a battle between rage and civility, defended with their eyes — Scott's that were mean and dark like caves that led to an abyss, a black hole, and Troy's that were soft and forgiving with the power to calm. Would rage or civility win out? Hard to say as the silence idled, their fragile reunion risking asphyxiation. More time passed. Then came Scott's languid shrug, not necessarily a peace offering but more a sign of indifference. "Have you moved here?"

"I was commuting." Troy's eyes dodged Scott's. "I rented a room in London, where I crashed several nights a week."

"You're using the past tense," Scott said, annoyed.

"After you left, Evan moved in. No, we didn't date. And shortly after I started my residency, Evan moved to Vancouver, so we gave up the lease."

"What about the place in London?"

"It was only ever temporary. Right now, I'm crashing on the sofa of another resident while I look for a place."

Scott poiished off his beer. "I'm sure you'll find something."

Dave appeared at the table to collect their empty plates. "Anything else, gentlemen?"

"Just the bill," Scott said.

When Dave returned a few minutes later with the cheque, Troy took it and followed him to the bar. Scott headed outside and waited for Troy on the sidewalk. They took another cab back to Scott's place, not saying a word until they stood by Troy's car.

Scott pulled his keys out of his pocket. "Thanks for dinner."

"My pleasure." Troy held Scott's searching gaze as another stony silence immured them, disrupted from time to time by the unnameable night noises that accompanied them. "Maybe we can grab a drink sometime? Or you could show me your new home?"

"Sure."

Scott didn't know how to react when Troy stepped forward and hugged him. Eventually he lifted his arms and loosely returned the embrace. They pushed apart and, without saying another word, Troy got into his car while Scott started for the house.

At the sound of the engine flipping over, Scott turned back towards the street and waved as the car pulled away from the curb. Inside, he wasn't sure what to make of the evening he had spent with Troy. He could still sense a wall between them, a wall he built and couldn't tear down. Something about Troy showing up when he did... Scott stiffened. It was something in those hazel eyes that, again, instilled equal measures of calm and suspicion. And just like on that first day they met, he wasn't suspicious as much as hesitant. Why? Because he knew. If given the chance, Troy would take on the lead role in one of his secret fantasies.

He ambled into the living room, tasted the warm glass of wine he had left there, winced, and made for the kitchen. He filled his glass with the remainder of the open bottle of the Willm Gewurztraminer Reserve, then made his way upstairs to his den to pack. This time he got to work, distracting himself from the chaos swirling about him and holding at bay his doubts that were, one more time, on the rise.

Reconciliation

SCOTT HUNG UP THE PHONE AND MASSAGED
the centre of his tightening chest. He'd just agreed to meet
up with Troy for drinks, and that made him nervous. Three
days after their reunion, the shame of how it had played out
still clung to him. He thought it would have been more open,
welcoming and loving. In that version of events, he and Troy
shared a long embrace that erased all their doubts and misunderstandings. Instantly, they were friends again. But that
was his imagination at work. Could anything break through
that tall, heavily reinforced wall that existed between them?
No, not when Scott was the one throwing up resistance. He
couldn't shake certain suspicions, too afraid to go where the
truth lied. But he owed it to himself, to Troy — to the friendship that was and he hoped could be again — to break down
that wall. Maybe meeting for drinks was the first step.

He ran into the kitchen and returned the onion and garlic
to the fridge. No time to cook, not when he promised to pick
up Troy in twenty minutes. He grabbed a honey-oat granola
bar from the cupboard and devoured it before he made it to
the car.

Seated behind the wheel of the platinum grey Passat, Scott
fixed his gaze on the dashboard clock. Seventeen minutes past
six. Parked at the curb in front of the Royal Arms Apartments,
he repeatedly made sure the doors were locked and kept
checking the side and rear-view mirrors. This area of the city,
in the east end, was scarier than his Malbeck neighbourhood.
It figured prominently on the evening newscast for break-ins,
night-time assaults and marijuana grow-ops. Scott flinched at

the knock on the passenger side window, then unlocked the doors.

Troy slid the seat back as far as it would go, pulled the door closed and looked at him. "It still smells like new."

Scott smiled faintly, flipped the engine and, once Troy fastened his seatbelt, shifted the car into drive. He drove westward, crossing the downtown core, and headed north of the financial district. In this older part of the city, known as Yorkview, each house had its own distinct look, unlike the new cookie cutter neighbourhoods popping up on the outskirts of the city limits. They came to a four-way stop with a park on the left and on the right, on the other side of the intersection, an elementary school. Scott hung a left, and they continued down the street for about a minute when he veered the car left again onto Miller Road. They came to a stop in front of a two-storey red-brick house.

Scott emerged first and, standing near the garage door, watched as Troy circled the car, eyeing it critically as if inspecting it for defects. When the inspection was done, they started up the walk. At the front door, Scott jammed his key into the lock and pushed. Entering the silent and empty house, he was overwhelmed by an unexpected rush of emotion — joy, panic, trepidation. He still couldn't believe that this was real, that *his* moment had finally arrived. Settling down ... was this really what he wanted?

"Wow," Troy said, venturing further into the house. "Proof-readers must make good money, no?"

"Not bad." Scott led Troy on a tour of the house, nonchalantly throwing out a comment about each room. "Forget about the colours," he said in the living room. "The painters are coming on Thursday." He left Troy standing in the middle of the red living room and walked through the dining area and into the kitchen. "I wasn't sure about the house until I saw the kitchen. That clinched it for me." Renovated a year ago, the kitchen, painted a light taupe, was bright and airy. A self-declared amateur chef, Scott loved the two wall ovens and the gas range, and it reminded him of the Saturday afternoons he'd spent baking with his grandmother. It inspired him to enroll in a baking arts course beginning in September. He was less enchanted with the elevated bar-counter at the end of the long island. He'd wanted an eat-in kitchen, but would have preferred room for a small table and chairs instead of the bar-counter. There was a fair size pantry and a large formal dining room with sliding doors that he never imagined using.

At the far end of the main floor level, on the front part of the house, they came to the large room that the previous owners had used as a family room. "I think this will be my office," he said and then led Troy upstairs. The master bed-room stretched the full length of the back half of the upper level, with a huge walk-in closet and an en suite bathroom. Troy particularly liked the master bathroom with its Jacuzzi bathtub that seated two and its separate slate stone shower. Scott wasn't sure what he would do with the two remaining bedrooms.

Back downstairs, they stood in the foyer, their eyes roving, and let an awkward silence dominate. Scott pulled an enve-lope out of his jeans pocket and held it out.

Troy stared at the sealed package. "What's that?"

"The money I owe you. Sorry it took so long."

"Scott..." Troy shoved his hands in his pockets. "Keep it. As a deposit —"

"Deposit? On what?"

"You know..." Troy let out a nervous laugh. "My first month's rent."

"You want to move in here?" Scott asked, his voice thun-dering with disbelief. "I mean, after —"

"It's not like you don't have the room. And I'm asking a lot, but I promise it'll be temporary. A couple of months while I look for a place."

"You said you were already looking."

"I am. I'm trying. There's not a lot of time right now, with my residency..." Troy bit down on the inside of his lip. "Crashing on Drew's sofa, well ... he and his girlfriend fuck all the time, and he's a squealer."

"Isn't that what you said about Janice's boyfriend, Tom? How is it that you always find the squealers?"

They laughed, a thoughtful laugh that peeled away a layer of awkwardness. Finally a small crack in that wall.

"Troy, please, take it." The stare-down was on, as if it were a battle of wills, and each of them standing their ground. Then Scott crossed to Troy, reached around him and shoved the envelope into his back pocket. He stepped back quickly, smirking at the defeat screwing up Troy's face. "A couple of months? You don't need to pay rent. You helped me out when I needed it. Let me do the same for you. Besides, I can handle your idiosyncrasies again."

Troy scrunched his eyebrows. "What idiosyncrasies?"

"The way the coffee mugs have to be lined up with the handles pointing to the right."

"I'm right handed," Troy said.

"The hand towels folded in three and hanging symmetrically on the towel bar."

"It's aesthetically pleasing to the eye," Troy quipped.

"Keeping your cereal in the fridge."

"It stays fresher."

Then a silence.

"This is temporary, though, right?" Scott had established a rhythm that suited a solitary life and he didn't want to make adjustments. He liked being alone, holed up in his own domain. "That didn't come out right."

"No more than two months," Troy said. "I'll find a place by October or November."

"All right." Scott extended his hand and could sense the relief when Troy gripped it. Even after everything they had been through and feeling as though they had been cut from each other's lives, this moment proved that they still mattered to each other.

They left the house, and as they neared the end of the stone walk Troy reached for Scott's arm. "Are you happy here? In Junction?"

Scott looked down. Lately, everyone was asking him that — his mother, Jacob, Leila when he announced he was moving, and now Troy. The question poked at him, tormented him. "I'm not unhappy." Scott levelled his gaze at Troy. "Being here in Junction has given me lots of time to think and analyze and brood. I'm just not sure what I want anymore. I thought I did, but I'm still here and then I'd think about you and what you're doing. You know, there's been this huge malaise hanging over my life, and sometimes I wonder if I should have made different choices."

"Like what?"

"I don't know." Scott's eyes roamed Troy's face. "Maybe I should have studied law, or social work. Maybe I —"

"Scott…" Troy cupped his hands to Scott's shoulders. "You've gotta do your own thing. Maybe it's writing. You're doubting yourself too much, and maybe that's holding you back from writing. And I know you love politics. Yes, I said it was crazy, but if you want to run for public office, do it. What I say or think shouldn't matter."

"You know it matters because I lo —" The word hung at the back of his throat. Could he say it? And mean it?

Troy's eyebrow arched. "You … lo —"

"You're right," Scott said quickly. "I keep doubting myself."

"Don't. Sure, we need a job so that we can eat, have a roof over our head, blah, blah, blah. Some people in this life have a higher calling. These are people who are called into service, and they're here on this earth to generously give of themselves to others. They're not worried about what's in it for them." He shook Scott gently and let his hands drop to his sides. "I think that you're one of those people. Maybe your calling is to write, or to run for office. Whatever it is, just give yourself over to it and stop throwing up resistance at every turn."

"I don't know."

"Don't think about it. Just do it."

Scott smiled faintly. Maybe Troy knew Jacob and, together, they had discussed his case and were planning an intervention. When Scott wasn't working, he read. Reading a book a week kept him occupied, even though he became somewhat of a hermit. Did he want to be a writer? Maybe. He could begin by sorting through the short stories and poetry he had written during his youth. He remembered the handwritten note on one of his rejected stories: *Characters need more development, but shows promise. Rewrite and submit again.* Back then, he'd shoved the story in a drawer. Now, was he ready to try again? What about politics? Not one for small talk, how could he manage canvassing door-to-door? First, he'd have to start giving back to the community, pick a cause and own it. That would help people discover him and what he stood for. Making his way around to the driver's side, he said, "Where should we go for that drink?"

Troy reached for the passenger door handle. "Manhattan's."

"Of course. You must be a regular by now."

"Fuck off."

Again, laughter.

Then at Manhattan's, they talked like they'd never been apart. The banter was, at times, cutthroat, but never left a scar. *He really is my best friend,* Scott thought as they stood to leave. He seemed confident, too, that neither of them would let their stubbornness and pride tear them apart again.

But they were men, still young and learning the ins and outs of life. And one lesson Scott had yet to learn was that pride often came before the fall.

Accession

AUGUST SLIPPED BY LIKE A HIGHLY ANTICIPAT-
ed second date after an unexpected, and unforgettable, one-
night stand — each day's energy flowing into the next with
the hope of recapturing the excitement of that first meet. A
month of goodness where everything happened smoothly and
without incident, where good cheer reigned.

Scott had moved into his Miller Road home, and Troy
along with him. As much as Troy's presence comforted and
proved that Scott was anchored to someone, it did something
else, too. It reminded him that he'd been on his own for too
long. So, it took time and patience for them to re-establish
an ebb and flow, to acclimatize to living together again. And
while Troy searched for an apartment, he returned from most
visits exasperated. Something wasn't quite right with each
place, or he claimed the landlord gave him bad vibes. Scott
finally said, "Then just stay here," a decision that brought two
friends together again, permanently, and restored a cherished
relationship.

Now it was the third Saturday in September, and Scott
roamed from room to room straightening photographs and
artwork, repositioning ornaments, scanning for dust bunnies.
His heart thumped in his chest. His parents were set to arrive
any minute, and he wanted the house to be perfect. Like his
childhood home that his mother kept immaculate, with everything in its place. He wanted her to be proud, and feel like she
believed in him.

The doorbell chimed. Scott ran from his office to the front
door, his hands shaking, breathless. He counted backwards
from five, then opened the door wide.

"Oh, Schnookums," Margaret said, lunging at Scott. She wrapped her arms around him and held on for dear life. After a moment, she pushed away and studied him. "You've lost weight. Are you eating?"

"Yes, Mama, a little, but it's a good thing. I'm running now."

"Just be sure to eat." She stepped past him, turning around in the space, her eyes finding every surface. "This is very nice."

Terrence, huffing, burst through the door. "You'd think we were staying a month." He set the two heavy suitcases on the floor next to the staircase. "Margie, did you bring the fridge and stove, too?" He shook Scott's hand. "Good to see you, son. And this is quite the house."

"Hi, Dad. Well, I'll give you the tour."

"Not until your father brings in the other bags," Margaret said, eyeballing her husband.

Terrence pursed his lips and left the house. Just then, Troy came around the corner.

Margaret brought her hands to her chest. "Well, look who it is. The Invisible Stretch."

"Hi, Momma D," Troy said in a whisper.

"Don't 'Hi, Momma D' me." She held out her arms. "Get over here and give me a hug."

Scott watched, relieved, as his mother and Troy hugged. His and Troy's fallout had brought about other repercussions. Two Davenport Christmases without Troy, and Margaret and Terrence constantly asking where he was. His mother tried to press him for information, but all he'd ever say was, "Troy's busy with med school," and walk out of the room.

Terrence reappeared, handing off several grocery bags to Scott. "They're filled with lead."

"Terrence," Margaret said with an edge. "Do you see how thin your son is? He's like a beanpole and needs that food."

"Well, lookie here…" Terrence set the remaining bags on the floor and advanced towards Troy. "It's the Invisible Stretch." They shook hands.

Scott chuckled. "Mama already used that line."

"She's always stealing my material." Terrence stared at Troy. "Where have you been, anyway? It's been a year and half —"

"Longer than that," Margaret cut in, and raised her hand as Troy went to speak. "Don't. Scott repeatedly said you were busy with med school. I didn't believe it then and I don't buy it now. But we'll get into that later." She turned to Scott. "I'd like to freshen up."

"You're taking my room," Troy said, moving to pick up one of the suitcases. "I'll show you."

Terrence blinked magnificently. "Your room? Are you two living together again?" He looked at Margaret. "The Bobbsey twins are back."

Troy flicked his eyebrows. "Who?"

"Dad thinks he's being funny," Scott said coolly.

Margaret's eyebrow arched. "You have to admit —"

"Don't start, Mama."

Margaret stiffened. "'Don't start, Mama?' Who, pray tell, do you think you're talking to?" She sucked her teeth. "Don't start, Mama? Well, this 'Mama' has no problem putting you over her knee, twenty-six years old or not. Don't start, Mama ... humph!"

Troy, trying to control his laughter, started up the stairs and said to Terrence, "Don't worry about the other suitcase. I'll come back for it."

Margaret, following behind Troy, pointed at the bags cluttered around Scott's feet. "Some of that needs to go in the freezer."

"Yes, Mama."

Scott carried all the bags into the kitchen and quickly put everything away. His mother had brought a month's supply of food — meat pies, shepherd's pie, cabbage rolls, beef stew, and three loaves of banana bread. He never liked cabbage rolls, never had the heart to tell her, but hoped he could pawn them off on Troy. One more time, the melodic ding dong rang out through the house, and Scott rushed to answer the door.

"Oh, wow," Janice Muller said, stepping into the house. "This is amazing." She hugged Scott and, standing in the foyer taking in the scene, added abstractly, "And you remember Tom."

Tom and Scott shook hands and followed Janice into the living room.

"This is for you," Tom said in his bearish voice, holding out the bottle of Wolf Blass merlot.

"Thanks." Scott took the wine, slipped into the dining room and added it to his collection. When he returned to the living room, introductions were underway between Janice and Tom and his parents. Again the doorbell, and he scooted to the door.

"Sounds like I'm late," Jacob said, glancing at his watch.

"You just like to make an entrance." Scott smirked. "Like most divas."

"Hey! Mariah Carey's a diva. I'm just her protégé." Jacob entered the house and handed Scott a gift bag. "It's not much."

"Thanks, but you know it wasn't necessary."

Scott led Jacob into the living room, another round of introductions, and then they all streamed out to the back veranda and the bright September sun. A few more people arrived for the unofficial housewarming, mostly Troy's colleagues from Junction Collegiate. An afternoon filled with good conversation, laughter, and his mother's delicious salmon puffs, seven-bean salad, brownies, and more. Scott hoped that his parents could see that he had come of age. And a familiar question poked at him: were they proud of him?

As people laughed and talked in small groups around the large rectangular patio table, Scott slipped into the house to replenish the tray of squares and cookies. The warm hand that cupped his shoulder startled him. He turned, his eyes locked onto those smiling nickel eyes that so easily saw through to his core. "You're not leaving yet, are you?"

"No." Jacob fidgeted with the cuff of his shirt. "I wanted to see if you needed any help?"

"No. It's all good, thanks."

A silence settled in as Scott arranged the peanut butter cookies on the silver tray, dodging Jacob's gaze. Being alone together now made him nervous. He didn't want anyone, especially his mother, dissecting their association. Too long away from the others, he knew she'd become suspicious and interrogate him.

Jacob took a step backwards and leaned against the kitchen counter. "It's a great house. I love what you've done with it."

"I just had it painted," Scott said cheekily.

"Well, you could have chosen ghastly colours, like mustard yellow or fire engine red."

"I painted to get rid of the fire engine red."

They laughed.

"I didn't know the party was inside," Margaret said dryly as she came into view.

"Just topping up the dessert tray." Scott looked at Jacob and rolled his eyes.

"I saw that," Margaret said.

Jacob scooped up the tray, as if on cue, and made for the back door.

When the door banged shut, Margaret stared down Scott. "Is he —"

"Jacob's just a friend." Scott took a cookie from the tin and bit into it. "Is everything okay, Mama? You seem ... I don't know. Quiet."

"I'm fine. This hot weather sometimes makes me tired."

"Maybe you should stay inside a bit." He chomped on the cookie. "Cool down."

Margaret advanced and placed her hands on the island countertop. "Maybe you should tell me what happened. I'm talking about with Stretch. You don't mention his name for more than two years, tell me he's too busy with med school to visit. Then you buy a house and he's living with you. And choose your words carefully, young man. I'm in no mood for any more cockamamie stories." She waited, drumming her red-painted fingernails into the countertop, but Scott remained silent. "What happened between you and Stretch ... was it that bad?"

Scott tied his face up in knots. "Was what that bad?"

"Scott..." Margaret tilted her head downwards slightly, as if peering over the top of her reading glasses, which she wasn't wearing. "Some people are made to be just friends. It may not have worked out romantically between you and —"

"Romantically?" Scott snorted. "Troy and I didn't date."

"You did something," Margaret said and, after a moment, gasped. "Oh, dear Lord." She fanned herself with her hand. "Oh, dear Lord."

"It was only one time," Scott said quickly.

"Oh, dear Lord."

"And it's not that it was bad. It just felt weird afterwards."

Margaret fanned herself faster. "Oh, dear Lord."

"But we're fine now."

"Fine?" Margaret's hand fell to her side. "How fine?"

"We're back to just being best of friends. We're fine."

"That's good to hear." Margaret sounded skeptical. "We were worried. Your father and I love you both, and you wouldn't talk —"

"We had to work it out for ourselves, in our own time, in our own way."

"By not talking to each other for two and a half years?"

"It wasn't that long," Scott spat.

"Watch your tone."

"Mama…" Scott looked down.

So much had changed since that first day he brought Troy home, his mother's reservations slowly peeled away by Troy's southern-style charm. And Troy shared Terrence's interest in old cars, which created a special bond between them. Scott, like his brothers, wanted nothing to do with that. After Troy started 'coming home' regularly to Ottawa, he spent hours with Terrence in the garage rebuilding that 1970 Plymouth Road Runner. Troy became a full-fledged member of the Davenport family, and Scott didn't initially realize how deeply their fallout had hurt his parents because they, too, ended up cut off from Troy.

Margaret approached Scott and took his face in her hands. "I wish you'd find somebody, open your heart to love. If not Troy, what about Jacob?"

"Mama!"

"He seems nice, decent looking. He makes you laugh."

"I'm okay being single."

Margaret pulled her hands away from Scott's face. "Stubborn. Like your father."

"That's why you love me so." Scott wrapped his arm around his mother's shoulders and, escorting her back to the veranda, added, "And you're sure you're okay?"

"I'm fine. And stop worrying about me." She raised an arm in the air. "I've got the Lord on my side."

The rest of the day flew by, Scott sitting back and watching how his parents interacted so easily with the young men and women around the table. Troy's beer-loving colleagues bonded quickly with Terrence, who drank them under the table, although that didn't endear him to his wife. There was something magical about the day, about Scott being surrounded by people who mattered to him, who gave his life meaning.

And later, when he crawled into bed, he knew he had arrived. He was home, at the beginning of a new and different journey, and ready for what lie ahead.

***

WHEN MARGARET ENTERED THE KITCHEN early the next morning, she found Scott seated at the island sipping coffee with his gaze fixed on the pages spread out before him. She stood in the doorway, trying not to make a sound, and watched her baby at work. But he was no longer her baby. He was a man and didn't seem to need her, didn't need her counsel. She leaned against the doorframe, studied him and thought about how he reminded her so much of a younger Terrence. Not so much his looks, but his determination and drive. "Good morning," she said and made her way towards him.

"Morning," Scott said, panic in his voice. He scrambled to collect his papers, shuffled them into a neat pile and flipped them over face-down on the countertop. "Sleep well?"

"Not bad, considering it wasn't my own bed." Margaret eyed the papers. "Do you always bring work home? And work on Sundays?"

"Not always. Just trying to keep ahead of things."

Margaret looked searchingly at her son, who held her gaze. *Is he telling the truth?* she wondered, but chose not to question him.

"I'll make some tea." Scott, clutching his papers against his chest, shot up off the stool and moved to the other side of the counter. He stashed the papers in the corner, on top of the breadbox, and plugged in the kettle.

Margaret slid onto a stool at the bar-counter. "This really is a lovely home."

"Thanks." Scott tore off the cellophane from the package of Earl Grey tea. "A nicer neighbourhood, too."

"Yes, it is." Margaret never liked the house in Malbeck, and when Scott told her about the break-ins, she wanted him to move out immediately. And despite whatever doubts she had about Leila, particularly her crassness, she was happy that Leila, even though it annoyed Scott, checked in on him regularly. It gave the impression that the two women were in collusion, and Margaret thought that that kept Scott on his toes and out of trouble.

"Sit down, Scott," Margaret said firmly when he brought her the steaming mug of tea.

Scott refilled his coffee and settled in next to her. "What's going on, Mama?"

Margaret tried to hold back the tears, but they pooled in her eyes and streaked down her cheeks. She opened her mouth to speak, the words buckling at the back of her throat.

Scott left briefly to get the box of Kleenex from the living room. When he returned, he remained standing. "Mama..."

Margaret dabbed a tissue at her eyes, and as the tears ebbed she looked at Scott. "It's your father. I didn't want to tell you yesterday at the party. It wasn't the time."

"Tell me what?"

"He doesn't want you to know, and we haven't even told your brothers..." Tears again stormed Margaret's eyes. "He's ... he's..." She wasn't sure she could say the words. Saying it made it real, more real. "He's dying." She moaned softly.

Scott blinked magnificently and placed his hand on the counter, steadying himself. Then he lowered himself back onto his stool and wrapped his arm around her.

Margaret rested her head on his shoulder, and they stayed like that for a time. She sat up abruptly, forcing Scott to withdraw his arm, and began to fix her face. "Your father has cancer." She kept her moist eyes trained on the crumpled tissue balled in her hand. "Initially, it was in his pancreas. Now it's metastasized. There's nothing the doctors can do but try to keep him comfortable." She lifted her eyes to Scott. "Like I said, your father doesn't want you to know, so no more trips home than usual."

"I'm not going to stay away if Dad's dying," Scott protested.

"He doesn't want you to remember him as weak and frail. He talks nonstop about how cancer ravaged your Aunt Carla. He doesn't want to end up like that." She lifted her unsteady hand to her face to wipe away the tears. "I'm praying, you know. I'm trusting that the Lord will bring him through."

Crying lifted that burden off her chest. She did not agree with Terrence's decision to hide his illness from the children. It was too much for her to bear on her own, and she had to tell someone, to not feel so alone. And of the three boys, she believed Scott could handle the truth best. At the sound of the heavy footsteps on the creaking staircase, Margaret again wiped the tears from her eyes.

Troy came into the kitchen. "Morning."

"Morning, Stretch." Margaret forced a smile, stood and, holding her mug, looked at Scott. "I'll go make sure your father's up. We're taking you boys out for brunch, and then shopping. That lumpy sofa that Stretch slept on has had its day." As she passed by Scott, she cupped her hand briefly to his shoulder and squeezed. She stopped at the doorway, turned and studied the two young men before her, tears exploding in her eyes, and left the kitchen.

Before mounting the staircase, she drew in several long, deep breaths. "Lord, I *do* believe, help my unbelief."

***

SCOTT, REACHING FOR HIS COFFEE, SHOT TROY a knowing look. "Don't act like you don't know."

Troy, after pouring himself a cup of coffee, occupied the stool Margaret had just vacated. "Cancer?"

"But Dad doesn't want us to know, doesn't want us to worry. So —"

"Not talking about it doesn't make it not real."

"I know that," Scott said with a slight edge. "For my mother's sake, let it alone."

They sat there, their arms resting on the countertop, hunched over their beverages and listened. The house was silent, and in between their own breaths they could hear a quiet moaning coming from upstairs. They looked at each other, panicked, but the panic quickly turned to relief. It wasn't *that* kind of moaning, but was immediately discernible as crying. Margaret was crying again. Scott imagined that she had cried a lot over the past few weeks and months. It did seem somewhat unreal. But his mother, no doubt, had been praying, gave it all over to God. And Scott was ready to believe that counted for something.

He closed his eyes, desperate to believe in the power of prayer and hoping that if there was any other moment more necessary in his life, now was the time for the Lord to manifest himself, *prove* that He was real.

Déjà-Vu

"WHAT DO YOU MEAN YOU'RE MOVING OUT?" Scott asked, his eyes wide with surprise. "You just moved in."

"It's been almost a year," Troy said in between sips of his Coors Light. "I told you it'd be temporary. Thanks for letting me stay this long."

"You don't have to leave." Scott looked in Troy's direction, but not directly at him. "It's been nice having you around. Reminds me of university."

"We're not in university now. And it's time for me to be on my own." Troy gently returned his beer to the table. "We've grown up, right? Look at you … a house, car, good-paying job. I kind of feel like it's my turn."

"Did you … did you buy a house?"

Troy let out a nervous laugh. "Kind of, yeah. Just waiting to hear back from the bank."

Scott locked his gaze on Troy. "When? Where? And why didn't you say anything?"

"I don't know." Troy dropped his head. "Really, we haven't seen that much of each other lately. I'm always at the hospital. You've been volunteering for that politician —"

"Peter Kilpatrick. He's a liberal and I know you don't approve. And I give him four hours a week on Saturdays. I didn't run off and join a circus."

"I just…" Troy looked up. "Things have been really good between us and I didn't want this to ruin that."

Scott didn't say anything for a few minutes, the chatter in the background on the rise. They were at Manhattan's, catching up after a busy week. And Troy was right. Things were good between them. Maybe that was because of their hectic schedules, which helped Scott to repress his love for his friend. Still not ready to trust, still not ready to take another chance on love. And the sparkle gleaming in Troy's eyes told him that maybe it was too late for *them*.

"Well, I'm happy for you," Scott said and meant it. "Now dish. Give me all the details."

Listening to that melodic voice deliver words in upbeat rhythms, tingling sensations pricked at his skin. The man seated across from him knew his ambitions, fears and hopes. The attraction had been there since the first day they'd met, when Scott was too young or too shy to realize it. And on that night when they gave into desire, the depth of their bond choreographed the lovemaking that left them spent, and Scott secretly hungry for more. When had he fallen in love with his best friend? *Fuck, I'm a fool.*

"Troy, there's something —"

"Am I interrupting?" the gravelly voice asked.

Scott blinked rapidly, studying the leggy man with jet-black hair ogling Troy.

"No." Troy slid sideways on the bench and then pointed at the open space. "Join us."

Seated, the guy held out his hand to Scott. "I'm Stuart."

Scott accepted the firm handshake. "Scott."

"Stuart is my b–boy–fr–friend," Troy said, his voice cracking.

"Boyfriend?" Scott threw a raised-eyebrow look at Troy. "And you were going to tell me that when?"

"To be fair," Stuart said, flexing his rugby-player's chest, "it happened pretty fast. And I'm sorry if I'm intruding, but I was heading back to my hotel, saw you through the window and wanted to say hello. I had to meet Troy's best friend."

"You don't live here," Scott said suspiciously.

"I live in Hamilton." Stuart looked at Troy and he grinned. "Here for the weekend."

Scott snatched his glass off the table, drained his drink and then slid to the end of his bench. "It was a pleasure meeting you, Stuart. Hope you two have a great weekend together."

Troy furled his eyebrows. "Where are you going? You had one drink."

"I haven't finished proofreading Peter's constituency newsletter." Scott stood and pulled out his wallet. "I promised it to him for tomorrow."

"Put that away," Troy snapped. "I got this."

"Thanks." Scott shifted his gaze between the two men, who exchanged coy smiles with each other, and winced. How did he not know that Troy was seeing someone? He stepped away from the table, only to turn back and focus on Stuart. "Listen," he said calmly, "my home is Troy's home too, and that means you're welcome there. Don't feel you need to throw away money on a hotel. It's an old house and the walls are thick."

"Oh, thanks." Stuart glanced at Troy, then held Scott's gaze again. "I appreciate that."

"Have a good night," Scott said somewhat restrained, then beelined it for the exit.

Walking home, Scott continuously forced back the tears eager to flow. He'd cut himself off from love because of Anthony Power. Now, the moment he was ready to take a chance, it *was* too late. And he'd screwed up. Big time. Troy had met someone. Was that why he was moving out? Were they buying a place together?

But this time, Scott had a choice: sit on the sidelines or let love lead him. Or maybe there was a third option.

***

THE EXPLOSION OF LAUGHTER MADE SCOTT stumble, and had his anxiety careening up and down his throat. He turned towards the house but quickly shifted his gaze back to the blooming perennials showcased in the late-afternoon sun. They were thriving, bursting with life, and totally contrary to his state of mind. He was still searching for a path forward, a purpose. Still afraid to take big risks and become who he dared to be.

And a month after Troy had moved out, the ground kept shifting underneath him and he didn't know how to cope. Like now. The laughter, the music, the conversations all set him on edge when, really, he should have been partying it up with the others. After all, everyone had gathered to toast Troy's new home in the south part of the city known as Welland Ridge. But Scott wasn't in a festive mood. How could he be? In the little over a year that Troy had been in Junction he'd built up a social network, and succeeded where Scott had, for all intents and purposes, failed. Troy had established himself in the community, and his decision to leave had struck a blow from which Scott had yet to recover. Not that Scott believed that they'd be roommates forever, but that he might have lost his only real chance at enduring love. Alone again, and no matter how silly it seemed, his biggest fear gunned straight for him: that he really was destined to live a solitary life.

Scott sipped his wine and continued his tour of the perfectly manicured yard. No one paid much attention to him anyway. Besides Janice and Tom, he didn't know anyone at the party. And why had Troy introduced him as 'an aspiring writer?' All that earned him were raised eyebrows and skeptical glances before people resumed their earlier conversations. Maybe being alone wasn't so bad. At least he'd be free to be as he pleased.

"Hello, Scott..."

Scott spun around, his eyes landing on the redhead approaching with his hand extended, but didn't react.

"I guess I deserved that," Evan said, his hand falling to his side.

Scott held Evan's gaze for a moment, then started to move away. He and Evan had been polar opposites that collided every time they met, forcing Troy or Janice to play referee. Scott wasn't in the mood for that.

"Scott..." Evan grabbed him by the arm. "Can we start over?" He followed Scott's eyes down to his hand and released his grip.

Scott didn't know what to say. They hadn't spoken since that night in his Gerrard Street East apartment when Evan revealed Anthony's unfaithfulness. Something else bothered him. He talked about wanting Junction to be home, yet he hadn't tried to make friends or genuinely be part of the community. Besides Troy and Jacob, no one knew him. He held them off. Now, here was someone reaching out to him, and he hesitated. "Troy said you moved to Vancouver." His voice was flat, almost robotic.

"I did." Evan lifted his beer can to his mouth. "Didn't work out."

"Sorry to hear that." Scott paused. "Now what?"

"I don't know." Evan bit down on his lip. "Troy's letting me crash with him until I get on my feet again."

Scott's eyes bulged. "You're planning on staying in Junction?"

"I kind of blew through my savings moving to Vancouver." Evan held on tightly to the beer can when a couple passed behind him. Then he drained his drink and squeezed the can, crushing it. "I'll go wherever I can find work."

"Something will come up," Scott encouraged.

"God, I hope so."

They scrutinized each other, probing for common ground, and perhaps something more meaningful: understanding. For the first time, Scott noticed the physical aspects that made Evan attractive. With his medium-length red hair and square face, Evan could easily double for Michael Fassbender. The way his full pink lips moved when he spoke, as if enveloping each word, had a hypnotic effect. His solid muscular frame allowed his nipples to stand out in his shirt. The confidence displayed in each movement. His stunning, pearly-white smile. His deep, from the pit of the stomach, laugh. Those intense copper-brown eyes that locked onto the recipient of his words. Then it hit him. Evan Lorde was, for the most part, the protagonist in the novel he'd written after his breakup with Anthony. What did that mean?

"Scott…" Evan ran his tongue over his lips. "Not to drag up the past, but I'm sorry about what happened with Anthony. I should have told you sooner that —"

"It's the past," Scott broke in, although Anthony Power was still a part of his present, still holding him back. "There's nothing for you to be sorry for, not when it comes to Anthony. I mean, you were an asshole in a different way. Wait, wait, wait…" Scott raised his free hand in the air. "So was I."

They laughed.

"We never really gave each other a chance," Evan said. "Back then I was threatened by you."

Scott scrunched up his face. "Really? Why?"

"You of all people know why." Evan rolled his shoulders. "I had a crush on Troy in university, and you were his best friend. Christ, the two of you were inseparable."

"I told Troy that but —"

"I was never his type," Evan interrupted. "Not like you."

"Let's not go there."

Again, laughter.

Evan held up his crushed beer can. "I need another."

"Me, too." Scott gulped the last mouthful of his wine and followed Evan towards the house. Everything kept shifting around him, and now he wondered if he and Evan could be friends? Then he had a strange thought. Maybe Evan, if he stayed in Junction, would be the person who'd help him anchor himself, feel settled in a new way. Or was he just kidding himself?

Once he'd refilled his wine, Scott spent a little time chatting with Evan, Janice and Tom. It wasn't long before he'd slipped away outside, taking refuge at the patio table on the veranda. Nursing his drink, he just wanted to block out the loud music and conversations crashing into each other. It reminded him of the Matrix, the new gay dance bar, that he sometimes frequented with Troy. No one ever seemed interested in him, and he didn't know quite how to act — like he couldn't understand how the rest of the world thought.

The patio door slid open, the music spilling outside, and for some reason Scott flinched. He flashed a nervous smile, then drained his wine.

Evan pushed the door closed and then sunk into the chair across from Scott. "At least you get to go home."

Scott chuckled. "This party shows no signs of slowing down, especially since most people seem to be having a good time."

Evan raised an eyebrow. "Most people? You're not having a good time?"

"I don't..." Scott sat up straight. "It's like high school. I was never one of the cool kids and always left to fend for myself."

"You seem pretty cool to me," Evan said.

Where did that come from? Scott wondered and glanced away as an awkward silence settled in. Then he checked the time. "I'm going to call it a night."

"How am I supposed to sleep with that racket going on?" Evan asked.

"Earplugs?"

"Funny."

"Well, if you want ... my guest room is free." *Did I really just say that?*

"Really?" Evan bounced out of his chair. "Give me ten minutes to throw some shit together."

"I'll meet you out front in ten."

After Evan raced into the house, Scott waited a few moments before returning inside. He poked his head into the living room and kitchen, scanning the faces. Troy was nowhere in sight. Scott made a final sweep of the downstairs before heading to the front door.

"Ready," Evan said as he neared the bottom of the staircase, a brown knapsack strapped to his back.

"Me, too." Scott pulled out his keys and that was when he saw Troy coming towards them.

"What's going on?" Troy asked.

"I tried to find you to let you know we were leaving," Scott said.

Troy's eyes narrowed. "We?"

"I'm crashing at Scott's tonight," Evan volunteered. "I don't think this party is ever going to end."

"Thanks for a good time," Scott said.

"You were like a wallflower," Troy spat. "We hardly spent any time together."

"You were busy playing host. I wasn't going to hog your time just because I'm socially awkward." Scott took a step towards the door. "Let's do drinks next week."

Troy folded his arms. "There were a couple of guys I wanted to introduce to you."

"No, no." Scott waved his hand. "Please, don't play matchmaker."

Then there was a silence that Evan broke with, "See you tomorrow." He squeezed past Scott and slipped out of the house.

Scott grabbed the door handle, but a warm hand on his arm prevented him from moving. He cranked his head to the right and held Troy's gaze. "What?"

"Is there something going on with you and Evan?" Troy scrunched his eyebrows, which made him look like an angry Doberman protecting its master.

Scott sucked his teeth. "Nothing's going on with Evan. He wants a good night's sleep. That's going to be difficult here. It's like an episode of *American Bandstand*."

"American what?"

"Never mind."

Troy let go of Scott's arm. "Don't be a stranger."

"I won't."

"Did you really have a good time? Because…"

Scott scratched the side of his head. "Maybe I was a wall-flower, but you know I've never been one for crowds. And some of your friends are just pricks. But I didn't come here to prove myself to them, or for you to hook me up with one of them." He offered a reassuring smile. "I'm really happy for you."

"Thanks."

Scott opened the door and, after crossing over the threshold, pivoted around, his gaze latched onto those mesmerizing hazel eyes. "Don't forget to call me about drinks." He didn't wait for Troy to reply and stepped onto the front porch.

As he made his way down the walk, he heard the front door close behind him. Were he and Troy really all right? He hoped so.

But then again, nothing in his life lately felt 'right.' His parents weren't saying much about his father's illness. He'd missed his shot at a romantic relationship with Troy, and now wasn't interested in anyone. And why was he still a goddamn proof-reader? Why wouldn't he act to live the life he imagined? Maybe he was broken.

Fifteen minutes later, Scott barged into his Miller Road home and made a beeline for the dining room. He snatched the bottle of Wolf Blass merlot from the wine rack and un-screwed the cap as he sailed into the kitchen. He'd just finished pouring two generous glasses when Evan came into the room. Sliding one of the wineglasses across the counter, he knew by the way Evan kept dodging his gaze that something had already changed. And when their eyes finally met, Scott recognized the look — the sense of loss gleaming in Evan's eyes, the hopelessness, the self-flagellation.

Scott took out the container of mixed olives from the fridge, then joined Evan, who'd already settled in at the bar-counter. "Are you okay?"

"I don't know." Evan traced his index finger around the rim of the wineglass. "I just never thought that, at this point in my life, I'd be starting over."

"God, Evan, you're twenty-seven."

"I just meant that I thought I'd be somewhat established by now," Evan said weakly. "You know, that I'd have a good job, that maybe like you and Troy I'd have bought a place."

Scott popped a Kalamata olive into his mouth, chewed thoughtfully and then discreetly discarded the pit. "You realize you have your whole life ahead of you, right? This is just a bump in the road."

Evan looked up. "How did you do it?"

"Do what?"

"Start over," Evan said with a hint of jealousy. "I mean, you left Toronto to come *here*. Almost everyone I've met calls Junction a hole in the wall, and it's like they're all trying to escape at the first possible moment. Yet you purposely came here and have made a home for yourself. How'd you do it?"

"It's the choice I made." Scott sipped his wine. "I needed a break and I couldn't see myself... At the time, I had to leave Toronto. That's all I knew."

Evan lifted his wineglass to his mouth and, before taking a sip, asked, "Do you see yourself staying here long-term?"

"Maybe. Who knows. I mean, I thought I'd be here a year. But since I don't know what to fucking do with my life..."

"Do you like it here?"

"When I accepted the job and knew I was moving here, I thought of Junction like a Kinder Surprise." Scott tossed another olive into his mouth. "I didn't know what I'd find inside, but I promised myself I'd find a way to like it and make it work."

"I wish I could have done that in Vancouver. Did Troy ever tell you why I left?"

"No. He and I weren't exactly speaking to each other then."

"It was the stupidest thing I've ever done," Evan confessed, the emotion scratching at the back of his throat.

Scott listened as Evan talked into his wine about the man named Reid Park, the sense of defeat rising in his voice. More than a trend, online dating was becoming the norm, and Evan had met Reid through Cuddlr.com. Since Reid was from Vancouver, the relationship progressed from online chatting to e-mail and then lengthy phone calls. At the time, Evan, originally from Vancouver, worked as a policy analyst for an opposition MPP at Queen's Park. With the MPP's election defeat, there was nothing else tying Evan to Toronto. He hadn't risked much in life and wanted to believe that Reid was 'the one.' He had nothing to lose by moving back to Vancouver. The one time Evan looked up as he told the story, his eyes glistened with disillusionment that made Scott cringe. That was how he felt after the debacle with Anthony. He had lived Evan's pain, nearly let the rage suffocate him. Would either of them ever be able to completely let go?

"I was pretty naïve." Evan fixed his gaze on Scott. "Actually, I was just stupid."

"You pulled yourself out." Scott tried to lift Evan's spirits, erase the sadness embedded in his face. "That counts for something."

"I guess." Evan didn't sound convinced. "It was great at first. Then I noticed money missing from my wallet. Reid stayed out late and came home drunk, or high. Half the time I couldn't tell the difference. The day I caught him snorting cocaine in the bathroom I knew I had to get out. I wanted to help him at first, but it was all too clear he didn't want help." He gave a nervous laugh. "I thought I could save him until I realized I had to save myself."

"You did the right thing."

"I felt ashamed." Evan blinked magnificently. "Maybe ashamed isn't the right word. I didn't want to admit that I had made a mistake. I didn't want people to know that I had failed."

"You didn't fail," Scott said emphatically. "Failing would have been staying in the muddle. You pulled yourself out. To me, that's victory. You did save yourself."

"You're the first person not to say, 'I told you so.'" Evan got up to get the wine bottle, topped up their glasses and then sat back down. "Isn't that the power of love?" He flicked his eyebrows. "It does seem pretty silly to fall in love over the internet."

"Yet it happens every day."

Evan leaned forward and rested his arms on the countertop. "Does Troy think you and I —"

"I made sure he understood that you're staying here because of the party," Scott said.

"Are you dating?" Evan asked.

"No." Scott gulped his wine. "After Anthony ... not that interested in dating. Still have a hard time trusting people, letting them get close."

"That's a shame. You're cutting yourself off from love when you have so much love to give."

"Love seems like an illusion."

"It's very real."

They sat in silence, sipping their wine and eating olives. There it was again, the movement underneath Scott's feet that had him questioning his worth. And what about Evan? Were their past misunderstandings suddenly forgotten?

Scott downed the last mouthful of his wine. "It's late." He stood and watched as Evan polished off his drink. Then, moving through the house and turning out lights along the way, he guided Evan upstairs to the room Troy had occupied. "Goodnight, Evan."

"Scott..."

Evan leaned against the doorframe. "Don't give up on love."

"Night," Scott whispered and headed down the hall. Closing his bedroom door, Evan's words came back to him. *Don't give up on love.*

Maybe he already had.

The Fallout

IT WAS ELEVEN DAYS LATER, A WEDNESDAY, and Scott and Troy had finally met up for drinks after it seemed like their 'busy' schedules purposely kept them apart. Seated on the patio at Manhattan's, they looked warily at each other, as if they were unsure of who they had become. Scott shifted his chair under the Coors Light umbrella, protected from the warm afternoon sun. The even better result was that he was no longer in Troy's direct line of sight.

"How come you and Evan are so buddy-buddy?" Troy sounded petulant. "During university, you couldn't stand each other. Now he's moving in with you?"

"He's renting a room." Scott reached for his wineglass. "It's only until he can save up enough money and get his own place."

"I told him he could stay with me," Troy snapped.

"That's between you and Evan." Scott returned his wineglass to the table. "Maybe he's a little uncomfortable with Stuart being there all the time, like he's in the way."

"Stuart's not there all the time." Troy leaned back in his chair. "Fine. He's there regularly."

"And I hear a bit vocal."

They laughed.

There was a silence that Troy broke with, "Are you and Evan sleeping together?"

"No!"

"Did you..." Troy drew in a deep breath. "Did you sleep with him?"

"No! Evan and me … we're working on being friends. I'm just helping him out like I helped you. God, do you think Evan's my type?"

"Your type? Got that it wasn't me."

"Oh, come on, Troy." Scott ran his hand over his face. "Let's not dredge up the past. And maybe you were my type, but I was too stupid to realize it. Now you're with Stuart, so it's irrelevant."

"Scottie…"

Scott's eyes locked onto the brunette approaching the booth. "Don't ever call me that. *Ever.*"

Jacob brushed the hair out of his face and slid into the booth next to Scott. He reached over the table and shook hands with Troy. "Is he always so temperamental?"

"Always," Troy said, avoiding eye contact with Scott.

Two minutes later, Evan appeared and sat down next to Troy. Scott listened while the three men talked spiritedly about the looming leadership contest for the federal Liberal Party. There was, between them, a natural alliance that made Scott nervous. Not nervousness exactly, but unease. Around the table were three of his friends, and with two of them he'd made mistakes, given himself over to desire. Each time it changed them, how they saw each other and, more importantly, how he saw himself.

"Assistant Chief of Staff," Jacob said, nodding. "For the mayor? What will you be doing exactly?"

"Build and maintain strong relationships with the community," Evan said, like he was reading from a script.

"He means, sleep with all the good-looking men in the city," Troy teased.

"Ha-ha!" Evan playfully shoved Troy. "I'll be representing the mayor and the city at events and meetings."

"Translation…" Troy burped. "He'll attend all the boring events that the mayor doesn't want to."

"Like my father, Troy thinks he's a comedian." Scott's eyes bore into Troy. "Don't give up your day job."

Laughter erupted around the table.

"Are they sending you to represent the city at the Junction Run this Saturday?" Jacob asked.

Evan waved him off. "Thankfully, I don't start until Monday."

"Then come cheer us on," Jacob insisted.

Troy, about to take a swig of his beer, pulled the beer stein away from his mouth. "Cheer who on?"

"Me and Scott." Jacob looked at Scott. "You didn't tell them?"

"No." Scott dodged the glances around the table. "It's my first race. I'll be happy if I don't come in last, or at least finish ahead of everyone in the over-seventy category."

"Some of those old-timers can run," Evan warned.

"Thanks for the encouragement," Scott spat.

Jacob cupped his hand to Scott's shoulder. "As usual, you're being hard on yourself." He removed his hand and looked at Troy, then Evan. "Scott's a good runner. I can barely keep up with him."

Scott pointed at Jacob's nose. "What's that brown stuff?"

Laughter.

Then came the moment, about an hour later, when Evan disappeared to the men's room and Jacob stepped away to take a call, leaving Troy and Scott alone again.

Troy leaned forward and spoke quickly. "What did you mean earlier?"

"I don't —"

"No, Scott." Troy slammed his hand on the table. "Don't play dumb. You said you were 'too stupid to realize it.' Did you —"

"You're with Stuart, remember?" Scott cut in. "That was a long time ago. And now —"

Troy flinched. "Now ... what?"

"I'm not interested in anyone like that," Scott lied.

"You're an asshole." Troy pushed back his chair, stood and walked away.

Jacob was back at the table. "Everything all right?"

Scott reached for his wineglass and polished off his drink. Then he signalled to their server, standing at the bar, for another. He held his gaze to his empty glass, unwilling to look at Jacob. How many times would he hurt his best friend, shove him away? *Coward. I'm a fucking coward.* But this time was different. Letting his heart rule him meant hurting others, tearing their lives apart.

He wouldn't do that. Not for a love that, maybe, had truly missed its chance.

The Confrontation

"SHOULD I GO?" STUART ASKED HESITANTLY.

Troy glanced at Stuart. "Go where?"

"Home," Stuart said askance. "You're anywhere but *here*."

They were loosely holding hands, seated on the deep black leather sofa in Troy's living room. It was Saturday night, a few minutes before nine and a month after Evan had moved into Scott's guest bedroom.

"I'm sorry." Troy stood and approached the large window, staring blankly into the dimly lit street. The quiet shuffle of feet against the floor shattered the silence like a roll of thunder. Then came the pressure on his shoulders, followed by the musky stench of Stuart's cologne that inundated his nostrils and burned his throat.

"I'm told I'm a great listener," Stuart whispered. And at six-foot-one, he balanced on his tiptoes to massage Troy's shoulders. His trim beard, speckled with grey, often had people thinking he was older. He was forty-one, a doctor, and worked in the emergency department at Hamilton General Hospital.

Troy twisted away and spun around. "I appreciate the offer but I'm all right. I'm tired. Let's go to bed." He grabbed Stuart's hand and led him upstairs to the bedroom. Once inside the room, he lunged at Stuart, driving his tongue down the back of Stuart's throat as they fell onto the bed. With his eyes closed tight, he made love fantasizing about the man he hoped would love him forever. That man was not Stuart McClellan.

***

STUART PUSHED ON THE ROUND WHITE BUTTON and swallowed hard as the muffled ding, dong, ding, dong rang out in the air. The door opened and he staggered. He remembered Troy mentioning that Evan was staying with Scott, but had forgotten until Evan came into view. Was that a game-changer? Troy didn't know he was here, and he didn't want Evan ratting him out.

"Stuart," Evan said with surprise.

"Is Scott here?" Stuart stepped into the house before being invited in.

"Yes." Evan closed the door. "Wait here." He disappeared down the hall, returning a short time later unaccompanied. "He's in his office. Take a left and then it's the last door on the left."

Stuart kicked off his shoes and walked determinedly to Scott's office. He knocked twice, entered the room and closed the door behind him with an unintentional bang. Forcing a smile, he strutted to the large maple desk and accepted Scott's handshake. Their gazes locked, Stuart chewed the inside of his lip as the silence grew awkward, unbearable. There it was again. The same raised-eyebrow look Scott had thrown at Troy when they'd met at Manhattan's. Troy introduced him as his boyfriend, but the hesitation and the way he said it — b–boy–fr–friend — made it seem conditional. And Scott's reaction had not gone unnoticed.

"I know it's late, but I needed to talk to you," Stuart said ruefully, fell into the chair in front of the desk, and crossed his left leg over his right.

"Troy and I haven't seen much of each other lately." Scott lowered himself into his seat. "Life's been a bit crazy." Not necessarily the truth, not necessarily an untruth.

"This may be none of my business, but…" Stuart uncrossed his legs and brought himself forward to the edge of the chair. "Is there something I should know about you and Troy?"

Scott, fiddling with his pen, set it down on the desk. "Like?"

"He talks about you a lot," Stuart said, exasperated. "*A … lot*. It's great that you're his best friend, it's just —"

"It's simple." Scott rested his arms on his papers. "A few years back, Troy and I had a one-night stand. He wanted more. At the time, I did not."

"At the time…" Stuart coughed, taking time to find the right words. "What does that mean?"

"It means I'm not a threat."

"Here's what I think." Stuart clasped his hands together. "Troy says you're like brothers. My gut tells me he loves you, and not like a brother. Clearly, he's hanging on to some adolescent hope that the two of you…" His voice broke off and he licked his lips. "It may sound crazy, because we've only been dating a few months, but I love him, Scott. He's stirred something inside of me, yet he's holding himself back. Because of you."

"Me?"

"Yes, you. He won't commit to me, to us, while you're in the picture."

"I'm not 'in the picture,'" Scott emphasized. "No matter what I feel for Troy, I won't come between you. I told him that."

"That's not good enough," Stuart countered.

"Not good enough?" Scott's voice boomed. "What do you want me to do?"

Stuart rose. "Let him go."

"You're asking me to give up my best friend? No way!"

"I'm not going anywhere," Stuart cautioned. "I'll fight for him, fight for us."

Scott fell back in his chair. "It's not a fight. You … can … have him."

"You don't see it. You don't see it at all." Stuart slunk to the door.

"I see Troy likes you," Scott called out.

Stuart opened the door. "It's a long road from like to love, especially when you're not the magnificent Scott Davenport."

"I'll talk to him." Scott's tone was urgent and conciliatory.

"Thanks. But, somehow, I don't think that's going to be enough."

Stuart stomped down the hall to the foyer, grabbed his shoes and stormed out of the house. He slipped on his shoes before sliding into the driver's seat of his black Mercedes sedan. Could he return to Troy's? He had sneaked out after Troy fell asleep, and going back there might mean explaining where he'd gone. Not an option, at least not now after his confrontation with Scott.

He jammed the key in the ignition and flipped the engine. *Go home*, he counselled himself, hoping that he hadn't messed up the best thing to happen to him in years.

***

PLUNKING BACK DOWN INTO HIS CHAIR, SCOTT covered his face with his hands and drew in long deep breaths. His own actions — or inactions — had brought him into a matter he desperately wanted to avoid. Yes, he loved Troy, but he wasn't a homewrecker. Never wanted to be the 'other man.' But Stuart couldn't expect him to, now, walk out on his friendship with Troy. They'd come back from the brink, were best friends again, confided in each other. Most of the time, anyway. That was the power of their friendship, their brotherhood. And just like he wouldn't be the other man, he wouldn't let himself be played as a pawn. He couldn't convince Troy to love Stuart. That was Troy's call. Or maybe…

Scott uncovered his face and flinched when his eyes met Evan's. "Jesus!"

"Are you okay?" Evan stood in front of the desk with his hands clasped behind his back.

"No, not really." Scott dropped his head. "I'd convinced myself that I didn't love Troy. When I was ready to tell him, fucking Stuart appears."

"At least you're finally admitting it," Evan said, matter-of-fact. "Took you long enough."

"You knew?" Scott's voice pitched high.

"Everybody knew. Everybody knows. No one understands why you've, how do I put it … why you've been an ass about it."

"Anthony. What he did and —"

"Troy would never do something like that. Not to anyone. Definitely not to you."

"I was never ready," Scott confided. "Never willing."

Evan raised an eyebrow. "And now?"

"And now…" A nervous laugh squeaked from the back of Scott's throat. "Maybe there's only one thing left to do." He leapt out of his chair, and charged out of his office and into the foyer. Thrusting his feet into his sandals, he leaned against the bannister when the room started to spin. His chest burned, the linguine with clams he'd had for dinner caught somewhere in the middle. The spinning stopped, but the tinny clams crept up his throat and he swallowed four times to force them back down. He snatched his keys off the occasional table and threw open the front door.

Halfway across town, flashing lights lit up his rear-view mirror. He navigated the car to the side of the road, shifted into park and touched his back pocket. "Goddammit!" No wallet. No driver's license. Sirens wailed, closing in on him, and then the police cruiser zoomed by. Scott exhaled a pent-up breath, then continued on his way.

Fifteen minutes after leaving his home, he stood on Troy's stoop, alternating between ringing the doorbell and pounding on the door. It took about two minutes for the outside light to come on, and then the door opened.

"Scott?" Troy rubbed his eyes "What are you doing here?"

"We need to talk." Scott burst into the house and waited for Troy to close the door. "I had a visit from Stuart earlier this evening."

"What? What are you talking about?"

"Stuart came to see me." Scott headed into the dark living room, then squinted at the sudden brightness. Facing into the room, he did a one-eighty. And when Troy came into the room, the light bouncing off his bare, muscular chest, Scott gasped.

Troy cupped his masculine hands to the back of his head, as if posing for a *Men's Health* ad. "Why would Stuart go to see you?"

"Because he knows." Scott staggered back a few steps until he bumped into the black club chair and straddle its arm. "He knows everything."

"I don't follow." Troy's arms fell to his sides. Shuffling to the sofa, he ran his fingers through his dark mane. "He knows everything about what?"

"That I love you." Scott hadn't planned on being so blunt, but at this point he had nothing to lose. "Whoa. Feels good to get that out." He fixed his eyes on Troy's right pink nipple. "I let Anthony ruin love for me. Never wanted to believe that someone else would love me and mean it. Never wanted to believe that being loved didn't mean getting hurt." He raised his head until he held Troy's gaze. "Never wanted to believe that I could love again. Too stupid, too stubborn, too pathetic to see *you*. You tried to tell me so many times, in so many ways, yet I —"

"Scott —"

Scott raised a hand, a tear streaking down his cheek. He slid his body fully onto the chair cushion, sitting erect and still, as if waiting for the portrait artist to begin. "Stuart loves you, loves you in a way I..." His voice faltered. Could he do this? Could he walk away? "Love him," he pleaded, lifted himself up and marched to the door. Before he could open it, Troy's hands were on him. Facing each other, Troy's head came down, but Scott turned quickly, the kiss avoided. Then he lifted his hands, placed them to Troy's chest and he shoved. But the warmth of Troy's smooth skin took Scott back to the night of their sex act. Troy's tenderness, the deep prodding of his tongue, his willing submission... Scott's pulse raced, his breathing heavy. *Walk away. Walk away now!*

Staring at Troy, this was the moment truth conquered Scott: he loved Troy but would never let himself live it. And without saying another word, he opened the door and slipped into the still of the night.

Part IV

August 2006 – December 2006

Nothing Will Ever be the Same

SPEED UP, SLOW DOWN, SPEED UP, SLOW DOWN. A vicious cycle filled with moments of panic at the near colli- sions as drivers switched lanes without signalling or checking their blind spots. The start of the Thanksgiving long week- end, and cars in both the eastbound and westbound lanes of the 401 crawled forward. The speeding up and slowing down mimicked Troy's temperament and frustrated him. There were times, and this was one of them, when life resembled the trees as they zoomed down the highway. A blur.

What had happened between January, when the doctors had declared Terrence cancer-free, and now? He barely re- membered what he had for lunch yesterday. Then fragments of the call with Margaret, and the unspeakable joy bubbling in her voice, floated in his mind. "The doctors can't explain it," she'd cheered. "The cancer just vanished. Poof! But I told them … it's a testimony to God's healing power." That was life travelling at lightning speed. Now it was August, and the cancer was back. "With a vengeance," was how Margaret put it. And life slowed to a crawl, just before rounding the final bend and soaring off a cliff.

The car lurched forward, and Troy along with it. He raised his hands to the dashboard, bracing himself, then fell back- wards. Traffic was at a standstill.

"Sorry about that," Scott said in a whisper. The words were swallowed whole by the silence, deafening — infused with a type of awkwardness that made stomachs churn and could crush a larynx in a single blow.

Troy cocked his head to the right and stared out the window at the trees. He worked to steady his breathing, push down the anger twisting and pulling at his insides. Because two months ago, Scott had admitted he loved him, then told him to love somebody else. Was that supposed to be some brave act of redemption? A way for Scott to set him free from a tormenting and unrequited love? And, now, what did it mean to be free? The anger held on, ravaged him, brought him to the breaking point. Not because he still hoped that Scott would change his mind, but because they'd so easily let go of each other.

The silence pressed down on Troy as they sat there, caught in the gridlock, neither of them willing to speak, to act in ordinary ways. He wanted to scream, tear his hair out. What had happened to them?

Scott shifted the car into park and eased his foot off the break. He turned on the radio and scanned the channels, stopping at one where the croaky voice explained how lanes in all direction on the 401 were closed at the 427-interchange due to a multi-vehicle accident. They looked hopelessly at each other, and the already fragile tension circulating about them became even more delicate.

Troy couldn't take the silence any longer. "How's your father really doing?"

"I don't know," Scott said with a hint of annoyance. "And it depends on who you talk to. It's confusing, too. I mean, Dad's ultrasound in April didn't show any growths. When he returned last month, they were everywhere." He glanced at Troy. "Mom's not handling it well. Some days, it's like she has him dead and buried already. Aunt Deidre was at the house last night, and listening to her you'd think that Dad is staging another comeback."

Troy grinned as Scott re-enacted the call with his mother the day before. Margaret was fixated on how frail and sick-looking Terrence had become in a matter of weeks. "'It's like he knows death is imminent,'" Scott said, mimicking his mother's scolding schoolteacher's tone. "'But I've given it over to God. I believe in His healing power.'"

"Maybe it's good that someone believes," Troy said.

"Maybe." Scott drummed his fingers into the steering wheel. "Thanks for making this trip with me. Dad will appreciate it."

"I'd do anything for Terrence."

"I know. But I'm concerned. You know we can't bring our issues into my parents' home. Dad doesn't need that kind of stress."

"We won't." Troy ran his right hand across his face. "We'll pretend like everything's fine."

"But everything's not fine," Scott said, his voice slow to rise. "We've hardly said a word to each other since we left Junction."

"I don't know what you want me to say!" Troy shouted. "This is weird. We haven't seen each other in two months. You only called because Terrence is sick. Now, we're trapped in a car together for seven hours. So, really, what do you want me to say?" He swung his head in Scott's direction, their eyes locked. Another showdown. He couldn't take it and looked away first. He closed his eyes, breathed deeply, and twitched at the loud, repeated honking of horns that came from behind. Then the car edged forward. They were moving again, gathering speed and soon enough flying down the highway. But Troy wasn't moving, not emotionally — stuck in the abyss, in a deep black hole that steadily tore away at his core. *Scott's right. Pretending like everything's fine between us is impossible, but we have to try ... for Terrence's sake. Even still, this is going to be hell.*

***

SCOTT HAD JAMMED HIS KEY IN THE LOCK just before the front door swung open. His mother rushed him, her trembling arms holding him in a clenching embrace. In that moment, he understood her fear and, forced back his tears. Calm and strong. For her. They pushed apart and he closed the door while his mother hugged Troy. When his gaze met his mother's again, he watched her smile fade, the pleasure and relief at seeing her boys drained from her face.

"I don't like this," Margaret said, matter-of-fact, looking at the two men. "I don't like this at all."

"Mama..."

"Don't Mama me." Her tone was stern, and that often gave way to her preacher voice. "You two need to fix whatever it is that's broken between you." She raised her hand in the air and pointed it at Troy. "And I know you're not thinking about interrupting me. Your father is sick and —"

"My father?" Troy asked. It had slipped out without him realizing it.

"Terrence." She threw her hands in the air. "You may be tall, white and lanky, but you're like a son to us. And Terrence doesn't need any more stress. The two of you right now with your pouty lips and gloom-and-doom looks … even the dumbest fool can see you're not getting along. It'd break your father's heart to see you like this. It breaks my heart to see you like this." She clasped her hands together as if she were going to pray and aimed them first at Scott, then at Troy. "Fix it."

"You didn't have to wait up for us, Mama," Scott said, eager to change the subject.

"Your Aunt Linda's here and in Frank's old room." Margaret stood with her left hand on her stomach and her right hand on top of her left. "You'll have to double up in your bedroom."

"I'll take the pullout in the den," Scott said.

"Your cousin Trevor has the den." Margaret stepped forward and kissed Troy on the cheek. After kissing Scott, she said, "We weren't expecting them. That's why I stayed up. Stretch bursting in on Linda would have been a ghastly scene." She and Scott laughed. "Don't stay up too late. There's a lot to do tomorrow and I could use your help."

Scott bristled. "What's going on tomorrow?"

"Heavens to Betsy." Margaret placed her hand on her chest. "Since Linda's here, your father's side of the family is getting together while he's still —"

"Go to bed, Mama," Scott cut in. "We'll deal with that in the morning."

"Goodnight, my babies." Margaret, starting up the stairs light-footed, added, "And fix it!"

Scott slipped into the living room, turned off the TV and made his way into the kitchen. He opened the fridge door and, desperate for a stiff drink, pulled out the orange juice carton. He had just filled up his glass when Troy came into view. "Do you want something?" All Troy offered was a blank stare, so Scott slid the glass across the counter towards Troy, then poured another drink for himself.

Clutching his glass, Scott headed towards the back door. Outside, the summery night air caressed his skin, the gentle breeze filled with the scent of burning wood. He loved that scent. It always made him nostalgic about his childhood trips to visit his grandparents in the country. Located on a large parcel of land with trees that lined three sides of the property, their home became a fortress. No harm could come to him there, or so he believed as a child. He craved that protection now. Not for himself. For his father. To keep him alive.

Scott walked across the deck, leaned up against the railing and looked in the direction of the door when it squeaked. He contemplated Troy, who approached cautiously.

Under the full veil of night, they were again immured in silence. Weren't they exhausted? Not from the drive, but from the emotional rollercoaster?

"I never meant to hurt you," Scott said, and downed his orange juice the way he sometimes did his scotch after a long day at the office.

"What did you think would happen?" Troy spoke quietly. "You said you loved me and then walked out on me. You never gave us a chance."

"You were dating Stuart."

"And that meant you had to cut me off? Badda bing, badda boom, and our friendship was done. That's what hurt."

"I was trying to do the right thing."

A long silence followed. The crickets chirping their melodies and the other unnameable night noises had a calming effect. They still couldn't look at each other, as if unwilling to peek over the wall that they had constructed between them.

"We have to figure something out," Scott said. "If we can't talk to each other, then maybe —"

"Maybe, what?" Panic rose in Troy's voice. "Do you want to officially end our friendship? Never see each other again?"

"No." Scott's shoulders slumped and he looked down. "I don't want to lose my best friend."

"I miss you. You were the one person I told everything to."

Scott lifted his head. "You kept a few things from me. Buying a house, dating Stuart —"

"Don't be an ass." Troy paced the veranda in a circle. "All I meant was … we understood each other. We cared and supported each other."

"You realize you're using the past tense, right?"

"I think we can be that way again. And you're not my grammar teacher." Troy stopped moving and looked at Scott. "There's a huge hole in my life because you're not in it. I don't like that feeling. And I'm filling the void with work or random hookups."

"What happened with Stuart?" Scott asked.

"Didn't work out."

"So, have you been tested for Chlamydia lately?"

Troy sucked his teeth. "Not funny."

"Wasn't meant as a joke." Scott started towards the house. "Take my room. I'll crash on the sofa." He opened the back door at the same time Troy grabbed his arm. They looked at each other but didn't say anything. He gently pulled his arm out of Troy's grasp and entered the house. Inside, he loaded the few dishes from the sink into the dishwasher.

"I can take the sofa," Troy said from the kitchen doorway. "I don't mind."

"No." Scott closed the dishwasher door. "Take my room. You'll need all your strength when it comes to Aunt Linda."

Troy leaned against the doorframe. "Why's that?"

"Aunt Linda is a phenomenon."

"You mean she's phenomenal."

Scott folded his arms. "No, I meant phenomenon."

"Scott…" Troy pushed himself off the doorframe. "Thanks for not giving up on us."

"Goodnight, Troy."

Their eyes were glued to each other until Troy backed up and disappeared.

Scott waited in the kitchen until the faint thud of his childhood bedroom door closing shattered the silence. He shuffled into the living room, collapsed onto the sofa and stared abstractly at the ceiling. He wasn't himself, didn't know who he was anymore or where he belonged.

The more important question was this: would he ever find his way home?

The Beginning of the End

"MORNING," SCOTT SAID WHEN HE WALKED into the kitchen. He ran his hand over his face and stretched to work out the kink in his back. On the hard sofa he had tossed and turned, a restless night with his mind also in overdrive. He woke up at seven when he heard his mother in the kitchen.

"Morning, Schnookums," Margaret said, getting up from the kitchen table. She turned on the coffeemaker, took a multicoloured striped mug from the cupboard and set it on the counter. "You look exhausted."

"I'm fine." Scott yawned as he moved to the fridge and retrieved the cream. "How long is Aunt Linda going to be here?"

"I don't know." Margaret's voice trembled, as it usually did, when she talked about people who got under her skin. Linda was one of those people who knew how to push her buttons, and did so almost gleefully. Margaret sat back down at the kitchen table. "Do I have to ask?"

"Troy and I are fine."

"Is that why you slept on the sofa?"

"Mama…"

"You know what your aunt is like. I don't want any more drama."

"Everything's fine. Really." Scott couldn't wait for the coffee to finish brewing and pulled the pot from the warmer pad. He filled the mug his mother had taken out for him, leaving enough room to add a generous amount of cream. "It wouldn't feel right if Troy and I didn't have a falling out at least once a year," he said and returned the carton to the fridge.

"You know, Schnookums…" Margaret, flipping through what had been her mother's *Purity Cookbook*, leaned back in her chair and contemplated him. "I don't know who you think you're talking to sometimes. The energy, bad energy, that you and Stretch were giving off last night was about more than a falling out. I could feel the hate."

Silence. Just the sound of the tick tock of the kitchen clock and Scott slurping his coffee. "A couple of months ago... I don't know when exactly, but I knew Troy *liked* me. And I —"

"And because of what happened with Anthony, you denied *your* feelings for Troy."

"How do you know that?"

"I'm your mother. Mothers see things." Margaret removed her reading glasses. "So, what happened? Did you tell him how you feel?"

"Yes and no."

"Oh, Lord."

"Mama, Troy had a boyfriend who really liked him. I didn't..." He sipped his coffee. "I told him I loved him, but that he should love Stuart because he could love him in a way I couldn't."

Margaret's head twitched. "What does that mean?"

"I've always thought of Troy as the big brother I never had. Mama, I don't want to have *that* talk today. But dating Troy would be, well, like ... like Rod and Charlotte." Rod and Charlotte were two of Scott's first cousins, and first cousins to each other, who eloped. "You said that was wrong."

"There's a big difference," Margaret said, preacher-like, "between Rod and Charlotte and you and Stretch. We treat Stretch like family, but he's not blood. There'd be nothing incestuous about the two of you —"

"You said you wanted me to date black men."

"That's not exactly what I said." Margaret put her glasses back on. "Humph."

Scott joined his mother at the table. "You'd be all right with me dating Troy? Really?"

"What I want," Margaret said with emphasis, "is for you to be happy. You've been alone for such a long time. You're such a handsome and successful young man, and you could have anyone you want. No one should go through life alone." She flipped the page of the cookbook. "Stretch isn't bad looking for a white man, and he's a doctor."

"Mama!"

Margaret raised her hands in the air. "I'm just saying…"

"Well, I screwed up," Scott said primly.

"What about that guy who was staying with you? Oh, what's his name?"

"You mean, Evan? Christ, no." Scott immediately dropped his gaze, and wanted to crawl into a corner and hide. "I'm sorry."

Margaret pushed her chair back from the table, stood and carried the cookbook to the counter. "Your children get an education, move away, and then think they can come back into your house and take the Lord's, my God's, name in vain." She looked up at the ceiling. "Lord, I know you're testing me, and I'm trying to do Your will."

Scott, holding his gaze to the floor, headed out of the kitchen and onto the back veranda. The sky was overcast, the morning air cool and crisp. Was the Lord, at this very moment, testing him too? And would he pass? Could he and Troy once again find purpose to their friendship? Was he ready to grieve for his father, or was he waiting, child-like, on a miracle? Would he find love again? *Focus on the present*, he reminded himself and returned to the kitchen to help his mother prepare for the inevitable Davenport onslaught and family antics from which he was already desperate to escape.

***

"STRETCH, BE A DEAR," MARGARET SAID, HOLD-ing out an empty silver tray. "There are more of the salmon puffs in the fridge in the white container."

"Stretch?" Linda, a formidable woman with skin the colour of molasses, was cutting the pan of lemon squares. "So, you're this Stretch I've heard so much about." She glared at Troy, her eyes sharp like a coroner's scalpel ready to cut open a corpse. "He sure is lanky."

Margaret chuckled. "I told you he was lanky."

"I'm not lanky." Troy made a sort of grunting sound.

"Turn around," Linda said, making a circular motion with her hand. "Humph. And no ass. Why is it that white men have no ass? Apparently, God does have a sense of humour. But we sure do need something to grab onto when —"

"Linda!" Margaret shouted.

The other women in the kitchen giggled.

Margaret, her knotted face expressing her displeasure, looked over the top of her glasses. "Stretch, the salmon puffs." She tried not to laugh with the other women as Troy stepped sideways to the fridge so that no one could stare at his backside. Laughter broke out again, but was instantly silenced by the stern look Margaret flashed around the room.

The house and backyard were crowded with members of the Davenport clan eating, laughing and retelling stories of childhood escapades that had been told a thousand times. A typical family gathering until Terrence coughed or sounded winded or looked fatigued. Then fear and concern displaced the joy and good cheer.

"My late husband didn't have much to grab onto," Linda said as she moved the cut squares from the pan to a platter. "But his package on the other side..." She fanned herself with the lifter.

"Linda!" Margaret stomped her foot on the floor. "First off, Don isn't dead. He's in Millhaven serving out his manslaughter sentence. Everyone knows that." She wiped her hands on her navy-blue apron. "Second, no one cares about his package. And it's certainly not a topic I want discussed in my house."

Troy, carrying the tray of salmon puffs towards the back door, said, "Momma D, Terrence said something about —"

"Mama, who?" Linda's head swung in Margaret's direction, then Troy's. "Did you just call her Mama?"

"Tell Terrence not to worry." Margaret shooed Troy towards the back door. "Everything's under control."

"She ain't your mama." Linda waved her hand in the air. "Where do you get off —"

"Where do you get off?" Troy spoke quickly, his voice cracking. "You don't know me or my story. And, frankly, it's none of your business." He pointed at Margaret. "Momma D's been a mother to me, more than my own mother ever was. So, don't tell me —"

"You don't just go around calling people 'Mama.'" Linda shook her head violently. "Especially when there's no blood between you."

"I don't recall asking for your opinion," Troy spat. "Big and loud doesn't make you right or important."

"Did he just call her big?" a voice whispered.

"Big *and* loud," a second voice confirmed.

"She's going to tear him apart," the first voice said, chuckling.

Linda set the lifter on the counter and placed her hands on her hips. "What did you just call me?"

"Big and loud." Troy, standing with his free hand on his hip, threw Linda a mocking look.

Linda untied the strings of her apron. "Those are fighting words."

"There she goes again," someone said with disdain.

Margaret moved to block Linda's path. "Stretch, outside."

"Young people today have no respect," Linda said, unable to outmanoeuvre Margaret.

"Don't get me started on respect." Margaret shot Linda a hard, threatening glare. "And what Stretch calls me is, like he said, none of your business."

Linda pointed behind Margaret at Troy, who hadn't moved. "He wants to see what big and loud is all about? Fine. I'm going to tear that scrawny white boy apart."

"Let's get one thing clear," Margaret said, her voice raised, and took a step towards Linda. "You're in my house. And in my house, Stretch is not only Scott's best friend, he's a part of this family. My son. And I expect you to treat him as such."

Linda tried to stare down Margaret but lost and took a step back. "Scott's best friend?" She reached behind her back to tie her apron strings. "In this house it seems everyone's too scared to speak the truth."

Margaret folded her arms. "And what truth is that?"

"That Stretch and Scott are lovers," Linda said. "Take the blinders off."

The back door swung open, and Scott slipped past Troy and into the kitchen.

With her apron strings tied, Linda pointed again at Troy. "Terrence talks all the time about how he and Stretch rebuilt that car. Stretch did this, Stretch did that." She gave Margaret a knowing look. "Those two jackals are doing the nasty together. You can tell by the way Stretch looks at Scott, like his loins are on fire." She picked up the lifter. "Best friends my shapely black ass."

Margaret unfolded her arms and pointed her long index finger at Linda. "I think you've said and done enough today. Get out of my kitchen."

"Sister, I'm just telling it like it is, like it needs to be told," Linda said unapologetically.

Troy, his face riddled with hopelessness, stormed out onto the back veranda, nearly dropping the tray of salmon puffs as he rushed through the back door.

"Then let's tell it!" Margaret slammed her hand on the counter. "Let's tell the world why Don is in Millhaven Institution."

Scott cupped his hand to his mother's shoulder. "Mama…"

Margaret twisted away from Scott and pointed at Linda. "You're so keen on telling it like it is, fine. Let's tell the world how Don took the plea deal so that no one would know what *you* did."

"Mom!"

Margaret stiffened at the wide-eyed stares locked on her and tried to calm down. But she was pumped.

Scott's eyes bore into Linda. "It'd help if you knew what you were talking about. No one appreciates a loud, attention-seeking, obnoxious … twit." He wanted to say, "Jackass," but censored himself.

Linda's comical mouth dropped open. Then she focused her furious eyes, wide and filled with total abhorrence, on Margaret. Despite everything, she expected her sister-in-law to come to her defense. "Are you going to let him talk to me like that?"

Margaret's hands shot up in the air, like she was surrendering to the enemy. "No, no. Once you start being big and loud, you're on your own. What's that expression? If you're going to dish it out, be prepared to take it."

"Amen," Scott said with the fervour of someone who actually believed, and returned outside.

Margaret eyeballed Linda who, after a time, finished arranging the lemon squares on the platter. This wasn't the way she wanted the day to go, but Linda liked to stir the pot, and Margaret wasn't going to stand for any more of Linda's shenanigans. She had almost let Linda break her, but was thankful that Scott pulled her back from the brink. This day belonged to Terrence, and to the future that was quietly slipping away from them both. *Be of good courage,* she counselled herself, drew in a deep breath, and headed into the living room to mingle.

***

"WHAT'S WRONG WITH STRETCH?" TERRENCE asked.

"Aunt Linda's at it again," Scott said.

"She's never been the same since Don went to jail," Terrence said with disappointment. "It's like it killed her spirit, turned her into —"

"The wicked witch of the west," Scott chimed in.

"Oh, you are your mother's son."

"No denying that."

They laughed.

"You better check on Stretch." Terrence pointed to the backyard. "I saw Trevor go after him and that's probably the last thing he needs."

Scott shared a look of understanding with his father before making his way towards the far end of the backyard. Troy stood near the seven-foot wooden fence while Trevor, a stocky blond, leaned against the maple tree that had been Scott's refuge during his youth. Nearing them, Trevor's deep monotone voice drowned out all the other noises. But Scott was too caught up in his own thoughts for Trevor's words to make sense.

"I told him not to take Linda seriously," Trevor said when Scott came into view. "She's unhappy and likes to make everyone around her unhappy." Trevor was Don's son from his first marriage, and Linda agreed to raise him while Don served a fifteen-year prison sentence. He had his father's mysterious blue eyes.

Scott looked blankly at Trevor. "I'd like to talk to Troy alone."

Trevor glanced at Troy, then he retreated towards the house.

Scott leaned against the tree and contemplated Troy. "Are you okay?"

Troy, his gaze fixed on the ground, shoved his hands in his pockets. "No. I, um…" As his voice broke off, he looked up, his eyes glued to Scott. "I don't know why I still feel —"

"Can we talk about this later?" Scott pushed himself off the tree. "I'm not trying to dismiss it, I just don't think I can deal with it right now."

230 • MARCUS LOPÉS

"Now, later ... it won't change how I feel about you," Troy called out.

Scott doubled back to Troy. There was less than a foot between them, and he was close enough to smell Troy's peppermint-scented breath. "You're being selfish right now. This weekend is about my father, not your silly crush."

"It's not a crush," Troy shot back.

"Then maybe I can't be your friend, Troy. Not like this. Not when..." Scott looked at Troy a moment longer, blinking magnificently, and then backed away. He made a beeline for the gate at the side of the house, marching like a soldier in a military parade to the front yard, and paced the walk for a few minutes. Then he bounced up the porch steps and flung himself into one of the Muskoka chairs. His heart raced as memories of that night at Millennium, when he punched Anthony, flooded his mind.

And now, like on that night when he couldn't outrun the rage, he wanted to hit someone.

***

IT WAS LATER THAT AFTERNOON, THE WARM October sun beaming onto the faces of those who had received Margaret's covert invitation to stay behind for a barbecue supper. It took some time for the reverberations from Linda's battle with Troy to dissipate, but a more festive atmosphere had finally prevailed. Margaret, surveying the backyard where everyone was now gathered, was heartened as she listened to the accolades bestowed upon Terrence. Maybe this wasn't an end. Maybe there was still time for a miracle. Losing him terrified her. She wasn't sure how she'd survive without him.

Margaret smiled encouragingly at Terrence, who winked before she made her way back inside. In the kitchen, she assembled the ingredients for a garden salad as the muffled swoosh of the toilet flushing and the squeak of the back door opening collided. Scott came into the kitchen, then Troy entered seconds later. She watched as they exchanged doubting looks, could see the hint of disgust joined by an absolute hate, and when they dropped their gazes her heart sank. Tired of their melodrama overshadowing the day, she said, "I thought this was fixed," as she sliced a tomato in half. Then silence.

She diced up the tomato and, wiping her hands on her apron, looked first at Scott, then Troy. "In the dining room." No one moved. She stomped her foot. "Now!"

Troy parked himself on the far side of the table. Scott fell into the chair his mother always occupied and shifted it on an angle so that Troy wasn't in his line of sight.

"Well?" Margaret stood just inside the entryway, working hard to remain calm as Troy and Scott still wouldn't look at her. "I better hear one of you talking soon or I swear, by the grace of God —"

"I love Scott," Troy blurted out, tears gushing from his eyes.

"I know you love Scott," Margaret said.

"And it's so hard to be around him when..." Troy rubbed his eyes, glanced at Scott and then bolted from the table.

"Troy Sebastian Muir!" Margaret hollered, pointing at the chair he had just vacated. "Sit down."

Troy froze, his tear-soaked face unable to camouflage his stunned look.

Margaret, who'd never called Stretch by his Christian name, smiled faintly. "Don't make me say it again."

Troy hesitated a moment, but collapsed onto the chair.

"Mama..." Scott, looking up from the floor, spoke cautiously. "This isn't the time —"

Margaret raised a hand. "I gave you time to fix this on your own. Now we're going to do this my way." She pulled out a chair and dropped onto it, studied the two young men before her who, in that moment, she wasn't sure she recognized. "You two have been friends a long time, been through a lot together. You're close, like brothers, and it's a very special bond. And don't either of you think about interrupting me." She paused, adjusting herself on the chair. "That type of bond is special. Sometimes what we feel isn't necessarily ... how can I explain it? Sort of like when puberty hits, and you're not sure what's happening to your body, the new emotions —"

"I'm not confused," Troy broke in.

"And I don't love him like I thought I did," Scott growled. "How are we supposed to be friends? He wants something I can't give."

"What did I say about interrupting me? Sometimes it really is like talking to a stone wall." Margaret pointed at Troy, then Scott, and her tone sailed from motherly to cutthroat. "I don't know why the two of you find it so easy to cut people out of your life." She glared at Scott. "I know I raised you better than that." She turned to Troy. "And I know, since you became a part of this family, that I didn't teach you that." She stood. "Terrence and I have repeatedly emphasized, in a world that is going to seed, the need to be kind and generous and loving. Right now you're both being selfish and insensitive, like you've lost your humanity. Take the time to work through this, no matter how hard it may seem. It may even seem impossible, but I believe your friendship is worth it. Certainly, neither of you deserve to be cut loose like a malignant tumour or unwanted growth." She sighed, her round dark eyes moist. "But hear me, and hear me well. Find a way to get along, for your father's sake if not your own. He sees what's happening between you, and the last thing he wants is to leave this world knowing that two people he loves, more than life itself, have fallen away from each other."

The back door opened and in came Linda carrying an empty pop bottle. "Everyone's starving," she said into the room, not addressing anyone in particular. "We should start the barbecue."

"I'll take care of that," Scott said and shot out of his chair.

Linda fussed over the vegetables on the counter for the salad, and Margaret knew exactly what she was up to — eavesdropping on her and Troy's conversation. But Margaret had had enough of Linda for one day and drew the sliding dining room doors closed. "I know you love him. I've known it for a long time. But you know how stubborn and proud Scott is. He likes things to happen on his terms."

"It feels like I'm in hell," Troy said.

Margaret stiffened. "I know you're upset, but in my house you mind your language."

"I'm sorry." Troy's eyes were dry now but ensconced with an agonizing devastation. "I want to be his friend, but I can't because I can't be around him because of how I feel. It's torturous. Christ, it's worse than hell."

"Language," Margaret warned.

"What am I supposed to do?"

Margaret moved to Troy and placed her hand on his shoulder. "Let go, let God. And if you want Scott in your life, you need to accept how he feels. I know that's not easy but it's the only way for you to hang on to him. And I know he wants to hang on to you."

"I'm not so sure about that." Troy rubbed his eyes. "Sometimes I wish we'd have never met."

"Oh, don't talk such rubbish." Margaret walked back towards the dining room doors. "You'd be lost without him. And he you. And if you hadn't met Scott you'd never know that your real name is Stretch, for the tall, lanky white boy that you are."

"I'm not lanky." A faint smile appeared on Troy's drawn face. "Momma D..." He waited until she pushed open the dining room doors and said, "Thanks."

"If you want to thank me, go outside and make sure Scott actually started the barbecue. Sometimes he's easily distracted when it comes to things he doesn't like doing, and barbecuing is one of those things." She patted him encouragingly on the back as he passed by.

"I knew he'd be trouble," Linda said after Troy left the house. "White men always are. I know. Everyone warned me about Don but —"

"Someone should have warned Don about you!" Margaret couldn't stop herself, couldn't bring the rage boiling inside her to a simmer. "What you did to Don ... don't you dare talk to me about white men being trouble. You're the one who couldn't keep your legs closed."

"Margie!"

"Don loved you, worshipped you. If you thought his 'package' was so great, then why did you have to test drive his cousin's? That's what broke Don, made him insane, made him kill his own cousin. And shut off those waterworks. Doesn't work with me." Margaret crossed to the back door. "Now pull yourself together. This is Terrence's day. No more drama, no more harassing Stretch or Scott. Or anyone else for that matter or I swear, as God as my witness..."

Linda, bug-eyed, went rigid.

"Now, be a dear. Finish that salad and come join us outside." Margaret, pleased with how she'd handled Linda, pranced onto the veranda. Her gaze immediately locked onto Terrence's, and they smiled. *Lord, don't take him from me yet. I'm not ready.*

Yes, she believed that God had it all under control.

***

SCOTT PUSHED DOWN A COUPLE OF TIMES ON the round red button. When flames flared through the grill, he took a step back and closed the lid.

"Stop right there," Terrence bellowed as he came towards the barbecue, balancing himself with a cane. "I do the barbe- cuing in this house."

"I just started it up," Scott said.

"All right." Terrence rested his cane against the patio table. "Make way for the master chef."

"Oh, Terrence," Margaret said disapprovingly as she neared the patio table. "I do wish you'd take it easy. Let the boys —"

"I'm not dead yet!" Terrence barked. Taking in Margaret's wide-open round moist eyes, he reached out for her hand. "I'm not overdoing it. But the good Lord is giving me a lit- tle more time. I just want to do some of the things that I'm good at while I still can." He took a step forward and kissed Margaret's forehead.

Margaret placed her hands briefly to the sides of Terrence's near skeletal frame, stepped to her right and said to Scott, "Don't let your father overdo it."

Scott and Terrence shared an understanding smile after his mother was back inside. He took the apron his father held in his hand, unfolded it, and looped it over his father's neck. Then he tied the aprons strings and patted his father on the back twice. "The master chef is good to go."

"Do the chef a favour." Terrence lowered himself down onto one of the patio chairs near the barbecue. "There's beer —"

"No." Scott spoke in the same sharp tone his father used to scorn him. "You're not drinking while undergoing chemotherapy."

"You know the chemo is just to make me comfortable. It's not actually fighting the cancer, not the way it did before." Terrence ran his hand across his high brow. "So, I'm going to live like I've always lived." He looked at Troy. "Stretch…"

Troy lifted his hands in the air as if to say, "Keep me out of it," and glanced at Scott. "I'll go get a couple bottles of water." He returned to the house.

"We want you around for as long as possible, especially Mama," Scott said, unable to squash the emotion in his voice. He balanced himself on the edge of the chair next to his father. "We haven't really talked, you and I, about this. I don't know what it's like for you, but I see what it's doing to Mama. She sees it every day. She needs you to fight, to not give up."

Terrence leaned forward and spoke in a barely audible voice. "There are days when I can't even go to the bathroom on my own. Now what kind of life is that? I can't drive. I can't…" Terrence ran his hand over his mouth. "I can't even *be* with your mother anymore."

"Oh, Dad!"

"Don't 'Oh, Dad' me. I feel like nothing more than an empty shell of a man, like I've been stripped of my masculinity." Terrence eased himself back in his chair. "I know this is hard on your mother. I know it's hard on all of you. But I'm standing on His word, and you should, too. God will take the pain away." He contemplated his youngest son with admiration. "I'm proud of you, Scott. I hope you know that. I haven't said it much, but it's true." A tear rolled down his face. "As much as we, your mother and I, would have liked you to have stayed in Ottawa, I understand why you had to leave. I know it wasn't easy, initially, for any of us, when you came out. But we did our best to understand, and I'm glad we didn't lose you like Norman lost Tyler. And I'm glad that you found someone to look out for you. Stretch is a good man. I hope you can see that."

Scott twitched. "We're just friends, Dad."

"I know," Terrence said with an air of disappointment.

Linda arrived at the patio table with the hamburger patties and hot dogs. She and Scott avoided eye contact with each other, and she quickly retreated to the house. Terrence struggled to lift himself out of the chair, but refused Scott's offer of help. Then, once he was standing, he slid the tray towards the edge of the table and opened the barbecue lid. Scott watched Terrence, who whistled while meticulously arranging the meat on the grill. That made him smile, that his father *was* living when they were both fully aware that soon darkness would reign.

Terrence stood in front of the barbecue and, at regular intervals, flipped the hamburgers and turned the hot dogs. Sure, Scott didn't want his father overdoing it, but taking it easy seemed like surrender. If Terrence stopped living, it would be like giving up and letting the cancer take complete control when it was already winning the race.

"Can't teach Stretch a thing about barbecuing," Terrence said playfully and looked at Troy.

Scott chuckled. "Stretch still needs a few more lessons from the master chef."

Troy, seated on one of the patio chairs, gave a languid shrug and sipped his beer.

"It's an art, you know," Terrence added.

Margaret came outside and rushed towards Terrence. Her eyes were wild and locked on Scott. "I told *you* to do the barbecuing. I know what your father said, but he shouldn't be overexerting himself." She took the tongs away from Terrence. "Sit down, you look flushed." She held out the tongs to Scott, but Troy reached for them instead.

"Take a break, old timer," Troy said as he stood. "Let a pro show you how it's done."

"Pro? You're a hoot. But I could sit down for a little rest." Terrence moved towards the chair that Troy had vacated, and just as he was about to sit down, scrunched up his face. "Who are you calling 'old timer?' I know you weren't talking about me." There was a light edge in Terrence's scratchy voice, but a moment later he and Troy exchanged smiles.

Margaret shot Scott another harsh look, but said to Terrence, "Drink your water."

"I could use a beer," Terrence said.

"Don't test me," Margaret warned.

Terence turned to Scott, who had his gaze focused on Troy's half-empty beer bottle. "Give me that, son," and held out his hand.

"I'll give you something," Margaret snapped, snatching the beer bottle from the table. She marched back towards the house.

"That was my beer," Troy said, sulking.

"Keep your eyes on the grill," Terrence said. "I don't like my hot dogs burnt."

Scott and Terrence laughed, Troy's eyes narrowed. There was something unique and comforting about this day that would be remembered for a lifetime. Scott couldn't say for certain what was in fact special about it. Wait a minute. Yes, he could. They were all at home and had, in a way, come full circle. *Does he feel the same way?* he wondered, sneaking a sidelong glance of Troy. Maybe Troy did, too, because of his deep need for family, for some form of acceptance. And on some level, he found it here in the Davenport home. Terrence and Margaret had welcomed Troy, treated him as if he were their child by blood. Scott knew Troy needed that sense of belonging. Still, why did he believe they had to let go of each other?

And something else. Scott understood that this would be one of the last times he would sit on the back veranda of his childhood home with his father. Soon all that would be left were his memories of the man who had taught him how to ride a bike, who was so proud of his youngest son for having gone to university for not one, but two degrees. He would never forget how his father, on the day of his graduations, fought back his tears.

Scott glimpsed his father, who looked a little peaked. "Dad, are you all right?"

"I'm feeling a little light-headed," Terrence managed to get out.

"Troy," Scott said urgently, "help me get Dad inside."

The tongs fell out of Troy's hand as he rushed to Terrence's side. Slowly, they lifted Terrence up and escorted him into the house. People, gasping and muttering, cleared a path to the living room. As soon as Terrence was seated in his leather recliner, his eyes rolled back in his head. He started convulsing, and involuntarily slid onto the floor.

Troy pressed his index and middle fingers to Terrence's neck, then bent forward so his cheek was just millimetres from Terrence's mouth. After about five seconds, he looked at Scott and said calmly, "Call nine-one-one." With one hand on top of the other, his fingers interlocked, Troy counted out loud while repeatedly pressing down on Terrence's chest. When he hit thirty, he blew twice into Terrence's mouth. No change. He began a new round of chest compressions.

Margaret rushed onto the scene, tears streaming down her face. "Terrence! Terrence!"

"The paramedics are on their way." Scott shoved his phone in his back pocket and worked to hold back his own tears.

The distant sound of sirens grew louder, and it wasn't long before the paramedics were in the living room.

"Hand me the defibrillator!" Troy barked at the pudgy brunette, then tore open Terrence's shirt. "I'm a doctor."

The pads were attached to Terrence's chest. About thirty seconds later, the mechanical voice commands started. "Stand clear. Shock advised."

Terrence's body spasmed at the shock. A pulse.

After assisting Troy and the paramedics to lift Terrence's body onto the gurney, Scott wrapped his arm around his mother. "Everything's going to be all right," he told her, although Troy's grim look contradicted him. They followed the gurney outside and helped her into the ambulance with his father. "We'll meet you at the hospital."

The family spilled out onto the front lawn and neighbours gathered on their doorsteps to watch the scene unfold. After the ambulance sped away, Scott bolted past everyone and into the house, racing into the kitchen to grab his keys and wallet from off the breadbox. Outside again, he instinctively tapped Troy on the arm. "Let's go!"

Blinking rapidly, Scott did his best not to cry as he climbed into the car. He sat there for a moment, staring blindly at the steering wheel, and, for the first time since he was a child, prayed.

The Send-Off

"AMEN."

Scott held his gaze to the tiny drops of water collecting on his black leather shoes. He raised his head and stared abstractly at the floral arrangement centred on the glossy dark brown casket. Blinked rapidly to force back his tears. This wasn't the time for him to cry, to crumble. Hadn't he cried enough? But there were no hard and fast rules for grief, or none that he had heard of. And the loss tackled him as if he were the ball carrier in a game of rugby. Only he couldn't prevent or release the loss. He couldn't dodge or sidestep it. He was, still, pinned down, possessed by the loss.

Like a flower deprived of sunlight and water, Terrence's collapse stole his energy, perhaps even his will to live. Too weak to climb the stairs, he slept on the pullout sofa in the den. And when it became too difficult to get himself in and out of bed without assistance, Margaret arranged to bring in a hospital bed. Terrence looked tired, and his eyes gleamed with the hopelessness of a man ready to surrender. Many speculated that he tried to hang on for Margaret's sake. Maybe that was true?

The minister read a passage of scripture and afterwards invited Scott to say a few words. Scott, lost in his thoughts, hadn't heard the minister call his name. Margaret reached for his hand and squeezed it gently. That startled him, and he looked down for a moment before standing. He took a couple of steps forward and touched his hand to the casket. He swallowed hard, then made his way to the lectern. The light rain that had fallen during most of the service had stopped, but the greyness of the day matched the mood of everyone gathered around the gravesite. Devastation.

Standing in front of the lectern, Scott reached into the inside pocket of his suit jacket for the notes he had prepared. He unfolded the papers and placed them on the podium. Tears banked in his eyes, blurring his vision and distorting the words on the page. He flipped the papers over and surveyed the crowd. The throng, which was nine or ten people deep around the two hundred chairs that had been set up, proved that his father had touched the lives of many. Through his construction business Terrence sponsored the community youth choir, and always provided prizes for the annual neighbourhood barbecue and fun day. But it wasn't until after Terrence died, and the calls and messages of condolence began flooding in, that Scott learned about his father's long-time, behind-the-scenes involvement with the provincial Liberal Party. Maybe that was why he was nervous and didn't know what to say. He hadn't expected to speak with the premier and several cabinet members, including the local MPP, among the mourners. And even more touching was that the inclement weather hadn't kept people from saying a final goodbye.

Scott looked at his mother, who nodded and offered an encouraging smile. "This all still seems a bit surreal to me," he said, his voice throaty with emotion. "I thought it would be easier because I knew how sick my father was and that there was nothing more the doctors could do. But when I saw the muscles in his face relax and that his chest was no longer rising and falling…" He rubbed his eye. "Knowing doesn't make it easier when I come downstairs in the morning and expect to see my father, seated in his leather recliner, reading the newspaper or watching Canada AM." Tears raced down his caramel cheeks.

Margaret rose from her seat, handed Scott a couple of tissues and wrapped her arm around his body. "Take your time," she encouraged, then sat down again.

Scott drew in a deep breath and waited for his vision to clear before continuing. "I loved my father. We didn't say it often. I don't think we had to. Dad showed up for all of my little league baseball games, shouting proudly, 'That's my son,' even though I always struck out. He drove down to Toronto to help me move into my first apartment. I spent my Sunday nights proofreading the invoices he sent out to his clients at the beginning of each week. Our love ... our love for each other was in our actions, in what we did for each other.

"You know, it's never easy being the youngest and growing up in the shadows of your older siblings. I think that's what made me a loner. In a way, maybe I still am. But Dad gave me, I believe he gave all of his sons, the space we needed to follow our own paths. He never tried to force me in a direction that was counter to who I am. I was always thankful for that. I'm not saying that Dad didn't have an opinion about what I was doing or how I was doing it. Most of us gathered here today know how free Dad was with his advice." Laughter. "But Dad let me live my life my way, and was there to listen and counsel when things didn't necessarily go as I had hoped."

He paused, and once again surveyed the crowd of mourners, studying their grief-stricken faces, the collective sorrow that bound them together. Something lifted him outside of that sadness, disconnected him from it. Even when he saw familiar faces — Evan, Jacob, Troy, Janice — he still felt outside of everything, outside of himself. "When I think about my father, I remember a man who had a passion for life, who loved to laugh and seemed to so willingly go with the flow. I witnessed firsthand Dad's love for my mother and how she lit up his world. He was just ... he lived *in* the moment, didn't seem to hold on to grudges. Maybe that was why, when we disagreed, we never let our differences come between us. Some days it seemed that my father was hipper and more attuned to today's generation than I was ... am." More laughter. "In the last couple of weeks, Dad had a final one-on-one talk with each of his sons." Scott bit down on his lower lip. "I don't know what Dad said to my brothers, but this is what he said to me.

"Family will be there for you, always. No matter what, no matter when." Scott fixed his gaze on his mother. "Remember the importance of family, of what family means." He turned his focus to the floral arrangement. "Dad knew I struggled, struggle, with the idea of faith and God, and encouraged me to, 'Just hold on.' He asked me to be open to God's will for my life, to let God be my help. I will try."

"Amen, brotha," someone said.

Scott smiled faintly. "I learned a lot about my father in the past couple of months. I got to know him a lot better, and over the course of his illness I think we became more than father and son. We became friends. During our *tête-à-têtes*, Dad encouraged me to not be naïve, that in this world, no matter what is thrown at me, I will always have a choice. He said it didn't matter if I followed the crowd or if I led it. But to inspire change, I need to let others see that change in me. Then he snorted and said, 'I may not have put it as elegantly as Gandhi, but you know what I mean.' I know exactly what you mean, Dad, and there, too, I will try."

"Praise God" and "Tell it, brother" and "Amen!" collided in the air.

"I don't know how to do this." Scott stared at his feet. "I don't know how to say goodbye or why I feel like I've been cut in two. I want to believe that Dad is resting among the angels, that there's something after this life." He stepped around the lectern and placed his hand flush against the casket. "While you are gone from this world into the next, may you be at peace. I will forever carry you in my heart, remember you in my deeds and, following in your example, live out my creed."

Scott took a step backwards and returned to his seat next to his mother, who grabbed his hand and held it tightly. There was another reading of scripture, and when the minister called on him again people exchanged curious glances. Only Scott, his mother and the minister were aware of Terrence's request that Scott sing his father's favourite hymn. He wasn't sure that he could do it, sing on such a day where his heart was broken and after so many years of not singing at all. Rising from his seat, he thought for a moment that his legs would give out on him. Standing beside the casket and again focusing his attention on the floral arrangement, he opened his mouth. Tears rushed into his eyes as his tenor voice filled the air as he sang, "I Surrender All." The soulful rendition moved many to tears. Through his blurred vision he saw Troy, who was seated to his mother's right, comforting her. The hymn was like the final act that made everything real. And as he sang through the final verse, the minister motioned those mourners sitting to stand as the casket was lowered into the grave.

Could Scott, too, surrender his all?

***

"SCOTT?" JACOB, WITH HIS BLACK SUIT JACKET slung over his arm, approached the maple tree at the far end of the backyard. The cool breeze sent a shiver down his spine and he put on his jacket. He looked up into the tree and there was Scott, seated on one of the thick branches and staring abstractly straight ahead. He didn't know what to do. He'd lost his own father to cancer five years ago. Then he wanted to be alone in his grief. *Maybe Scott wants the same thing now?* He started to back away.

"You don't have to go."

Jacob froze and, after a moment, advanced towards the tree. "I wanted to see how you were before I head off," he said when Scott came into view again.

"I'm all right," Scott spat.

"Not very convincing." When Scott looked away, Jacob inspected the tree, trying to figure out a way to scale it. He chuckled at the discovery of the small pieces of wood nailed into the bark that formed a ladder. He peeled off his jacket, folded it in half, and placed it on the top of the fence a few feet away. Breathing deeply, he climbed up the makeshift ladder and moved slowly, painstakingly, as he balanced himself on a branch that was about level with the one that Scott was on. "Phew," he said, his hands flush against the tree to hold himself in place.

"Acrophobic?" Scott teased.

"Yes." Beads of sweat covered Jacob's forehead. "And it's not funny."

"It's hysterical. You're five feet off the ground." Scott's sides cramped, and he tried to check his laughter but couldn't. "I'm sorry…"

"No, you're not."

"Just sit there and don't look down."

Jacob looked down. "Jesus!" Resting his head against the branch curving out behind his head, his throat constricted, his heart raced. He didn't move and, to calm himself, silently counted backwards from fifty. "Is there anything I can do?"

"For God's sake don't fall!"

"Not funny."

"Seriously, though, I'm fine. I just wanted to be alone for a bit."

"I get that," Jacob said with a strain. "But you're not alone. You know that, right?"

"I do." Scott checked the time. Almost seven, and voices still carried from the house to the back of the yard. A car door banged shut. Another loud boom that sounded like a car back-firing but it could easily have been a gunshot. "I could use a drink. A real drink. Not my mother's Kool-Aid punch."

"I'm game," Jacob said.

Scott swung his legs around and balanced himself on the branch. He eased himself forward, dropped to the ground, then spun around and looked up at Jacob. "You coming?"

Jacob's eyes widened. "That's how you get down?"

"Just do it and don't think about it."

Jacob took his time moving into position, again his breathing slow and deep. He finally pushed himself forward and let out a high-pitched shriek as he fell to the ground. Scott was, by this point, suffering convulsions of laughter.

"What about Troy, Evan and —"

"No. Just you and me." Scott rubbed his arms. "No one will even notice that we're gone."

Jacob snatched his jacket off the fence and followed as Scott led the way to the gate, down the driveway and into the street. They left behind the mournful laughter and quiet sobs, swept up in a new and necessary peace.

But they never made it for a drink. Jacob wanted to stop at his hotel on Rideau Street to lose the suit. Bare-chested, hunched slightly as he rummaged through his suitcase for a T-shirt, when he stood up straight he saw Scott wipe the tear from his eye. He knew that feeling — empty, demoralized, lost — as if he'd just been garrotted with cheese wire. That look... Nothing could hold him back. He cautiously approached Scott and hugged him. Almost instantly, Scott's warm hands cradled his back. Seconds later, their mouths were locked, their tongues dancing over each other. In no time, they were stripped naked and on the bed.

"Oh ... my ... God..." Jacob lay perfectly still, his left arm wrapped around Scott's neck while gently stroking his own cock with his right hand. His mouth was close to Scott's ear, but he was breathless and couldn't say another word. Scott was still inside him even though they had both come, and he savoured the full weight of Scott on top of him. They stayed like that, in a clenching embrace, until Scott had gone soft and pulled out.

They cleaned up a bit, enough to prevent Jacob's come from drying in his chest hairs, and climbed back on top of the bed. The silence that dominated was awkward, and they avoided eye contact with each other. Jacob stretched out, his hands cupped to the back of his head. Scott sat with his legs crossed and drew the bedcovers into him to hide his crotch.

Jacob removed his hand from behind his head and placed it on Scott's exposed knee. "Let's not make a big deal out of it. It happened. Let's not…" He cut himself off when Scott's hand covered his, gasping at the matching pressure. But it didn't last long.

Scott slid off the bed and started to dress.

That ache was on the rise, squeezing his insides, while he watched Scott put on his clothes. Deep down his wish was that it could be more than a one-time thing. Scott still stirred something inside of him, feelings that were very much alive and true. If given the chance, he'd love Scott completely. He sat up and drew his knees into his chest. "I know it's none of my business, but are things okay with Troy?"

"There's a wall there."

"Is that because you're still in love with him?"

"I guess that secret's out." Scott adjusted his tie. "But that wasn't much of a secret, was it?"

"Not really."

"I'm not in love with Troy. Not anymore. Or I don't think I am. Fuck, I don't know." Scott moved to the door. "I'm sorry, Jacob. This shouldn't have —"

"We're good, Scott," Jacob said with a tinge of disappointment. "And you and Troy will figure things out. You mean too much to each other not to."

"Has my mother recruited you for the 'Save Troy and Scott's Friendship' campaign?"

"No, but —"

"Sometimes," Scott interrupted, "I wonder if the best thing you can do for the person you love is let them go?" He wrinkled his nose. "I'll give you a call when I'm back in Junction.

We'll grab dinner." He opened the door just enough to squeeze through and disappeared into the corridor

Jacob fell back into the bed as the door closed. Even after sex, he hadn't succeeded at getting Scott to confide in him, not in the most intimate of ways. And Scott rushing off like that, so detached from what they had just done, made him think of himself as a predator Scott was desperate to escape. But Jacob wasn't a predator. Remembering how much the world spun around and made him dizzy after his father's death, he wanted to be a refuge. Like he had done, Scott would only end up trying to escape from one person. Himself. And he'd never succeed.

But no matter what, Jacob would be there for Scott, be his friend.

***

A FEW MINUTES PAST ELEVEN, SCOTT EASED open the front door to his parents' house. Lights were still on but the house was eerily quiet. He closed the door, trying not to make a sound as he slipped off his shoes, then started light-footed up the stairs.

"Scott Christian Davenport," Margaret called from the living room, her imperious tone compelling him to retrace his steps. "Where have you been?"

"I needed a breather." Scott rounded the banister and stopped at the entryway. *Christ, this isn't good.* His eyes landed on Janice, seated on the sofa next to his mother, then crossed the room to Troy in the recliner, and finally Evan on the loveseat.

"I was worried sick." Margaret spoke harshly. "I tried your cell phone and you didn't answer. That's when I started to worry, that something had happened."

"I'm sorry —"

"Thankfully Janice, Evan and Stretch stayed with me." She looked at Troy. "Stretch assured me that you were all right."

"We should go," Janice said and stood.

Margaret lifted herself off the sofa, stepped to hug Janice and then Evan. "Thank you for keeping me company." She looked first at Troy, then at Scott. "You don't know how much this hurts me, how much it hurt your father, to see the two of you still acting like fools. You're family, and you don't turn your back on family." There was a silence. "Don't either of you have anything to say?"

"Sometimes things end," was Scott's blunt assessment. "And life goes on."

"When did you become so cynical?" Margaret folded her arms across her chest. "Maybe you were simply putting lip service to what you said this afternoon about the importance of family. Oh, no, you didn't just roll your eyes at me?"

"Mama..."

"Your father would be so disappointed."

Tears streaked down Scott's face. "Mama, that's not fair."

Troy, whose position had been repeatedly vetoed, strode to Margaret and hugged her tightly. "If you need anything —"

"You know what I need," Margaret cut in and sighed when Troy looked away. "You two are hopeless. One day you'll see how foolish and stubborn you're being, and you'll regret it. I just hope and pray that by then it won't be too late." She escorted Janice and Evan to the door and followed them outside.

Scott turned away from Troy, who stayed behind a moment but never said a word. After the visit when Terrence collapsed, they had, one more time, retreated from each other — their friendship declared dead, and no attempts were made to resuscitate it. It should have saddened Scott, wounded him deeply, but it didn't. Was his mother right? Had he become cynical?

With the front door open, the banging of car doors and the roar of an engine turning over seeped inside. A short time later, his mother was back in the living room, and they looked searchingly at each other.

"Of all days," Margaret said bitterly, "you could have shown Stretch a little compassion. Your father loved him like a son, and today you made it seem like he didn't exist, like he didn't matter. What's happened to you?"

Scott couldn't hold back the tears that were again pooling in his eyes. "I don't know. I just ... I can't..."

Margaret rushed to Scott and took him into her arms. "Oh, Schnookums, you have to let it all go. Get out of the past and into the present."

Scott stayed in his mother's arms until he stopped crying, which seemed to go on forever. When he finally pulled away, he wiped his face with his hands. "I'm going to try to get some sleep. Goodnight, Mama."

He had started up the stairs when Margaret rushed into the foyer and said, "Open up your heart to forgiveness. It's the only way to free yourself from past hurts."

"I don't think forgiveness is the problem," he said in a barely audible whisper and staggered up the stairs.

No, it was something else entirely.

The Reprieve

HIS HANDS IN HIS POCKETS, SCOTT STOOD IN front of the living room window with his eyes closed trying to block out the sounds bombarding him from all directions. The rain smashing into the window. The raspy voice of the radio host reading the headlines. His mother's humming streaming from the kitchen. Alone, they were each trying to keep busy, as if that would numb the sense of loss, make them immune to it. Being together yet separate in that quietude was comforting, and for the first time in days Scott could hear himself think.

He opened his eyes, walked across the room and yanked his hands out of his pockets. He collapsed into his father's leather recliner and, staring at the ceiling, a tear strayed from his eye and rolled down his cheek. There it was, that sense of loss burning in his chest.

Margaret, carrying a mug of tea, came into the living room and made herself comfortable on the sofa. She took a sip and set the mug down on a square pewter coaster on the coffee table. "How's my baby these days?"

"I'm fine," Scott said, blinking magnificently.

"You don't seem fine. You look lost."

"Maybe I am." Scott looked at his mother. "It hurts so much."

"I know it does, sweetie." Margaret's voice cracked. "I know it does. But it's just like you said. Your father is resting among the angels."

Scott wiped the tears off his face. "When Dad and I last talked, he said he knew I was different since I was about three years old. Did you know he thought that?"

Margaret reached for her tea. "Yes. He didn't know how then, but your father just sensed something different about you. Terrence was convinced that, in some way, you were going to make Davenport a household name." She sipped her tea and set the mug down again. "You were happy and curious as a child, unlike your brothers who were cranky and cried all the time. Your father always said you had this special sparkle in your eyes. And he was right."

"I never wanted to disappoint —"

"And you didn't," Margaret interrupted. "Your father was very, very proud of you. Don't you dare think otherwise."

"What about you, Mama? Have I disappointed you?"

Margaret looked down, pulled a tissue from the box on the side table and dabbed it at her eyes. "I know my reaction to you being gay was dramatic, and I hurt you, but I..." She raised her head, locked her eyes on Scott. "All a mother wants is for her children to be happy and safe, and in a world where there is still so much hatred and ignorance, I was so scared for you. Oh, Schnookums, I'm not saying I understand it all, but I've learned that it's not my place to judge. But I do believe in a loving God, a God who loves us all no matter what. And I love you, Scott Christian Davenport, and I am very, very proud of you."

"I love you too, Mama." Scott rubbed his eyes. "It's been a hard couple of months."

"Yes, it has. But it'll get easier."

"I hope so."

"Are you seeing anyone?"

Scott's eyes widened. "Where did that come from?"

"You've been alone such a long time." Margaret slid backwards into the sofa. "I don't think you're a loner. I do think that you've closed yourself off from love, too afraid to get hurt again. Don't you think it's about time for you to open up your heart again to love?"

"I'm not really interested in dating," Scott said dismissively. "And being in a relationship isn't the only way to be happy. And —"

"And what?"

"I'm not desperate. I'm not afraid to be on my own."

"I'm not saying that being in a relationship will make you happy. But you have to be open to love."

Scott shifted in the recliner. "It doesn't seem like people talk about love nowadays."

"What do you mean?" Margaret asked.

"When I look at the profiles on the various dating sites, there are a lot of guys who are 'advertising' for long-term relationships. But no one's talking about their hearts going pitter-patter, or meeting someone who makes them smile on the inside. They want to know if you're financially and emotionally stable, what you like in bed."

"Something should be a surprise. And that's not something I need to know."

"It's hard to be open to love when everyone's chasing after it, like an addict looking to score." Scott pursed his lips. "All I'm saying is that love should find us, surprise us, make us jump."

"What does it mean to 'smile on the inside?'" Margaret rocked her head gently from side to side. "And, really, if you want to be loved, be lovable. You seem so closed off from love and the world."

Scott's body went rigid. "What does that mean?"

"Every time we talk on the phone, all you talk to me about is your work or your running. It seems like all you do is work and run." Margaret's expression seemed uncertain, but then gave way to a wry smile. "You're young, and you should be out enjoying life, meeting people. And, no, I don't mean drifting from one bar to the next, getting drunk and having random sex. But there's a whole world out there to see. You used to be so active as a child, curious as a cat."

"Well, I … I'm running my first half-marathon at the end of the month."

"Why didn't you say anything?"

"It didn't seem like the right time, with Dad…" Scott blinked back his tears. "I didn't want you to be disappointed in case I don't finish the race, or if I don't do well."

"Why are you doing it? I mean, why are you running the race?"

"I'm doing it for me, to step outside my comfort zone."

"Then it doesn't matter if you don't 'do well,' whatever that means. Success will come in doing your best on race day. Whether you finish the race or not, I'll be proud of you."

Margaret blew on her tea before taking another sip. "And by the way, I'm coming to watch my baby run the race."

"Mama…"

"I think you'd want someone there at the finish line cheering you on. You can book my train ticket online before you go. I've never been good at that type of thing." She tapped her fingers against her mug. "Now, what about Stretch?"

"Mama, please," Scott said, exasperated. "I don't want to talk about Troy. It's over. *Finito*."

"I remember that first day you brought Stretch home." Margaret grinned. "I wasn't sure what to think. Were you dating? How did you possibly meet when you seemed like polar opposites? You were artistic, Stretch was scientific —"

"What time is the insurance guy supposed to be here?"

"You can pretend all you want like it doesn't matter, but I know you miss him." Margaret paused to sip her tea. "He's been a good friend to you, and for you to have so ruthlessly cut him out of your life was wrong."

Slouched down in his chair, Scott checked the time. "Was it one? Because it's almost one now."

"Sometimes you're as stubborn as your father." Margaret stood. "Do we have all the right papers?"

"Yes."

"Gosh, I can't remember his name." Leaving the room, she stopped by the recliner and cupped her free hand to Scott's shoulder. "Let love be your guide. Let it show you the way."

"I'm not really sure what you're trying to say."

Margaret tightened her grip. "Love is the pathway to forgiveness."

"Or the gateway to hell," Scott quipped. He was about to laugh until he saw his mother's knotted face and turned away.

Margaret, mumbling unintelligibly, disappeared into the kitchen.

Scott remained in the recliner, closed his eyes and listened to the rain still crashing against the window. There was a certain calmness about the room, a sort of presence that gnawed at his heart. Maybe his mother was right, that he wasn't doing much outside of work and running, and half-heartedly trying to launch some type of writing career. An emptiness that kindled his uncertainty about the future and what he wanted. Could he believe that God was at work in him? Not when he couldn't feel that presence *in* him, uncertain of that life-changing power. But he was doing his best, as he promised his father, to 'just hold on' and believe that God was there. Maybe that would make his faith easier, reconnect him, let him once again believe in something … anything.

Don't Bother

AFTER YANKING THE KEY OUT OF THE IGNITION, Scott remained in the car with his seat belt fastened. His head, slightly cocked to the left, rested against the headrest. He contemplated the grey stone house from across the street with a new heaviness. He had returned to Junction three weeks after his father's funeral and threw himself head first into his work and his running — on his own at last and able to grieve, really grieve, in a way that had not been possible in Ottawa.

It was mid-December now. Snow blanketed the ground and grey, sunless days were the norm. The sub-zero temperatures, frequent snowfalls and icy roads made it easy to hibernate. And this was unexpected, for Scott to find himself parked outside Troy's house and trying to summon the courage to get out of the car. He hadn't thought about what he'd say, but he was starting to believe that, as his mother said, love was the pathway to forgiveness. There had always been a type of love that existed between them. A brotherly love that was, to Scott, the purest and truest love that could exist between them. But, now, was it more than that?

But how had he ended up here, parked in the street in front of Troy's house? Partly because of his mother, with whom he spoke to almost daily and who always asked after Troy. He sensed his mother's determination when it came to some form of reconciliation between them, her babies. When they spoke, his mother acted like she never heard from Troy, but Scott often caught her in a 'lie,' making reference to something that gave away the fact she did talk to Troy regularly. But her 'nagging' had worked — forced him to think about the long and deep friendship they'd shared, their closeness. That love.

Regret, as his mother suggested, dogged him. Had he been too swift and harsh, too ruthless, too heartless?

Scott undid his seat belt and exited the car. Approaching the house, this unexpected feeling of uneasiness overtook him, and now he doubted his course of action. Despite his misgivings, he and Troy had to find a way to either hang on to each other or let each other go *une fois pour toutes*. He rang the doorbell and waited.

The door opened, and Troy stood in the doorway but didn't say a word.

"It's pretty chilly out here," Scott said. "May I come in?"

Troy kept his eyes on Scott as he stepped aside.

"Is this a bad time?" Scott asked and unbuttoned the top button of his charcoal grey wool jacket. At Troy's lethargic shrug, he added, "I thought we could talk."

Troy shoved his hands in his pockets. "What? Is this the moment when you start being honest with me?"

"We've been through a lot the past few months and —"

"Stop it, Scott," Troy cut in. "I know about Jacob, and what happened between you the day of Terrence's funeral."

"That was ... unfortunate. But if there's anyone I'm going to love, it's —"

"No, Scott. You were right. We end this now."

"I never seriously considered your point of view," Scott mumbled.

"You were never interested in my point of view."

"Troy, I —"

"We're done, Scott. You said you couldn't be my friend. That's fine." Troy pulled his left hand out of his pocket and checked the time. "I have dinner plans, so..."

Scott stepped towards the door and spun around. "Troy, I'm sorry..." His voice trailed off because the contempt radiating from Troy's eyes told him no more apologies, no 'second chances.' "Take care of yourself." He opened the door and left the house. In his car, he sat there, still possessed by the loss of his father's death, horrified by the sudden realization that he was sleepwalking through life. He hoped that by reaching out to Troy, and consequently reconnecting with him, he'd wake up — prove that he hadn't lost his humanity. But Troy rejected him, and now nothing seemed to matter, nothing at all. He inserted the key into the ignition, flipped the engine and headed for home.

But where was that?

***

"YOU SHOULD HAVE SEEN MY BABY RUN," Margaret sang-spoke, as if she had just been moved by the Holy Spirit. "He came around that final turn, put the pedal to the metal and was moving so fast people thought it was Jesse Owens all over again."

Scott chuckled. "Not quite."

"They were eating his dust," Margaret insisted.

"And what about the two hundred and ten runners who finished ahead of me?"

"All that counts is that I'm proud of you," Margaret said. The race had taken place almost two months ago, at the end of November, but Margaret spoke like it had happened yesterday. She turned to Tyler, who'd moved back to Ottawa after Norman's death in the hope of reconnecting with his family. "Twenty-one kilometres in one hour and forty-three minutes."

"That's impressive," Tyler said. "I remember my mother talking about Dad and Uncle Terrence running a race once."

"Really?" Scott looked wide-eyed at his mother. "I didn't know Dad was a runner."

Margaret placed her hand to her chest as her shoulders shook. "I'd forgotten all about that." She touched Scott's arm. "You were three or four at the time. It was a couple of months after your Aunt Carla died. They decided to run for the cure and showed up on race day, having not trained, and took off like cheetahs chasing after their prey." She couldn't stop laughing. "At some point during the race, Norman got a charley horse and your father sprained his ankle. We were all wondering what had happened." She wiped the tears off her face. "Everyone had crossed the finish line, even those who had walked. I was beginning to panic, and then, off in the distance were two sorry-looking men, holding each other up as they hobbled towards the finish line. That was the end of their running careers."

"Well, we really should get going so I don't miss my flight," Scott said to Tyler.

"Don't worry, Aunt Margaret." Tyler picked up Scott's suitcase. "I won't speed." He opened the front door and headed outside.

Margaret rushed at Scott and drew him into her. "You'll call me, right?"

"I'll call you once I'm home." Scott pulled out of the embrace.

"No, I want to hear from you every day while you're in New York."

"I'll call you when I'm home." The cold, blustery air entered the house, and Scott leaned in and kissed his mother on the cheek. "I need to get going."

"I want to hear from you from New York, not when you get home. Don't make me come down there after you."

"Now that I'd love to see." Scott flashed a smile on his way out the door.

"I mean it," Margaret called out. "Call me." She pushed the door closed, hustled into the living room and stood in front of the window. She waved until the car disappeared down the street. *So stubborn,* she thought, smiling, as a tear came to her eye. *And so much like his father.*

Epilogue

May 2007

Moving On

THE WARM MAY AIR CARESSED SCOTT'S SKIN as he wrote in the black hardcover notebook at the patio table on his back deck. He had not completely thawed out from what had been a long and 'empty' winter. He was, four months after his trip to New York City, shaken to his core. The size and robust energy of the city had amazed him, made him feel alive. He wanted to be a New Yorker, one of those people unscrupulously chasing after big dreams. He was still uncommitted, uncertain of his talent and doubting his ambition. At the writers' conference, he'd met some famous authors and others who acted the part with their bravado and football stadium-size egos. In that ocean of possibility, he was the little blip on a radar screen before the signal was lost.

New York had changed him, changed the way that he saw himself. Maybe it was the other writers at the conference, and how their lively and polished prose intimidated him. *If only I could write like that,* he thought a lot. Perhaps it was the way he blended so effortlessly into the city, like it possessed him — a sort of magic in the air that rekindled childhood dreams long forgotten. Yet some days he wavered between writing and a life of public service. Was he crazy to want them? Choosing one or the other didn't seem fair, but he couldn't see how to balance those two different worlds. And by not committing to either, he'd just keep dodging his vocation, sidestepping his real self. Wouldn't that be the real tragedy?

He'd tried establishing a routine, writing for an hour before putting on his proof-reader hat and running in the evenings two to three times a week. But the writing didn't stick, not so far anyway. Maybe that was because things had changed.

Troy was 'gone' from his life. Hooking up with Jacob on the evening of his father's funeral had created a sort of wedge between them too. They still ran together, now just on Saturday mornings, but didn't confide in each other the way they used to. Evan, perhaps accidentally, became a more trusted confidant. They seemed to get along naturally, found a way to talk to each other that surprised them both. Yet it didn't fill the void created by Troy's absence and left Scott aching for something more.

Winter was that never-ending stretch of highway that had the potential to lead nowhere, and nowhere was exactly where Scott was headed. Sometimes he wondered if he should try again with Troy, be more forceful, but always dismissed the idea. He 'accepted' — despite his mother still pressuring him to make amends — that he and Troy had lost each other. Permanently. Like an amicable divorce where the other's imprint lingered but didn't necessarily intrude, and life continued, and them along with it. But there was an intrusion, and life didn't just go on.

Ding, dong, ding, dong carried lightly through the house and out onto the back deck. Scott set his pen down on his notebook, rose and returned inside. He moved about cautiously, trying not to make any sudden movements or be seen. Last thing he needed was to be trapped into talking to some religion pusher. At the kitchen doorway, he slowly leaned forward like a spy trying to glimpse the person he was tailing. Unable to see anyone through the glass in the front door, he tiptoed into the living room. When he saw the long brownish hair blowing in the wind, he bolted for the door and opened it wide. "Hey," he called out to the tall figure heading down the walk as he stepped out onto the front step.

Janice spun around. "I'd given up." She retraced her steps towards the house.

"I was out back," Scott said when they were inside and led her into the kitchen. "Are you playing hooky?"

"I called your office and the receptionist said you were off for the rest of the week." Janice pulled out one of the stools and plopped down. "I was going to invite you out to lunch, but finished up early instead. Want to grab a drink?"

"I have some white wine chilling in the fridge. And the bar is stocked if you want a more girly drink."

"Don't start with me," was Janice's playful response.

Scott retrieved the wine bottle from the fridge and then slipped into the dining room to secure the wineglasses. He returned to the kitchen, divided the remainder of the Kumeu River chardonnay between the two glasses, and suggested retreating to the patio. Outside, the sun burned brighter since the clouds had moved on, and he slid one of the patio chairs into the shaded part of the deck while Janice was more eager to soak up the rays. Letting the quietude have dominion, they sipped their wine, their eyes roving the backyard.

Janice was the last person who Scott expected to show up at his door. Happy to see her, or perhaps indifferent, she had been more Troy's friend than his. The early years of his and Troy's close friendship made him and Janice accidental friends. Although they never hung out on their own, there was a mutual respect and solid alliance whenever they were together.

"It's probably no secret as to why I'm here," Janice said after tasting her wine. "How long has it been?"

"Since before Christmas," Scott said, matter-of-fact. He always appreciated Janice's directness, but he wasn't in the mood for her to play analyst with him. "It's what he wanted. I reached out to him, tried to tell him... It was too late, too goddamn late."

"If you think it's what he wants, you're wrong," Janice said. "He's miserable. I know. I see the way he mopes around like a zombie. It's gotten better. I convinced him to see a therapist so he could deal with his feelings for you. And I think he has ... dealt with his feelings for you, I mean. But he needs you in his life, Scott. The two of you are fated to each other. I've never seen that type of connection between two people, deeper than twins. I think of Tom as my soul mate, but when it comes to connectivity..." She looked both disappointed and impressed. "We can't touch what you and Troy have."

"Had." Scott ran his index finger back and forth along the base of his wineglass. "I don't know what to do at this point, if doing anything would make a difference."

"Scott..." Janice adjusted her skirt, pulling it down over her knees. "You have to talk to Troy and make him listen, make him believe that you want the two of you to be friends again. Oh, don't look at me like that. You miss him, too."

"First Jacob, and now you." Scott took a huge gulp of his drink. "Seems like my mother's been rallying the troops."

"Maybe that's because we care," Janice said bluntly.

"I don't miss him." It was part truth, part lie, and he wasn't sure that Janice believed him. "Yes, sometimes I wonder how he's doing and I hope that he's happy." He drained his drink and set the glass on the veranda floor next to his chair. "It's been good to be on my own, to not feel smothered. All right, that's not the right word. But I don't know how to put it." He sidled his eyes to the blue jay parked on the high fence to his right. "Maybe Troy and I were too close."

"What does that mean?" Janice sounded petulant. "Are you trying to somehow negate your entire friendship with him?"

"No." Scott shifted in his chair, crossed his left leg over his right. "Maybe I depended on him too much. I don't know why I..." He censored himself. He was about to say that he didn't understand why Troy had been his only friend, why he had never succeeded at establishing similar associations with others. And for some reason Evan and Jacob didn't count. "It's been kind of freeing to be on my own. Maybe I've become a hermit, but it's been good for me. It's helping me figure things out."

"Figure out what things?" Janice sat up straight. "Be specific, Scott."

"My life, what I'm doing, where I am," Scott said, his voice rising. "Ever since my father died I've felt lost."

Janice stood and slid her chair closer to Scott's. She eased herself down and placed her thin hand on his knee. "Losing a parent is hard. It's like you've lost a part of yourself, and that's normal. But haven't you cut yourself off from the people who love and care about you?"

Scott uncrossed his legs, forcing Janice to remove her hand from his knee. "I don't think I'm there yet, ready for some type of reconciliation. It'd be forced and wouldn't last."

"Sometimes we're not ready for something until it's thrust upon us. In your quest for truth, have you drawn any conclusion yet? Figured out the 'why' to life?"

"Don't patronize me." Scott tried to dodge the critical look Janice threw at him, and when he couldn't, he stared into his lap. "I learned I had to stand on my own, prove that I didn't *need* anyone," he said with conviction and looked up. "In a way, I had to reclaim my life. Not from Troy but from that whole ordeal with Anthony Power that I let possess me. Troy and me … we became a casualty of that. Perhaps unintended, but —"

"Then fix it," Janice pleaded. When Scott didn't say anything, she continued, her voice ripe with frustration. "Then maybe *you* should see someone. Don't look at me like that. I mean a therapist. You say your father's death has left you shaken, questioning everything about your life, so maybe talking to someone will help. I know a good psychologist who specializes in grief counselling. I could make a call and she'd probably see you next week. Think about it." She glanced at her watch, took one more sip of her wine and rose with the grace of a ballerina. "Tom has one of his union meetings tonight, so I have to pick up the twins from daycare."

Scott lifted himself out of his chair, took Janice's wineglass from her and set it on the patio table. After Janice looped her arm through his, they made their way down the veranda steps and towards the front of the house. In the driveway, she withdrew her arm and they stood facing each other.

Janice reached for Scott's hand and held it tightly. "We live in a time when we readily chuck away anyone and anything that, all of a sudden, doesn't seem to fit. Or maybe it's because we think that we've outgrown the thing or the person, or that we've changed. We've become ruthless and selfish, and not in a good way. Please don't become one of those people. Don't toss Troy away like he's that rotting apple tucked away in the back of the fridge."

This was the first time that Scott had really taken notice of Janice, who was almost his height and who Troy had often described as determined. She was pretty with her round blue eyes and thin pink lips. "Thanks for stopping by."

Janice made a sort of grunting noise and released Scott's hand. She got into her car, started the engine and rolled down the window. With her seat belt fastened and her hands gripped to the steering wheel, she said, "No wonder you and Troy got along so well. You're both incredibly stubborn."

"Ha-ha." *Now she's trying to bait me.* Scott tried to remain Zen, let the comment wash right over him. "Drive safe."

Retracing his steps back to the veranda, his mind was in an awful tumult. Maybe he'd already become one of those ruthless and selfish people Janice feared ruled the world. Maybe he did miss his best friend, but he was too much of a coward to have his apologies thrown back at him again. Maybe he'd just never been that good of a friend.

Seated again at the patio table, he picked up his pen but nothing happened. His hand locked, the words gone ... nothing. *Fuck, she's good.* His hand slowly opened and the pen dropped onto the notebook. He'd been a fool. What had his father said to him before he died? *Remember the importance of family, of what family means.* Troy was family. That hadn't changed. Massaging his temples, Scott swallowed back that metallic taste in his mouth. Could he prove that he'd always be there for his family, no matter what? After staring blankly at the blue sky for about twenty minutes, he collected his notebook and pen and trudged into the house.

Scott fell into his desk chair, his focus trained on his phone. *You can, and should, do this,* he thought, hesitated, but then powered it on. The knots in his stomach tightened as he scrolled through his contacts. When he found Troy's, his finger hovered over the 'Call' button. *Christ, what the fuck do I say?* He couldn't think about it anymore. He had to just do it, touched the screen and waited.

"Hello," came after the third ring.

"Hi, Troy." Scott's throat constricted, and it gave him enough time to figure out what to say next. "It's Scott. I know it's been a while, but I really think we should talk. Can we grab a coffee?"

Scott's heart careened into his throat while the soft breaths filtered through the line. The silence stretched on, and he wasn't sure if the line had gone dead.

"I think about you every day," Troy said.

"Then let's meet."

"Things have changed, Scott."

"I just..." Scott's voice cracked. "I miss you. Life hasn't been the same without my big brother."

"Right..." Troy drawled, which was followed by his savage laugh. "I'm in the middle of my shift. God, I hope I'm out of here by eight. How about a late dinner, say, nine at Manhattan's?"

"Perfect. See you then."

Scott ended the call and returned the phone to the desk. Then he pulled open the top drawer and rifled through the papers until he found the photo stashed there. It was the one of him and Troy taken during their first year of university. Their lips stretched into broad smiles, their arms wrapped around each other, and their free hands waving the peace sign. In their eyes gleamed the joy of an enduring, shatterproof friendship. It had shattered, but this was the first step in putting it back together. And the shy, socially awkward eighteen-year-old didn't exist anymore. Troy was right. Things had changed.

For the first time in years, Scott was ready to love again, give himself completely to someone. Was that someone Troy? No. They had to focus on just being friends and learning to trust each other again. But searching for love wasn't his priority. If it happened, great, but he believed what he'd told his mother. He had to be patient and let it find him.

Now was his time to chase his dreams. He hadn't been totally honest with Janice. He'd figured out a few things, prepared to test the limits of his ambition. All of which would, he hoped, never leave him broken again.

Acknowledgements

I am, as always, grateful to Dave Taylor of thEditors.com, whose insights helped me make this book the best it could be. Adam, Arynn and the team at Frostbite Publishing always deliver. Thank you!

Writing can be a solitary journey, but the unwavering support and encouragement from Heather-Anne Gillis and Myrtle Gillis carries me through the lonely hours, days, and weeks. Special thanks to John Fortier, for always showing up with notebooks and pens just when I need them — and for tolerating my cluttered workspace.

I am forever indebted to you, my readers, for sticking with me along this journey. Thank you!

Can I Ask a Favour?

Thank you for reading *Broken Man Broke*.

We truly appreciate the time you've invested in this book when you had so many other options available. It means a lot that you've chosen to read and hope you enjoyed it.

We'd be very grateful if you took a few minutes to post a review — good, bad, or ugly — on Amazon, Goodreads, Twitter, Facebook, and your website or blog. We'd consider you a superhero if you also told your friends, family and colleagues about this book. Word of mouth is power!

About the Author

MARCUS LOPÉS is the author of *Everything He Thought He Knew, The Flowers Need Watering,* and, most recently, *The Visit.* An avid runner, blogger and actualizer of dreams, he lives in Toronto. For more information, you can visit his website at marcuslopes.ca.

Printed in Great Britain
by Amazon